To Peg,
Enjoy the Adventures
of Lex Stall.
Best Wishes
Mark L. Dressler

DYING for FAME

A Lex Stall Mystery

Manhattan's tenacious female detective

MARK L. DRESSLER

Dying for Fame is a work of fiction. Names, characters, organizations, places, events, and incidents are either the product of the author's imagination or are used fictitiously. Any resemblance to actual persons, living or dead, or events is entirely coincidental.

Published by Satincrest Press, USA
ISBN: 978-0999062326

Previous novels by Mark L. Dressler
DEAD and GONE - published 2017
DEAD RIGHT - published 2019
Two mysteries set in Hartford, CT
Featuring Dan Shields
(The detective who breaks all the rules)

DEDICATION

Dying for Fame is dedicated to all my friends, supporters, my Weaver High School classmates of 1964, and the entire alumni.

ACKNOWLEDGMENTS

Advisors: Ann Horan, Joellen Adae, Patricia Grigaitis
Editor: Heather Doughty – HBD Edits
Proofreader: Joshua Suhl
Formatting: Liz Delton

Cover designer: Jeanine Henning
Author photo: Jessica Smolinski

Thank you, Joyce Ogirri – Production manager, News 8 WTNH TV, New Haven
Thank you, Teresa Dufour – CT STYLE host, News 8 WTNH TV, New Haven
Thank you, Stan Simpson – Real People host, Fox 61 WTIC TV, Hartford
Thank you, Carole Goldberg and Steven Goode – Hartford Courant

Thank you, Lynn Sheft for your contributions to this story, and your continued support.

Special thanks to Laurie Bompart and her staff at Barnes & Noble UCONN Hartford Bookstore for contributing to my success.

To the personnel at the Boston Children's Hospital. Thank you for the wonderful work you do.

CHAPTER 1

It was strangely quiet on East Seventy-Seventh Street at 12:45 a.m. Fredrike Cambourd peered out a window from his basement art studio, barely able to see the brownstone across the way. The near-total darkness was haunting, but the conspicuous absence of sounds from rats clamoring around trash cans, and the cadence of stray cats patrolling this Manhattan neighborhood cast an ominous shadow on the night.

Chilled air seeped through the window's edges, as he closed the curtains. Returning to his chair, the artist glanced at a palette that had several paint globs spread across it, picked up a dry brush, dabbed it into a burnt umber dollop, and stroked the color onto a waiting canvas. The eyes of the unfinished portrait stared at him, but they couldn't warn him of the danger lurking on his doorstep.

Suddenly, the silence was broken. One footstep, then another, landed on the concrete stairs leading to his workshop. Cambourd turned as the doorknob slowly twisted, and in walked a familiar person. Resting the wet brush on the pallet next to his chair, Cambourd took a deep breath and uttered, "You nearly scared me to death."

"I'm sorry, but I had to see you, and it couldn't wait."

"What the hell is so important?"

The intruder glared menacingly at the startled man and harshly declared, "I think you know."

Cambourd replied, "I must."

1

The angry caller moved closer to him, "I can't let you. And you know what I want."

The artist grabbed his cane, pointed it at the hostile trespasser, and abruptly shouted, "Never!"

"Never is right, you old man." The uninvited visitor revealed a gun, aimed it at the obstinate artist, and fired a shot. Cambourd stumbled back, his chest spewing blood. The gun wielder raised the weapon and again pulled the trigger, sending a bullet into the wounded victim's head. Cambourd fell to the floor, his chair crashing into the wooden easel and unfinished painting that landed beside the fallen body. Pivoting swiftly, the assassin walked up the stairs, and disappeared into the ghostly night.

Fredrike Cambourd was dead. Dying wasn't the worst thing that could have happened to him.

CHAPTER 2

NYPD Detective Lex Stall and her partner Gil Ramos slipped through curious bystanders, walked under a string of yellow tape, and stepped into the crime scene. Low hanging ceiling lights, brick walls, and iron barred windows gave the place a prison-like aura.

The veteran detectives approached a uniformed officer. "The victim's name is Fredrike Cambourd," the sergeant said. "We're still knocking on doors. The building super and other tenants are upstairs. They're all pretty shook up." Pointing to a room at the rear of the studio, the policeman stated, "There's a man back there you need to see. His name is Jerry Davidson. He called it in a little over an hour ago at nine-eighteen."

"What's his story?" Lex asked.

"Says he walked in and found the body."

Lex studied the room noticing dust and specks of blood on exposed pipes. She saw the corpse sprawled in a pool of red fluid, and spotted wire-rimmed glasses resting against a blood-soaked chair where the victim must have been sitting. There was an unfinished portrait and broken easel on the stained drop cloth. The female subject's face was covered with red streaks; her eyes the only ones that witnessed the killing. A few feet from the dead man were a beret and stained shelves that stored paints, brushes, and other artist's implements.

The stench of excrement filled the room. They stepped

3

toward the victim and Gil gagged. He whispered to his partner, "Smells like crap in here."

Lex replied, "We've been in worse places. Hold your nose, big boy."

Medicolegal Examiner Pam Bruckman faced them. "Nice way to start the day, isn't it?" she said.

"What's it look like?" Lex asked.

"Two shots. One to the head, one in the chest," she responded as her pale-faced trainee stretched a cover over the dead man. Pointing to her left, Pam warned, "Be careful of the vomit. I don't think it's my assistant's." She turned to her right. "Hers is over here."

"Got a ballpark?" Lex asked

"I'd say he was shot sometime during the night. Judging by the body temp, probably six to eight hours ago."

"Thanks. Have fun," Lex said.

A Tiffany-style lamp rested on an antique table. Two portraits hung a few feet above the lamp. Having been to several museums, Lex recognized the faces of Claude Monet and Auguste Renoir. A 2014 calendar taped to the wall had the first 17 days of March checked off. Nearby was an old wooden desk, its right leg resting atop a thick yellow phonebook. On top of the rickety desk was a wallet secured in a plastic baggie. "I'll ask Rusty about it. Looks like he's been over here." Both drawers were open and empty. "It seems the killer found what he was looking for."

Gil said, "This trash basket has a pile of paint-splotched rags."

Leaning against the wall furthest from the victim were three large blank canvases. The detectives moved toward a dented four-drawer metal cabinet that didn't appear to have been disturbed. Noticing something interesting up against the side of the cabinet, Lex said, "Take a look at this cane. It's tagged."

Eying the silver handle, Gil said, "Looks expensive."

She examined the object closely and snapped a picture. "Those red spots aren't paint. Blood. This cane must have been moved."

The detectives approached lead Crime Scene Investigator,

Rusty Brainerd. Yellow markers labeled "1" and "2." were on the floor. She bent at the knees to get a close look at shell casings that appeared to be .38 caliber when she heard Rusty shout, "Don't touch anything until we're finished."

That harsh warning got Lex's dander up. The arrogant, smart-assed runt had botched one of her cases several months ago. She sternly replied, "You forget who's in charge here? I know how to do my job. You better get it right this time." Rusty didn't flinch, but Lex knew her stinging remark irked the pint-sized investigator. "Any sign of forced entry?" she asked.

"No," he grunted.

"What about the wallet on the desk?"

"Wallet is empty, except for a driver's license that expired five years ago. We dusted the desk."

"Was that cane up against the metal cabinet when you got here?"

"Yeah, why?"

"Because it looks to me like that cane was near the victim when he was shot, and it was moved. There's blood spatter on it. Why would the killer pick up a bloodied cane and move it?"

Rusty spun around. His eyes met hers, and he huffily retorted, "You figure that out. You're the detective."

Lex glared at him while her burly, forty-two-year-old partner tugged her arm. "Let it go," Gil said, steering the agitated detective away from the investigator's view.

Approaching the back room, the detectives passed an open pocket door, and Gil remarked, "I've seen bigger bathrooms on airplanes."

Lex neared the policeman standing at the back room door. "When we arrived, the guy inside was dazed; said he threw up and had to sit. I brought the man in here, and the EMTs took a look at him."

She studied the room. There was a settee abutting the rear wall. On top of an oval table were an empty wine bottle, two long-stemmed glasses, and a plate of cheese and crackers. "The victim certainly had a friendly visitor."

"The glasses," Gil added. "Female?"

Careful not to pick them up as she examined the rims, Lex said, "Hard to say. I can't tell if there's lipstick on either one. Rusty will have to check these out. The food looks barely touched."

Lex rotated toward Jerry Davidson, whose head was bowed while he sat in a cushioned armchair. Wearing a blue, pin-striped suit, a white dress shirt opened at the top button, and loosened paisley tie, he raised up. The clean-shaven man, appearing to be in his mid-forties, had beads of sweat covering his forehead. "I'm Detective Lex Stall. This is my partner, Detective Gil Ramos. Mr. Davidson, we understand you discovered the body."

"I can't believe it," he said in a broken voice. The shaken man took a handkerchief from his coat pocket and wiped his brow. "I can't imagine who would have done this."

Lex fetched a pad and pen from her purse. "Tell me about this morning, sir."

Clutching his damp handkerchief, the man gravitated forward. "I got here around nine, opened the door and came in." He momentarily closed his eyes. "You saw what I saw. Fredrike was obviously dead."

"I'm sure it was quite a shock," Lex said.

"I vomited and called nine-eleven."

The Rolex on the man's wrist was an indication he was no pauper, and his expensive looking attaché was leaning against the chair. "Mr. Davidson, may I take a look inside your briefcase?" Gil asked.

The distressed man presented it to the detective. Inside was a small laptop and a day planner. There were also business papers tucked into a manila folder, so Gil closed the attaché and gave it back to Davidson. The businessman checked his watch and abruptly rose. Standing eye-to-eye with the five-ten male detective, Davidson wiped his brow again, opened his wallet, and handed Gil a business card. "I have to get to my appointment."

Lex wasn't pleased with the man's brazen attempt to make a sudden dash for the door. *Where the hell does he think he's going?* The tenacious thirty-seven-year-old, auburn-haired detective glared at him and put her hands up, stopping him in his tracks. "Mr. Davidson. Why don't you sit back down!" she commanded. "Now, who is it you are meeting with?"

He took his seat. "I was going to visit Marcus Worthington. He's the director at the museum."

"Which museum?"

"The Metropolitan Museum of Art."

Lex nodded. "Under these circumstances, I'm sure Mr. Worthington will understand if you delay your visit. Wouldn't you agree?"

Caught off guard by Lex's order, he had no choice but to obey her, pull out his cell and delay the meeting.

She studied him while he avoided eye contact with her. When he ended the call, she said, "I believe you said you opened the door. So it wasn't locked?"

His eyes reluctantly met hers, and she saw a glassy look. "He never locked it and often worked until dawn."

Lex digested that statement and it was obvious to her Davidson knew Cambourd would likely be working in the studio very late. "What was your relationship with him? How often do you come here?"

"We had a business deal. I placed his artwork in local galleries. Sometimes I drop in on him, like I did today."

"When was the last time you were here?"

"About a week ago."

Lex zeroed in on the empty bottle and leftover snacks. "Do you like wine?" she asked sharply.

Davidson raised his voice in protest. "If you're asking if I drank that wine with him, the answer is no, and I don't eat cheese because I'm lactose intolerant."

"Mr. Davidson, you seem quite nervous. Is there anything you

7

need to tell us?"

He rested his head in his hands before looking up. "Hey, I found my friend shot to death, and you want to know why I'm tense?"

"I understand." Lex replied. She calmly asked, "When you came in, did you notice anything out of place? Anything missing?"

Davidson clasped his hands, and asserted, "No. Christ sake. He was dead, and my head was spinning. What are you getting at?"

"Nothing, sir, but if robbery was a motive, then you may have noticed something missing."

"Well, I didn't. What the hell would anyone take? You saw the studio."

"I did," Lex replied. "Money is always a motive."

"He wasn't exactly a rich man. He was a miser, lived upstairs in apartment two, but he spent most of his time here."

"Did he rely on a cane to get around?"

"The cane? He had fallen a few months ago. Left him with a slight gimp, but he was okay. He liked the cane; thought it was distinguishing."

"You wouldn't have picked it up and moved it, would you have?"

"What kind of a question is that?"

Disturbed by Davidson's earlier attempt to leave the scene, Lex didn't give him an answer, and homed in on the rattled man. "Do you mind telling us where you were last night and earlier this morning?"

"Where do you think I was?" he said as he shifted his body, clearly ruffled. "I was home sleeping."

She upped the heat. "Do you own a gun?"

Looking away from her deep gaze into his eyes, he slammed his fist on the chair's arm. "No! What the hell? You think I shot him?"

Lex ignored the hostile response. "Tell us about Mr. Cambourd. Did he have family?"

Davidson grabbed his handkerchief again. "It's hot in here, I need some water." Gil walked to the bathroom where he found a cup, filled it with water, and returned. The detained man drank the liquid, set the cup down on the table, breathed hard, and began to regain his composure before answering Lex's question. "He wasn't married."

"Are you saying he wasn't presently wed, or he was never married?"

"I don't think he was ever married. I know he has no children."

"What about relatives, friends, acquaintances?"

"I can't say. If he had relatives, they're probably still in France. As far as friends, he had me and I believe a few at the museum." Davidson wiped his sweaty brow. "Look, he came here from Paris about forty years ago when Marcus Worthington offered him a job as conservation director at the Met." Lex kept writing as Davidson continued. "Fredrike had retired not long ago. He wanted to devote all of his time to painting and pursuing his quest to become famous. As I said, I've been helping him sell his artwork. Several of his paintings are at the Heinrich Altman Gallery."

Lex paused before pushing on. "You said he painted late at night. Are you aware of anyone else who might have known his habits?"

Davidson threw his hands up. "Beats me. I suppose his landlord and neighbors knew." Raising his brow, he uttered, "Fredrike didn't have an enemy in the world. It could have been anyone. Some robber might've seen the lights."

Lex icily stared at her subject. "I don't think this was a random act, do you?" She moved closer. "I'm quite sure Mr. Cambourd knew his killer."

Davidson bristled at the insinuating remark and angrily barked, "What kind of bullshit is this? Anyone could have walked in here. That sounds like an accusation. Do I need a lawyer?"

Lex felt her partner's nudge, and she backed off. "Calm down, sir," she said. "You don't need a lawyer. This is just a friendly discussion."

"Really?" he angrily replied as he grabbed his briefcase. "I think this conversation is over." Davidson stood. "I'm leaving now."

Lex smiled at the businessman, and handed her card to him. "Don't lose this. I'm sure we'll be talking again soon."

Davidson swiftly buttoned his shirt, pulled up his tie, checked his inside jacket pocket, and headed to the front door with his black briefcase in hand.

Lex kept her eyes on him as he exited the studio. She'd clearly put a target on his back.

CHAPTER 3

D on't forget the back room!" Lex yelled to Rusty as she and Gil left the crime scene and headed outside. The horde of onlookers had dispersed, and the detectives walked a few feet to the steps that led up to the slain artist's living quarters. Another patrolman was at the entrance. "Anyone upstairs?" Lex asked.

"One of our guys is still up there," he said while opening the door.

The detectives entered the first-floor. Mail slots occupied one wall. A rusted wall-mounted fire extinguisher hung on the opposite side next to a flight of stairs. Lex looked up the staircase and saw a door at the top of the landing. The floor creaked as she and Gil continued walking down the gray walled corridor. Lex spotted a familiar uniformed officer standing with his arms crossed outside apartment two. "Hey, Pete, how's it going?" she asked.

"Great. How's Bonnie and Clyde today?"

Lex smiled broadly at him. "Nice to see you too. Anything suspicious up here?"

Pete pointed to the inside of the victim's living quarters. "Can't say for sure. This isn't the neatest place I've ever seen. Take a look-see."

Glancing inside, Lex saw clothes slung over chairs and an orange tabby asleep on top of the clutter. She asked, "Any neighbors hear or see anything?"

"Not that we can tell but go talk to the landlord across the hall.

11

He's pretty upset. Likes the TV loud too. Hear it?"

"Sure do," Gil said.

Lex tapped Pete's shoulder. "We'll be back. Keep an eye on the cat."

Across the hall, landlord Norman Stillwell's door was closed, so Gil rapped on it. He knocked again before an unshaven man, dressed in suspendered jeans and a white tee, opened the door. Lex flashed her badge in front of his sullen eyes. As he shook his head, his long, unruly hair fell in place. "Mr. Stillwell, are you alright?" she asked.

Judge Judy's voice resonating from the large TV was deafening. Lex stood in front of him while Gil eyed the rest of the apartment. "Do you mind lowering it a bit?" she requested.

Stillwell picked up the remote and lowered the volume. "Better?"

Lex nodded. "Much."

The landlord retreated to his rocker and puffed a cigarette. The distinct aroma of marijuana was mildly masked by the smell of tobacco. Lex repeated her question. "Are you alright?"

He shook his head and hoarsely answered, "Not really. Fredrike was a good, peaceful man."

"Do you know if anyone was up to Mr. Cambourd's apartment yesterday, this morning, or within the past few days?"

"He was always in the studio. I took care of the cat most of the time. Even cleaned that stinky litter box."

"Did you see or hear anything last night?"

"That's what the other cops asked me."

"I know, sir, but would you mind if we ask you about last night too?"

He glanced at her. "Go ahead."

"You never heard or saw anything?"

"Just my TV."

"What about the other tenants?"

Stillwell rolled his eyes. "Them? Have you met them? I have a collection of oddballs living here. They wouldn't be fazed by a

12

nuclear explosion."

Lex thought that answer a bit strange. "Why would you rent to a bunch of eccentrics?"

The slim landlord got up, extinguished his cigarette, and picked up the full ashtray. A box of Pall Mall's was on the table. "Because the government supports them, and the state gives them a rent subsidy. I get paid like clockwork. No worries having to evict anyone. Go visit them like the other cops did." Stillwell stepped into the kitchen and emptied the ashtray into a trash container.

"We'll be back," Lex said.

The detectives knocked on the next apartment's door. When it opened, a man who identified himself as Fabian, wearing a plaid shirt and shorts was standing before them. Lex saw a wagon filled with plastic bags that contained cans, and the man said he was a Vietnam veteran making a few bucks by cashing in the empties. Gil asked, "How long were you in Nam?"

"Long enough to lose half my arm," he replied.

"I'm sorry, sir." Lex offered. She then asked, "Did you see or hear anything last night?"

"Didn't see nothing," he said. "Only thing you can hear around here is Stillwell's TV."

No one answered the door at the adjacent apartment, so the detectives proceeded down to another unit. Gil knocked on the door, and the detectives were greeted by a man appearing to be well into his seventies, maybe eighties. He had a breathing apparatus attached to his walker and wore thick glasses. "Sorry to bother you," Lex said. "We're checking to see if you may have heard or seen anything last night."

The man shook his head and nodded without saying a word. Gil said to Lex, "Let's move across the hall."

She rapped on the door and a woman wearing a long apron over her dress, opened the door. The aroma of something good filled the room. Her husband strolled over in his wheelchair. "Sorry to bother you," Lex said. "We're following up to see if you may have seen or heard anything last evening."

The woman replied, "We didn't. A couple of officers were here earlier. It's a shame. I never would have imagined anything like this happening here."

The detectives had one more unit to check on this floor, but it had a "For Rent" sign on the door. They headed back to the landlord's apartment and again heard the loud TV. Stillwell quickly toned it down again. "We noticed one apartment was vacant, and no one answered number four," Lex said. "We're going upstairs now."

"Wait," Stillwell said. "You can't. It's boarded up."

"You mean it's vacant?" Lex asked.

"Kind of. There's four places up there but we had some damage due to water leaks…and a small fire. Anyhow, the insurance company refuses to pay. I had to let the tenants move out and can't afford to have the units fixed up. Everything is boarded up."

Lex said, "So tell us about the empty place down here."

"That old geezer died a while back. Haven't been able to rent it yet."

"Who lives in apartment four?" Lex asked.

"Lorena Tufts. Hard to keep track of her; she's a nurse at Mid-Manhattan." Stillwell picked up a cigarette, lit it, took a puff, and rested his smoke in the ashtray. "That's not all. She's a he, I mean was a he. You'd never know, but she went the whole way." He hesitated, "Had the operation."

Gil shrugged and said nothing.

"Was she here earlier?" Lex inquired.

"Haven't seen her in a few days," the landlord responded. "Mail is still in her slot."

"Do you have a key to her apartment? We'd like to take a quick look," Lex stated.

Stillwell picked a keychain off the kitchen table, and escorted the detectives to the apartment. They entered the unit. Gil commented, "Neat and clean."

"Never said she wasn't tidy," Stillwell mumbled.

14

Lex saw a calendar taped to the side of the refrigerator. "Looks like her work schedule."

Stillwell opened the fridge. "Milk's fresh, leftovers look good."

There was a magazine on the kitchen table. Gil said, "Look at this. *Guns and Ammo.* She's got a subscription." He opened the periodical to the earmarked page that had checkmarks next to three different firearms.

Lex asked Stillwell, "Do you know if she owns a gun?"

"Beats me," the landlord answered.

Gil said, "Either she does, or she may be about to buy one."

Lex suggested, "Let's take a look around, but unless a weapon is openly displayed, we can't take it without a warrant." She asked Stillwell, "Does Lorena have friends or family?"

Scratching his head, he replied, "Haven't got a clue. Never mentioned family and as far as I know, I'm her emergency contact."

"Do you know where she's from?"

"Never asked. All I care about is getting my rent money, and she's no problem."

"Do you have her cell number?"

"It's in the book on my kitchen counter."

Two pictures in photo frames were on a table. "Either of these her?" Gil asked.

"Yeah, both…before and after."

The detectives took a quick look into the bedroom. It was neat like the rest of the place. "We need to come back with a warrant," Lex said. "Never know what might be hiding here."

"For sure," Stillwell said. "That's why I know she had the surgery."

"So, you snoop in everyone's apartment?" Lex remarked.

Stillwell furrowed his brows. "Snoop? I am the janitor too. Fixed her toilet a while back, and well, let's just say, I've seen a few things in here."

Lex eyed him. "A few things?"

He shrugged. "It's a small place. Have to check everywhere. We get roaches you know. Nasty critters."

The detectives and Stillwell headed back to his apartment. The landlord opened a black address book, picked up a pencil, and wrote Lorena's number on a piece of paper before handing it to Lex. Gil took out his cell phone. "Let me see that. I'm calling her." His attempt to reach Tufts failed because her voicemail box was full. "No answer. Can't leave a message," he said.

"We need to find her," Lex replied. "Thanks, Mr. Stillwell. We're going back to Cambourd's."

Pete was still standing at the apartment entrance. "You can take a potty break now," Lex kidded.

"Not now. I wouldn't want to miss anything. You guys get anywhere?"

"Not yet," Lex said. "One tenant is missing, and she may be a person of interest. The landlord hasn't seen her, and it appears she may own a handgun."

The detectives entered the cluttered living quarters, and Lex took a quick look around the small apartment. In the corner of the main room was an antique secretary drop-front desk. Most surprising was that the walls were barren, except for a coat of gray paint. No artwork. No Monets. No Renoirs. Not even a Cambourd. She glanced into the galley-style kitchen and saw a dented toaster and rusting microwave on part of the counter. Moving closer to the appliances, she flinched as a cockroach crossed her path. "He's right," she said. "There are critters in here."

Lex returned to her partner. She noticed him staring at an old phonograph and radio that were in one corner of the room. "Pretty old stuff. So is that vintage RCA TV on that wobbly table," he said.

"I don't see a computer and didn't notice one in the studio," Lex said. "We haven't seen a cell phone either. I wonder if Rusty bagged one. All I remember seeing was a landline in the studio, same as here."

The cat leapt off a chair, headed into the bathroom, and a few seconds later a pungent odor wafted toward the detectives. "This is why I have a dog, Lex," Gil said. "You wanna empty the litter box?"

She peered at Pete while pointing at Gil, and said to the officer, "You want to shoot him, or should I do it?"

"He's all yours, Annie Oakley."

Gil got the message and walked toward the bathroom. Upon reentering the main room with clean hands, he mused, "Like I said, I'd rather have a dog. I'm gonna see what's in the desk?" He opened it. The two top shelves were crammed with books, and there were several small compartments. "Lex, this is a little strange. There's nothing in here except for a couple of rows of books that appear to be in French."

She approached her partner and removed a book from the top shelf. "I remember reading this is school, *The Hunchback of Notre Dame*." Lex slid the bottom drawers open and saw several old black and white photos. Other items in the drawers included a few Parisian newspapers and several maps of the city. "Let's hit the bedroom," Lex suggested.

She saw the grin on Gil's face as he said, "Love to, my sweet. Not sure my wife would approve."

Lex poked him. "Try thinking with that thing above your neck."

The detectives entered Cambourd's bedroom where the bed was unmade. She opened dresser drawers. "Underwear, socks, nothing unusual."

Looking under the bed, Gil commented, "Nothing here." He opened the closet. "Not much of a dresser. Small wardrobe and two pairs of old loafers. Wait, the top shelf has a few shoe boxes." Pulling them off the shelf, he removed the lids. "Papers, receipts, all kinds of stuff. What do you think?"

"Leave them. We'll be back. Let's wrap it up."

Lex went across the hall to see the landlord. "We're going now, but we'll be back tomorrow. By the way, there's at least one roach in Cambourd's place."

"Damned things. Nabbed one here too. Gotta spray again."

"Thanks for your help," Lex said.

She turned to Gil and Pete. "We're done for now."

CHAPTER 4

Jerry Davidson breathed easier after escaping Lex's grueling interrogation because he knew he'd been less than truthful with the detectives. It was 11:25 a.m. when he started walking toward Fifth Avenue. Feeling somewhat relieved that what he'd taken from his dead friend's desk was safely tucked inside his coat pocket, he continued on to his destination. Oblivious to pedestrians and vehicle traffic, he was nearly struck by a cab as he approached the enormous Metropolitan Museum of Art. Climbing the steps alongside several patrons, he opened the door, and proceeded inside.

Familiar with the path to Marcus Worthington's office, he walked up a bank of stairs to his extreme right. Entering the director's workplace, Jerry looked at Marcus. "I have very bad news," the distraught businessman said.

The seventy-nine-year-old Worthington, whose gray hair was sparse, said, "Are you okay? You look like you've seen a ghost. What's wrong?"

Jerry's eyes were glazed. "It's Fredrike." After a long pause, he exclaimed, "He's dead!"

Marcus gasped, and his jaw dropped. Sitting in his high-back chair, stunned by the unbelievable news, he sighed, "Dead? He's dead?"

Jerry sat on one of the two armchairs in front of the long mahogany desk, setting his briefcase on the red and black oriental carpet. "He was shot." The businessman looked skyward and then focused on the stunned director. "I walked into his studio and found him. It was horrible. I can't get the sight of his bloodied body out of my head."

Marcus set his silver-rimmed glasses down, and uttered. "Killed. Oh my God! Who the hell would have shot him?"

"I don't know. You know he never locked his door. I warned him many times to do so."

"I need a drink," Marcus said.

Jerry continued, "I puked my guts out and called the police." Shaking his head, he grimaced. "Two detectives questioned the shit out of me. That female bitch went up and down me as if I had killed Fredrike."

Sadness was written on Marcus's face, and he teared up, grabbed a tissue, wiped his eyes and put his glasses back on. "This is unbelievable. Why?"

Jerry lowered his head and became silent while Marcus went four steps back to his credenza and poured himself a drink. "You should have one too."

The businessman looked up when he was handed a glass of bourbon. The director moved back to his chair and chugged his alcohol. "My staff will be shocked."

Jerry wiped sweat from his forehead, held the shot glass but didn't drink. "We still have the Impressionist exhibit to discuss."

Marcus opened a folder. "We have commitments of forty masterpieces from several museums, and the artwork will start arriving soon." He looked at his consultant. "You have to go to London to visit a few private collectors, and there's one in Boston with a few interesting pieces."

"I know. I will soon."

Marcus's demeanor suddenly shifted. "A funeral, what about a funeral? He has to be buried. He has no family. We need to take care of his final resting place. I know the perfect setting: a cemetery on Long Island, not far from my home."

Jerry picked up his briefcase. "We'll need to wait until they release him from the morgue. I have to be on my way."

Marcus sighed. "I have to break the devastating news to my staff."

Passing Monet and Renoir paintings on his way out of the building, Jerry lamented, "Fredrike treated these as if they were his own."

When the businessman reached the street, he began shaking while sticking his hand out to hail a cab. He got into the yellow vehicle and told the driver where to take him. It wasn't home.

Chapter 5

Alexis Maitland Stall, a twelve-year veteran of the NYPD, was the only female detective at the Nineteenth Precinct. Her curvy, five-nine figure was always a welcomed sight.

With renovations taking place at the Nineteenth Precinct on East Sixty-Seventh, Captain Vernon Pressley's crew were operating out of the already remodeled Central Park Precinct, whose primary function was protecting eight hundred acres and fifty-eight miles of Central Park pedestrian paths. The two-level structure, originally a stable, now featured a magnificent glass ceiling atrium lobby. The small, modern facility housed mounted police, foot patrol and administration officers, paddocks, and a few cells that were occupied most of the time by drunks and muggers. The relocated detectives occupied an empty portion of the second level. Four six-foot tall, open, half-glass and half-wall boarded partitioned cubes were on one side of the squad room. A conference space, an interview room, and two bathrooms were across from them. Five, soon to be six, detectives paired to share three workspaces. The empty unit served as a snack area with a coffee maker and treats available to the detectives. A door behind the work area opened into a small storage space.

Entering the squad room, Lex and Gil headed to the captain's office. Their path took them by Stanley Hutchinson, a portly detective who often reminded the shapely Lex that she was the only female around. His partner, Frank Starsky was a subdued officer closing in on retirement. The duo was known as Starsky and Hutch. Their wall displayed a racy swimsuit calendar that Lex tried to ignore. She neared Hutch and saw him staring at her. "Keep your eyes on your work!"

Captain Pressley, fifty-one, took over the detective division nine years ago. His glassed office was enclosed. The door was etched with his rank and name. The captain's desk displayed family pictures along with an encased bullet that sat in one corner; the same shell that a decade ago had been removed from his chest. That incident left him with a four-inch scar as well as occasional migraine headaches, and sensitivity to light.

She and Gil stepped into the captain's office. Pressley peered over his gray tinted glasses and pointed to the two chairs opposite him. "What have you got?"

Lex placed her notes on the desk. "The victim's name is Fredrike Cambourd. He was a retired museum curator and artist, shot sometime during the night in his art studio. His friend Jerry Davidson, a businessman, found him and called it in. To me, the man seemed awful edgy and, at times, hostile. We have our sights on him."

"She really ripped him," Gil said. "Lex may be right, but I'm not entirely sure. I don't know how I would react if I found my best friend shot to death...And we have no weapon."

"Gee, thanks," Lex said. "True, we don't have a weapon, but he could have ditched one."

Gil replied, "He said he didn't own a gun."

Lex readdressed Pressley. "It appears the victim had a social visitor earlier in the evening. There was an empty wine bottle and snacks in a back room. I sent Rusty to check out the evidence. We'll have to wait to see if the lab comes up with anything." She flipped to a blank page. "We went upstairs to Cambourd's apartment; spoke with the landlord and tenants. There's a missing female neighbor named Lorena Tufts. A person of interest. It appears that she may own a weapon. We'll need a warrant to search her apartment, and we'll take another look at the victim's studio and living quarters."

"I'll get on the warrant. Should have it by the time you guys get here in the morning." Peering at his detectives, Pressley said, "Detective Trevor Benzinger will be here soon to team with Epstein. He's young, so don't abuse him."

"Right," Gil said. "We'll let Hutch do that."

Lex and her partner went to their open cube to the left of the captain's office. "You're fixed on Davidson. That's obvious," Gil said.

She appreciated the window with a view of the park. Their well-lighted office had desks, each with new computers, multi-functional phones, and leather executive chairs. The detective's stations were divided by a short partition. A shared table and printer were behind them. Gil's desktop displayed photos of his wife RayAnn and their twin teenaged sons Darryl and Dwight, along with framed, autographed pictures of retired baseball players Darryl Strawberry and Dwight Gooden.

Photographs of her father, daughter Liz, and a box of Kleenex that Lex regularly pulled tissues from to hand to her partner, whose face often had doughnut crumbs, were on her desk. Seated, she thought about Davidson's attempt to abruptly end her questioning, and it set off a large red flag in her mind. Lex said, "He sure was sweating and nervous. He's hiding something."

"You think he might be protecting someone?" Gil asked.

"Maybe," Lex responded.

"What about Tufts?"

"Interesting. We'll have to see where she leads us. Never know."

"How about Stillwell? A real character," Gil said.

"Pothead, too, but harmless. Let's get out of here," Lex said.

"I'm right behind you."

Gil nearly always rode the subway from his home in Queens because he hated to drive into Manhattan. However, there were times when he'd had no choice but to get in his Chevy Malibu and make the trip.

He headed for a train, while Lex went down the back stairs to the small parking lot. Stopping at the stable, she peeked inside, saw Butterscotch and walked to the animal's nook for a brief chat with her friend. Lex then got into her two-year-old Corolla and drove toward her Greenwich Village residence, making the twenty-five-minute trip home while listening to her favorite Fleetwood Mac disc.

Parking was usually scarce on her street, but this time she found a space two houses from her residence. She walked up four steps to the front door of her brick townhouse, retrieved her mail, and entered the small foyer. Lex kicked off her shoes and opened the French doors to the parlor. She often read and watched *Jeopardy* with her fourteen-year-old daughter, Liz, in this room. Bookcases were on both sides of the gas fireplace. A half bath, laundry, kitchen, and pantry made up the rest of the first floor. Upstairs included a full bath and two recently painted bedrooms.

Lex moved back to this house, the same place she'd been raised, after her bitter divorce. Her mother passed a few months later, leaving the home to Lex. Her father died when Liz was four, and Lex's closeness with him left a huge void. She was his little girl who could do no wrong. More importantly, she could always talk with him. Lex's mother was more of a taskmaster and never understood her. They didn't have the same strong bond that Lex had with her dad.

Entering the kitchen, Lex saw Liz and the girl's best friend, Shannon both fixated on the computer screen. The curious mother asked, "Schoolwork or Facebook, young ladies?"

Liz clicked off the desktop and swung around to her mother. "School, of course."

"Okay, you two. Please be careful what you post."

Shannon grabbed her backpack. "I have to get going."

The helpful teenager often started preparing dinner before Lex got home, but this was not one of those days. "Can we get pizza?" she asked.

Lex responded, "Not tonight, I'm going upstairs to change. I had a busy day. How about boiling water and get pasta started."

Liz hid her disappointment and happily obliged.

While they ate dinner at the kitchen table, Lex stared at her daughter, and it gave her chills. Liz was blossoming into a young woman. Lex had pictures of herself at that age, and the resemblance was remarkable.

"Why are you staring at me?" Liz asked.

Lex smiled. "You're so much like me and you're growing up so fast."

The truth was that there were skeletons in Lex's closet. She knew she'd have to talk with the teenager at some point about those demons. The last thing the protective mother wanted was her daughter making those same mistakes. Especially, losing her virginity at fifteen.

CHAPTER 6

Lex entered the squad room with her Starbuck's in hand, and immediately encountered Hutch who was on his way to the coffee machine and box of doughnuts. The boisterous detective usually brought in the treats, courtesy of pool money. The only person not contributing to the fund was Lex because she never ate the calorie-laden snacks and she detested in-house coffee.

She saw Hutch eyeing her black pant suit. "Don't say it, grab a doughnut."

"Give me a break, Lex. I was going to say how nice you look today."

The half-full coffee mug on Gil's desk was sacred. The New York Mets souvenir had been signed by Tom Seaver. There was a chocolate doughnut beside it. Lex sipped her latte and peered into Pressley's office. "That must be the new guy," she said.

"Pretty young, if you ask me," Gil said before taking a bite of his doughy pastry. "Tall one too."

Pressley stepped into the squad room behind Epstein and introduced the rookie, Trevor Benzinger to his comrades.

As soon as the captain got back to his chair, Lex and Gil approached him. Pressley reached into his two-tiered tray and passed her the requested warrant. "Thanks," Lex said. "We're going back to the tenement now."

Pressley held up a manila envelope. "Remember the firefighter who died in that arson fire?" The detectives each nodded. Pressley continued, "Sometimes, I think their job is tougher than ours. Starsky and Hutch have hit a dead spot with that case. They're sure they know who is responsible for setting that laundry ablaze, a drug dealer named Sollie Briggs. They think the bastard sent his young son, Dray, to set the fire. Witnesses identified the boy who was riding a bike. One person stated he'd seen Sollie arguing with the shop owner a couple of days before. Dray and his mother, Arnetta disappeared." The captain gave the envelope to Lex. "We're making a donation to the Firefighters' Fund."

Gil opened his wallet and shoved the only cash he had inside, a ten. Lex opened her purse and placed another ten into the envelope. Pressley dismissed his detectives, and Lex and Gil neared Hutch. "I underestimated you, big guy," she said. "Nice gesture with the firefighter."

Starsky faced her. "We know the kid's father put him up to setting the fire, but all we can hang on that bastard is drugs, and he's been there and done that before. We need to reel his ass in for good. That firefighter didn't have to die. Where you off to?"

"The artist's place. We have a killer to track down," Gil said.

Lex nudged her partner. "See if you can find a couple of boxes in the storage room."

Gil came back with two cardboard cartons. "These should do."

They exited through the rear precinct staircase to the stable and parking lot. Gil headed toward the unmarked squad car they were assigned. Lex said, "I'll be there in a minute." She walked back to see Butterscotch. "Hey, girl, how you doing? Going for a walk in the park today?" She scratched the horse's head. "See you later."

Gil waited inside the vehicle until Lex opened the passenger door. "How's the old nag today?"

"You are talking about Butterscotch, right?"

"Funny, Lex."

"She's fine. Wants me to bring her a bag of carrots."

⚓

28

Arriving at the brownstone, Lex and Gil walked up the front steps to the outside door. Gil rang the bell. Seconds later, a voice shouted, "Open it. It ain't locked."

The detectives proceeded to Stillwell's apartment where the landlord was standing by his open door. The marijuana odor was strong, and Lex saw the weed stick in an ashtray. "How are you today?" she inquired. "Another smell wafted in the room "Did you spray for roaches?"

Still unshaved, wearing a pair of old shorts and pajama top, he stroked his hair. "Yup, should keep them away for a while. Only had enough killer to do my place. I have to get some more. I suppose you want to take another look around Tuft's apartment."

"We do, and we have a warrant to search it. Have you seen her?" Lex asked.

"No. Want me to bang on her door?"

"Bring the key." She paused. "By the way, is that outside door always open?"

"Yeah. I put the 'ring the bell' sign out there to make people think it's locked. Tenants know."

They proceeded to Tuft's apartment and Stillwell knocked on the door. There was no answer, so he unlocked it. Lex presented him the warrant, and the detectives entered the unit. With Stillwell hanging around, Lex asked, "Can you get her mail? I want to check it." The landlord left to do his chore.

Lex turned to Gil. "Ready to hit the bedroom?" She smiled at him, knowing he wasn't about to say anything smart.

They went in, and Gil checked the closet. "Mostly work outfits, not many dresses or blouses."

Lex opened Lorena's dresser and saw underwear. "I don't believe it. Her bra is larger than mine."

"Not too late for implants, you know," Gil smugly responded.

She glared at her partner. "You see something wrong with me? No one else is complaining."

Wisely changing gears, Gil said, "She's got a few pairs of shoes and purses. I don't see any luggage."

"Why the quick departure?" Lex asked.

"I'd disappear real fast if I killed someone," Gil replied.

Lex opened another drawer. "Look at this. A gun permit. She's got a registered Glock Forty-Two, a pocket Glock. I don't see the weapon, but here's ammo, thirty-eights. Six missing. Same caliber that killed Cambourd." Picking up the box of bullets, she said, "She's certainly a person of interest." Lex grabbed the permit, and they reentered the living room.

A cigarette butt was resting on the edge of an end table. "I'm gonna bag this," Gil said.

"That's odd," Lex noted. "I don't remember seeing a cigarette here yesterday."

Stillwell reentered the room with the mail and placed it on the table next to the gun magazine. "Junk and a couple of bills," Lex said, thumbing through the short pile. The landlord caught her attention when he lit up another butt. "Mr. Stillwell, were you in here after we left yesterday?"

He froze. "No."

She turned to Gil. "What kind of cigarette did you just bag?"

"Same kind my mother used to smoke. Pall Mall."

Lex stared at the landlord because she had seen a red and white cigarette box on his kitchen table. "Why were you up here? This cigarette is yours, isn't it?"

Stillwell's mouth opened wide. "Okay, you got me. I ran out of milk, and I knew hers was fresh, so I came and took it."

"You do that kind of thing often?"

"Already told you I fix stuff. I'm in and out of places all the time."

"Did you ever see her and Cambourd together? Talking or in each other's place?"

"Never noticed. They obviously knew one another. It is a small building."

"What else can you tell us about Lorena?" Lex asked.

Stillwell shrugged. "You think she killed him?"

"I can't say she did or didn't. All we know is she has a gun, and she's missing. Does she have a car?"

"No one here does."

Lex walked a few steps to the kitchen and glanced at the calendar that was on the side of the refrigerator. "According to this, she last worked a couple of days ago, but oddly there's no other notations." She flipped the page. "Nothing here either."

"Interesting," Gil said.

Lex took out her cell and called Pressley. "Captain. Lorena Tufts has a Glock Forty-Two. Thirty-eight caliber. She's a registered nurse at Mid-Manhattan. We need to talk to her employer." Lex put the phone back into her purse and asked the landlord, "You said you were her emergency contact. Do you remember her boss's name?"

Stillwell placed his hands under his chin and thought for a few seconds. "It's Simona or something like that."

"You can lock up, but if you see or hear from Lorena, call us immediately. We'll be back to finish up here." Lex motioned to her partner. "Let's go."

⏶

The detectives approached the sliding glass doors of Mid-Manhattan Hospital and entered the facility, walking to the information station. Gil showed his ID and said to the clerk, "We need to speak with the head nurse. I believe her name is Simona."

The employee responded, "Nursing administration is on the second floor. Her name is Sedona Cortez. Follow the blue line and take the elevator. You'll see signs when you get out."

"Thank you," Gil replied.

Heeding the instructions, they entered an elevator and exited at level two. Lex saw a sign and Gil followed her to the office. She opened the door, and Sedona Cortez glanced up from her computer.

"Ms. Cortez, we're with the police department." Lex presented her badge to the nurse. "May we sit?"

"Yes. What's this about?"

Lex said, "It's about an employee named Lorena Tufts. When was the last time you saw her?"

Sedona had a worrisome look on her face. "What's happened?"

"Maybe nothing, but we can't locate her. When did you last see her?"

"A couple of days ago. She worked second shift. Got off at midnight. Why?"

Lex replied, "I don't mean to alarm you. We want to talk with her about a crime she may have witnessed. Her landlord said he hasn't seen her recently. We were at her apartment, and it looks like she may have gone somewhere. When is she scheduled to work again?"

Sedona brought up the schedule on her computer. "She's on duty, day after tomorrow."

Lex thought it odd that Lorena was scheduled, yet the calendar on her refrigerator didn't have any indication of future work. She asked, "Do you know if she's close to anyone: friends, coworkers, or family?"

"Lorena was a loner." Sedona opened a drawer and retrieved Tufts' personnel file.

"May we see it?" Lex requested, hoping that Sedona would disregard the privacy laws.

"I'm afraid not. There are rules we have to follow."

"We understand," Lex said. "Can you tell us where she worked before you hired her? And by the way, her landlord clued us in on her gender transition."

"You know we can't discriminate. In fact, we have to bend over backward so we don't get sued by some civil rights organization," Sedona stated. "Lorena previously worked at Woodland Hospital in Hartford, Connecticut." Closing the file, Sedona put her hands together and interlaced her fingers. "This is such a touchy and awkward subject." She shook her head and took a deep breath. "Lorena seems distant at times. She's a good nurse, but I think, in a sense, she feels out of place."

"How so?" Lex asked.

"I think she is too conscience of her gender identity."

"Did she ever talk to you about it?" Lex wanted to know.

"She did once, but I told her it had no bearing on her job. She doesn't trust anyone. She thinks everyone looks at her as being odd. She thought coming here would be different than Hartford." Sedona paused. "I told her I thought she should continue therapy, but she said she was tired of psychologists."

Lex was silent for a few seconds. *The gun. Killing Cambourd doesn't make any sense. Is she unstable enough to commit suicide? Worse yet, could she be planning an attack against her coworkers?* Lex gave her card to Sedona. "Please let us know if you hear from Lorena."

The detectives left the hospital, and Lex placed her hand on Gil's shoulder. "We need to talk to Pressley. I'm concerned about Lorena. She may be suicidal or on the verge of an attack at the hospital. That's a huge concern, especially if she harbors bad feelings about her coworkers. It looks to me like she had no intention of returning to work."

▲

They headed back to the precinct and marched into Pressley's office. "What's up?" he asked.

Lex said, "We could have a very unstable person on the loose. I'm concerned Lorena Tufts may be planning an attack on her coworkers, or she may be contemplating suicide or both."

Pressley jumped up. "What? Are you serious? Do we need to secure the hospital with uniforms?"

Lex shook her head. "I don't think we should do that until we have something more concrete to go on. All we know is that she has a gun and might be unstable. We know she came here from Hartford, worked at Woodland Hospital. Don't you know someone in Hartford?"

Pressley nodded. "Yeah, Captain Harold Syms and I go back a way."

"Think he can help us check out Tufts?" Lex inquired.

"He might. I'll call him right now, and you can explain." Pressley picked up his phone, and called Syms. As soon as he heard a voice, Pressley said, "Harold?" A few seconds later, he responded, "Sorry to hear that, Detective Shields. I'm putting us on speaker so Detectives Lex Stall and Gil Ramos can join in." Addressing his employees, Pressley said, "Syms is out, had an emergency appendectomy. This is Detective Dan Shields."

Lex explained the situation and asked Dan to find out all he could about Lorena Tufts. He agreed to investigate. "Thank you," Lex said.

"I'll get back to you when I get some info," Dan replied.

"Please do. She may be armed and dangerous."

"So am I," Dan said.

Pressley chimed in. "Give Harold my best."

"Will do."

Lex sighed. "I don't have a good feeling about Lorena Tufts."

Chapter 7

Hutch arrived with doughnuts, and Gil nudged Benzinger. "Hold it. I have seniority." After taking a jellied, he said, "Go for it, rook."

Hutch grabbed the young detective's hand. "After me, pal."

Benzinger finally picked his doughnut, and Gil sauntered toward Lex. When he entered their workspace she shook her head. "What is it with you guys and doughnuts?"

He took a bite. "Have to keep up the public perception."

"Of what? Fat cops? How about upholding the perception that you solve crimes?"

"I felt that one, Lex." He set his once bitten food on his desk. "Let's get to work."

Lex used the desk phone and called Stillwell. He answered, and she heard a yawn. "Hello," he said.

"Mr. Stillwell, this is Detective Stall. We need to come back and take another look around Cambourd's apartment and studio."

"What time is it?"

"Ten of eight." She heard him yawn again.

"I just got up. Have to find that damned cat."

"May we come over now?"

"You know how to get in."

▲

Less than an hour later, the detectives entered the building, and Lex heard a loud TV. "He's definitely up."

Gil knocked on the door. Stillwell, wearing pajamas, opened up. With a cup of coffee in one hand and an unlit cigarette in the other, he said, "What's it like out? I need to get some shopping done. Gotta pick up roach killer too."

"Nice day," Lex replied. "We'll leave when we're done. Good luck shopping."

Stillwell retrieved keys. "Here you go; square one is the studio."

The detectives walked across the hall and Gil unlocked Cambourd's door. They entered the apartment and Lex flicked on the light switch. She went to the kitchen and didn't see any creepy crawlers. Then she opened a cabinet and swatted away a big one. Inspecting the cupboard contents, she said, "Not much here: a few dishes, glasses, and cups."

"Nothing in or under the pile of clothes on this chair," Gil said.

Lex moved toward the refrigerator, stepped on a small rug, heard a hollow sound, and felt the floor give. Bending, she drew the rug back. "Look what we have here. A hidden compartment with a wooden box inside."

Gil approached her to take a look. "What the heck? Open it."

She slid the lid off and saw several yellow envelopes stacked upon each other. Opening the top one, she said, "Cash, looks like all hundreds." She counted. "Five grand." She opened a second envelope. "Same here. Fifteen in all." She opened the others and counted. "All the same."

"Holy smoke," Gil said. "Seventy-five grand?"

"My God," Lex said as she placed the envelopes back inside the box and closed it. "I don't get it. Didn't Davidson say Cambourd had no money?"

"I'm not sure he said that. I think he said the man wasn't rich. That's a lot of money stashed away for a rainy day."

Lex handed the box to Gil. "Do you think there may have been more money downstairs that the killer made off with? Do you

36

suppose Davidson knew Cambourd wasn't a poor man?"

"I checked his briefcase."

"Right, Sherlock. He wouldn't have had anything suspicious in there. It's possible he shot Cambourd, stole money from the studio, went home, and returned there knowing he would call it in."

The cat appeared and sidled up to Lex. "Hey, kitty, you look hungry. I saw your food in the cupboard."

Lex reached in and spotted another roach, this one appeared to be dead. She grabbed a can of food and fed the kitty. "Stillwell better spray this place when he gets back."

Gil carried the money box and they headed to the workshop. Entering the studio, Lex saw her partner wince. The cleanup team had disinfected the place. However, strong chemical odors remained, enough to cause Gil to cover his nose. "The room reeks. Can't stand bleach."

"I guess you don't do the laundry. I'm sure RayAnn uses bleach. You have clean underwear, don't you?"

"I won't if we stay here too long." Gil pointed to the blank canvases and paint supplies. "What do you want to do with this stuff?"

"Can't see taking them," Lex said.

"When we get back, I want to check with Rusty. He must have the cane, wallet, and wine glasses. I assume he's doing his job checking for prints and DNA."

Lex looked at her partner. "You are talking about Rusty, right?"

Gil eyed her. "You can't let it go, Lex. Everyone screws up. We're not perfect either."

Ignoring the snarky comment, Lex said, "A killer went free because of him. You're right. I can't let that one go. We had that murderer, and the DNA gets contaminated? Rusty forgot gloves? He should have been fired."

Gil shook his head "Okay. I get it." He stepped to the metal cabinet and opened a drawer. "Hard to tell if this was rifled through or if anything is missing. I see files with artist names and museums."

"If money was the motive, then it probably was in the desk," Lex said. "Those two drawers were empty."

Gil closed the cabinet drawer and pulled open the bottom one. There he found a couple of notebooks. "Looks like he kept an inventory of his own paintings. Let's take this stuff." Lex paced the room, and Gil waited for her to stop. Then she faced her partner. "Out with it," he demanded.

She stared at the scene of the shooting. "Two shots were fired at close range, and there are no signs of a struggle. He definitely knew his killer. That brings us back to Jerry Davidson. He said the artist had few friends. So, what happened? Were he and Davidson arguing? One minute, friends and the next minute, bang…dead? The open desk drawers and the empty wallet suggest robbery as a motive, but it doesn't add up, unless Davidson was playing coy by telling us Cambourd wasn't a rich man."

"What about the cane?"

"You know what? In some sort of weird move, was placing that cane against the cabinet a form of respect for him? An apology? My gut keeps telling me Jerry Davidson knows more than he told us."

"Whoa," Gil said. "I know you don't like the guy, but we have no proof or timeline for that matter, and we haven't found a murder weapon. He could be innocent."

"Pam said two shots. Either one would have instantly killed him. You know what that means?"

Gil put his fingers together. "It usually means a vendetta or some type of self-satisfying hostility."

"But there seemed to be a friendly meeting," Lex responded. "That's the puzzling part. Wine and cheese in the back room. If that friend intended to kill Cambourd from the get-go, it doesn't make sense he waited until the artist was at his easel with a paintbrush in his hand before shooting."

"I need to get a box from the car," Gil said.

A couple of minutes later, he came back, and several items were placed into the cardboard container. "Let's get back to the precinct with all this stuff," Lex said.

"We'll have to log the money and stop at the Nineteenth to bring it to Kelly in the property room before getting back to Central Park." Although they were housed at the Central Park Precinct, the booking and evidence safekeeping processing was still done back at the Nineteenth Precinct on East Sixty-Seventh Street.

Gil placed all the taken items inside their vehicle's trunk and closed it.

About to get into the car, Lex noticed a store that drew her interest. "There's a wine and cheese shop on the corner. I bet that's where Cambourd purchased his supply. Come on. I want to check it out."

They proceeded to the neighborhood shop. Inside, she saw a variety of cheeses and a nice selection of wine. Lex showed her badge to the elder-looking white-haired man at the counter. "Looks like a good selection," she said.

"Election?" he replied.

Lex noticed the hearing aids in his ears and spoke louder. "I said you have a nice wine selection. What's your name, sir?"

"Allard Kelstrom."

Lex asked, "Was Fredrike Cambourd a customer?"

Kelstrom adjusted the volume on his ear devices. "That's better. What did you say?"

"I asked if Fredrike Cambourd was a customer."

"Comes in from time to time."

"Do you remember when he was last here?"

Kelstrom was silent. Lex could see him thinking. "Memory isn't that good. Sort of comes and goes. Don't remember."

Lex asked, "Did he pay with cash?"

"Always gave me a hundred-dollar bill and let me keep the change."

A young employee was wheeling a cart of wine boxes. He stopped at the counter. "These are cops," Kelstrom said.

Duane was the name on the employee's black shirt. "We were

asking about Mr. Cambourd," Lex said.

"Nice man. Shame."

"Do you know when you saw him last?" Lex questioned.

"I think it was a few days ago."

"What did he purchase?"

"As I recall, he only bought cheese. He usually buys wine, too, but he didn't this time."

Lex asked, "Did he say anything?"

"No, he never talked much."

"Thank you," Lex said, handing her card to the employee and one to Kelstrom. "Have a nice day," she said.

The detectives headed back toward their car, and Lex stopped in front of Stillwell's building. "Wait here. I have to do something."

"Here's the keys," Gil said. "He can have them back."

"Thanks. I hope he's there."

She headed inside. Ten minutes later, Lex exited holding Van Gogh and a bag containing cat food. "Stillwell finished his shopping, and he's happy to be rid of the cat. Liz wants one, so we're adopting it."

Gil shook his head. "You realize we have to drop off the money with Kelly and then take box of Cambourd's stuff to our office?"

"I do. Drive so we can get it done."

"And what about the cat?"

"I'll take it home with me."

Chapter 8

Van Gogh and the cat food were in the back seat of Lex's Corolla. Driving toward Greenwich Village, she thought about Lorena Tufts. *No one merely evaporates into thin air. If she is in Hartford, I hope Shields is able to find her.*

Entering her home, Lex carried in the adoptee, her purse, and the cat food. She placed Van Gogh on the floor. The feline stretched and magically scooted into the kitchen. Lex followed, and Liz, who was sitting at the computer, jumped from her chair. "Mom. A cat!" Liz knelt to pick it up. "He's so cute. Where'd you get him?"

When Lex took the cat from the apartment, she discovered Van Gogh was more like Mary Cassatt, a female. "Put her on the floor and get a bowl. I have cans of food in the bag. Get some water too. Her name is Van Gogh, and she was orphaned. We need to get a litter box. In the meantime, go get the Rubbermaid basket and some newspaper."

Liz did as she was asked. A few minutes later, Van Gogh was dining, and her new bathroom was in place. Liz took a picture with her cell and texted Shannon, *We got a cat.*

Shannon replied, *Awesome! Maybe my mom will let me get one.*

Liz texted back, *You can meet the her after school tomorrow.*

Shannon replied with a happy face emoji.

Lex was on her way upstairs to change. "You want to eat out? There's a pet shop on Bleecker. We can stop there too. Let me put on jeans and then we can go." Lex didn't need an answer, she knew

Liz would never object.

The mother-daughter duo headed to Washington Square and ate at Panera before walking to the pet shop. After purchasing a litter box and litter, they continued their walk home. Lex detoured to a place she often visited. Approaching an old record store that her late father once owned, Lex moved close to the window while Liz placed herself on a street bench. Staring inside as if her father were there, Lex silently said, *Hi, Dad. I'm fine. Liz is growing up too fast. She's a lot like me, and I know I gave you some trouble.*

Lex listened to her dad's voice. *Yes, dear, but you grew up to be pretty good.*

She replied, *Thanks. I wish you were still here. Love you.*

Imagining him talking again, she heard, *Love you too.*

Lex tapped the window before she and Liz continued toward home.

▲

With the new litter box in place and *Jeopardy* about to start, Liz, Lex, and Van Gogh gathered on the couch to tune in to Alex Trebek. When the show was over, Lex stared at her young daughter, knowing there were things she'd never told Liz.

The truth, as Lex alluded to while chatting with her father, was that she smoked her share of weed in high school, and her first experience with alcohol at age fifteen had cost Lex her virginity. She was at a friend's sweet sixteen birthday party when it happened. To this day, she wasn't sure if she'd been raped, but back then she knew she couldn't tell anyone that she had sex, except her closest friend. Lex dreaded telling Liz about this experience.

There was another dark secret that she'd kept from Liz. Lex had told her about Corey Randall, the man she thought she would marry. She'd met him while they were at NYU. He was a star hockey player at the college. Lex spent a lot of time with him attending hockey games, smoking pot, and studying as well as doing other things with

42

him in his dorm room. One of those things led to Lex's getting pregnant, but she'd subsequently lost the baby.

Then he was killed. It was a snowy, November night when Corey walked Lex home from school, and stopped at the drugstore on his way back for a pack of cigarettes. That's when he and the store owner, Mr. Linton were killed by robbers. Corey was the reason Lex decided to become a cop.

Liz was ready to walk to the kitchen. "Wait," Lex said. I think it's time we had a chat about life." The proud mother placed her arm around Liz.

"Mom. I know about the birds and bees."

Lex smiled at her daughter. "I'm sure you do, but this is about me. I was your age once, and I made a few mistakes along the way when I was a little older than you are. Especially one or two involving those birds and bees."

Thirty minutes later, Liz hugged her mother. "Mom. Don't worry about me."

Lex smiled at her pretty daughter. "You have no idea. We always worry about our children. I have to trust you."

CHAPTER 9

After stopping at Starbucks, Lex placed her expensive latte in the car's center console. Arriving at the precinct, she parked in the small lot, got out of her Corolla with her purse in one hand, and grabbed the hot drink with the other. When she shut the door, her cup slipped, and hot liquid splashed the pavement. *Nice going, Alexis. At least you didn't get any on your shoes.* She picked up the empty container, tossed it into a trash can outside the stable, and stopped to say good morning to Butterscotch. "Hey, hope your day is going better than mine."

Lex entered the squad room, and Hutch said, "You look frazzled."

"Better believe it. Four bucks down the drain. My latte is all over the lot."

"Dig in and join the rest of us." Hutch lifted his mug. "Grows hair on your chest."

"Thanks, just what I need," she replied approaching her desk.

"No latte?" Gil noticed.

"Don't ask. I'm going to the ladies' room. I'll grab a cup of our free stuff on my way back."

Returning to her office, she sipped the awful coffee, then said, "Lorena Tufts. I doubt she had anything to do with Cambourd, but I'm sure she is up to something bad."

"Suicide?"

"Maybe, but I think if she's suicidal, she also might be intent on

44

killing someone else. If it was simply suicide, then why run away? Why not just do it? I'm curious to see if Dan Shields has come up with anything." She called the Hartford detective, placing him on speaker. "Hi, Dan. This is Lex Stall."

"Hi, Lex. I was about to get back to you. I went to Woodland Hospital and spoke with Lorena Tufts' old boss. He said she went through a rough two years before her surgery. Get this: her birth name was Leonard Tufton. I have an old address and checked it out. None of her neighbors even knew she had gone to New York. Anyway, her father died five years ago, and her mother sold the house and moved to Florida. No other relatives that I can find. I'm checking hotels to see if she's registered anywhere."

"Thanks," Lex replied. She glanced over at Gil as he took the last bite of his doughnut, and she grabbed a Kleenex, handing it to her partner.

"Lucky me, a wife at home and another one at work," he commented.

She shook her head and passed him another tissue. "You missed a spot. Let's not waste the rest of the day. I'm thinking we should contact Marcus Worthington. He might have a few things to say about Davidson, in addition to Cambourd."

With a clean face, Gil called and spoke with the museum director. After disconnecting, the detective said, "We can drop in anytime."

Lex clutched her purse. "Let's go."

"Wait. You forgot something. You gonna call Rusty?"

Lex momentarily closed her eyes and picked up the desk phone. Rusty answered. "To what do I owe the pleasure of this call?"

Detecting sarcasm in his tone, Lex said, "Okay, knock it off. Any progress on prints or DNA?"

"We're processing. I'll let you know when we have something."

"Did you find a cell phone?"

"No. All we have are the wine bottle, glasses, cane, and wallet."

"We never found one either. Thanks. Let me know when you

have some results."

"Will do. Are we good now?"

Lex paused. "Perfect. Thanks."

She turned to Gil. "They're still processing the evidence, no phone. I'm ready for the museum."

With the Met only a few blocks away, they walked toward the historic building. Lex's pace was slower than usual. Even so, it didn't take long before they were front of the enormous facility. Halfway up the stairs, she looked to her left and froze while staring at the very spot her cheating bastard, ex-husband had proposed to her. It gave her chills.

Gil took her arm. "I know what you're thinking. Let's go inside. We have work to do."

They stopped at the information station to get directions to Marcus Worthington's office, and the director was advised the detectives were on their way up.

They entered the office. "Please sit," Marcus said.

Lex took a notepad and pen from her purse before she spoke. "Tell us about Fredrike Cambourd. How he came here, what he did, who his friends were, any other little tidbits about his life."

Marcus pointed to a picture on his desk. It was himself standing in front of the Musée d'Orsay in Paris. "That's quite an interesting story. My wife, rest her soul, and I vacationed in Paris many years ago." He smiled at the thought of that trip and flashed back to it. "We were on our way to that museum. There was a gallery a few blocks away that we visited. I saw paintings I would have sworn were Monet and Renoir masterpieces. A young lady, the gallery owner's daughter, told us the paintings were done by Fredrike Cambourd." Lex saw Marcus's eyes widen. "The finest replications I'd ever seen. If Monet and Renoir's signature had been on them, they could have passed as theirs. The woman told us Fredrike worked at the Musée d'Orsay.

"We got to the museum, and I asked to meet him. He spoke English fairly well and served the museum as an assistant curator. A year later, I was named director here, we had a need to hire a new conservation curator, and I reached out to him. He informed me he'd always wanted to come to New York, so it was a match that was meant to be. He accepted the job."

Lex and Gil were intently listening to this story. Marcus continued, "He took exceptional care of our vast collections of artwork. When he retired, I hated to see him go, but he wanted to paint again and make a last attempt at becoming a famed artist."

Lex saw the change in Marcus as he frowned. The director was overcome with emotion. He adjusted his glasses. "Now he's gone, tragically gone, and no one knows why. When Jerry Davidson told me Fredrike was dead, I thought I was going to have a heart attack."

Lex kept writing and asked, "When did he tell you? Jerry was with us when he called to cancel his appointment with you."

"I got his brief message, and he came here after leaving the studio."

"Was he visibly upset?"

"I could see Jerry wasn't himself and after he told me about Fredrike, we both shed tears and shared a moment of silence."

Lex felt the vibration of her phone in her purse, and took a quick look. It was her lawyer, Creighton Manning and she let the call go to voicemail. Focusing on Worthington, she asked, "Were you aware of his friends, people he may have been close with?"

"You could say Fredrike was a loner. It's not like he was a total recluse or an unfriendly sort. Several coworkers respected him, but I don't believe he had many friends."

Lex saw the director's computer and pointed to it. "Would he have used a computer here?"

"Only if he had to. He hated them."

"What about cell phones?"

"Hated them too. Sometimes it was like he was still living in the sixties."

"Do you mind telling us what he earned while he worked here?"

"You mean salary?"

Lex nodded. "Yes."

Marcus leaned back. "You know, curators are fascinating people. It's about being in a make-believe world. They love to be in the company of the great artists' works. Cleaning and restoring masterpieces makes them feel as if they were the real artists. Fredrike had a fantasy friendship with Mr. Monet, Mr. Renoir, and several other dead masters. He often worked in isolation, which was the nature of his job." Lex saw that sparkle in Marcus's eyes again. "Money is secondary. Fredrike earned ninety-eight thousand in his last year."

"I assume you have a new curator," Lex said.

"Edward Gastone was his understudy. He succeeded Fredrike as the head conservator. They worked well together, but I wouldn't say they were especially friendly. The only ones who seemed to be confidants were Jerry Davidson and myself."

"How often did you visit Fredrike?"

"His place wasn't far from here, so once in a while, I would stop by to say hello. I would often bring him a bottle of wine."

"When was the last time you were there?"

"I'd say about three weeks ago."

"Did he act any different or say anything unusual?"

"No. We just drank the wine and chatted."

"What did you talk about?" Lex asked.

"I don't remember specifically, but he enjoyed talking about his days in Paris."

Lex turned the page in her notepad. "And Mr. Davidson? How did they meet?"

"I introduced them, but I don't know much about their personal relationship. I do know that Jerry had an arrangement with him. Several of Cambourd's paintings are for sale at a high-end gallery. Heinrich Altman's, I believe."

"You're right," Lex said. She switched gears. "What do you know about Jerry Davidson?"

"He's an independent art consultant. He's helped us with several exhibits, and he's working with me now on our planned Impressionist exhibit."

"Any reason to think Jerry and Fredrike weren't getting along?"

Marcus leaned forward. "What do you mean? Jerry respected the man."

"Any reason to believe he needed money?"

"Money? He has money. Buys the best clothes. His condo on Park is more than I can afford. He's been around the world more than Columbus."

Lex closed her pad. "Thank you for taking time to speak with us." Both detectives got up and shook Marcus's hand.

When the detectives exited the museum, Lex opened her purse and took out her cell phone. "It vibrated when we were sitting," she told Gil. "It's my lawyer, Creighton Manning." She listened to the voicemail. "All it said was to call him as soon as possible. He probably wants to tell me he's gotten a response from Jon's attorney about back child support. I'll call when we get to the precinct."

▲

When she got back, Lex immediately called Manning. The attorney's secretary put her on hold for a minute before he picked up. "Hi, Lex. Thanks for calling back so soon."

Lex listened, expecting him to tell her that the back child support payments would be coming. Suddenly, her face became ashen and she shouted, "Are you serious?" She slammed her fist on the desk. "How the hell can he do that? He owes me," she yelled into the phone before ending the call. Facing her partner, she said. "I'm being sued. My ex is filing a custody suit."

Gil placed his arms around her, and Pressley rushed in. "You all right?" he asked. Lex angrily huffed, and the captain said, "Let's go to my office."

She followed him, and he closed the door. Her hands were clammy as she told the captain what had happened. "I'm being served, probably tonight. I have to see my attorney in the morning."

Pressley clutched her hand. "Go home. If there is anything I can do, I will."

Lex was shaking as she left. "Thanks. My gun is loaded. Line up a good criminal defense attorney."

CHAPTER 10

Lex was seething and distracted while driving home. She nearly side-swiped a bus before regaining control of herself. *I swear, if Jon thinks he's taking Liz from me, he better think about getting a new set of balls because I'll shoot off the ones he's got.*

A

A white Volvo was parked in front of her residence, and Lex walked past the vehicle. She climbed the front steps to her entrance, retrieved the mail, and went inside.

Checking the time, she knew Liz would be home within the hour. Lex threw her purse and mail onto the kitchen table and then heard the doorbell. Peering out a window, she saw a suited stranger holding an envelope in his hand. She had no doubt what this visitor was doing on her front steps, so she begrudgingly opened the door. "Are you Alexis Stall?" the marshal asked.

"I am," she replied. "You don't have to tell me what that envelope is."

She accepted the summons and watched him walk back to his vehicle. Lex gritted her teeth, clutched the envelope, slammed the door, and walked hastily to the kitchen to open the letter. *What am I going to tell Liz?*

The divorce with Jon was nasty. He was a two-timing husband who had affairs with fellow teachers, so Lex walked out of the marriage. Initially, the two agreed to an amicable split, but their lawyers sidetracked it into a heavyweight fight. Lex wound up with Liz, child support, and alimony. Jon got the house since the deed was slyly in his name only. She moved back to her childhood residence to live with her mother and daughter.

Sitting in the kitchen with the summons, Lex heard the front door open and Liz enter. Lex stared at her daughter. "What's the matter, Mom? Did I do something?" Liz questioned as she set her books on the table.

Lex stood and hugged her. "No Lizzie, but I have to tell you something. See this paper? It's a summons."

Liz asked, "Summons? For what?"

Lex put the paper back inside the envelope and went with her daughter into the parlor. Sitting beside Liz, and a busybody named Van Gogh, Lex placed her arm around the teenager. "Sweetheart, this is about us; me and your father," Lex sighed. "He's seeking custody."

Liz frowned. "Why? We're good."

"I don't know yet. I'm meeting with my attorney tomorrow morning. You can ask your father if you want to."

"I don't understand."

"Neither do I, but I had to let you know. Don't worry, my attorney says he'll take care of everything." Lex knew she couldn't be sure of that. "C'mon, Lizzie, let's get a pizza. We can be back in time for *Jeopardy*."

They walked seven blocks to their favorite place. Lex barely ate, and Liz carried leftover slices in a cardboard box as they walked toward the record store. Lex gazed into the window and stood silently for a moment, drifting off into another world. Her lips were moving. *Hi, Dad. Came by to say hello and to let you get a look at your granddaughter. If you haven't noticed, Liz is a lot like me.*

He answered, *I know, dear. Love you both.*

Lex frowned. *I need to tell you something, Dad, but not now. I'll be back soon.*

She listened and her mind heard him. *Whatever it is, Alexis, I'll be here.*

Liz and Lex began walking. "Mom, why do you always stop and stare inside? Grandpa isn't there anymore."

Lex squeezed Liz's hand. "Someday, you'll understand."

CHAPTER 11

L ex was awake at dawn. Wearing her bathrobe, she went down to the kitchen, made coffee and read the summons again. She sipped the liquid and waited for Liz to come downstairs.

At 6:30 a.m., Liz entered the kitchen and said, "You look tired."

"I've been up a while, and I think somebody's ready for breakfast."

Van Gogh meowed. "I'll feed her," Liz said.

"Thanks. What do you want to eat?"

"I'm not that hungry. I'll take a granola bar with me."

"Okay. I'm going up to shower and dress. I'll see you later."

Lex was soon on her way to Manning's First Avenue office, a place she'd been a few times, so she knew where to park. Entering the lobby with its gleaming marbled floor, she got into an elevator, exited on the eleventh floor, and hesitantly approached the glass door with the name *Creighton Manning* stenciled in gold. When she walked in, Manning's secretary greeted her, and Lex identified herself. "He'll be right with you Ms. Stall."

The dapper attorney opened his door and invited his client into the office. Lex remembered the view of Manhattan visible from the window to her left. Perched atop the simulated fireplace mantle to the rear of his chair, was his Harvard law degree. The attorney's executive desk displayed paperweights with likenesses of Muhammad Ali and Joe Frazier. Never married, the only photos in the room were of a Ferrari and thirty-foot boat.

"Thanks for coming, Lex. I know this is difficult." He pointed to the coffee maker in back of her. "Would you like a cup?"

"Thanks, I'll pass. I already had two." Lex nervously opened her purse and handed him the summons. "What the heck happened?" she asked. "I thought you had reached an agreement with Jon and his attorney on the back child support."

"We did agree. As you know, Jon had been out of work for six months, having been fired for striking a student while disciplining him. Jon was subsequently rehired. The board hastily fired him and did a shoddy investigation. The allegation was fabricated, and the student finally admitted it never happened. The board should only have suspended him in the first place. He'll be collecting his full salary minus whatever he got from unemployment."

"What's the problem then? He should be able to make up the payments."

"I agree, and you'll get the money, but that has nothing to do with the custody suit." Manning read the summons. "That little attorney, Asino, is a snake in the grass. He'll need to come up with a lot of dirt in order to prove that Liz is better suited to live with her father."

Lex had a blank look. "How absurd. You know how crazy I am right now? Tell me this custody thing won't fly."

Manning leaned toward his client. "Look, Lex. This isn't going to be easy, but I've been to war before. I need to find out what Asino has up his sleeve."

Lex got up. "Sleeve? He better protect what's in his pants."

Manning rose and tried to ease his agitated client. "Calm yourself. Let me do my job."

Lex took a deep breath. "I'll calm down when this is over. Standing face-to-face with a murderer would be less stressful than this."

"I understand," Manning said. "Please let me handle it. I'll call you when I have something more to tell you."

Lex shook her head. "Okay. Call me."

She left the attorney's office and headed back to her car, all the while seeing dollars in legal fees starting to pile up. *Got no choice, Alexis. Have to pay the piper to fight this one.*

▲

Lex entered the squad room and Pressley stepped out of his office. "How'd it go?" he asked.

She tried to hide her emotions. "I'm okay. Manning will get me through this."

"Good," the captain said as he retreated to his quarters.

When Lex approached Gil, she could tell he saw right through her. "I can see you're not okay."

Lex grabbed a tissue. "You're damned right I'm not. I'll be right back."

Returning minutes later from the ladies' room, she declared, "I'm ready for work."

"Not so fast," Gil said. "Exactly what happened?"

She explained what Manning had said, and then she shifted into detective mode without skipping a beat. "Jerry Davidson is going to have to come up with a solid alibi before I let him go. Listen, we know what Worthington said about him, but I want to know exactly where Davidson was before the killing and drive a truck through his alibi. How about calling him? We need to talk to him again, and he might be more cordial to you."

Gil smirked. "Might be? I think that's an understatement." He retrieved Davidson's card and made the call.

"Put him on speaker," Lex whispered.

The businessman answered. "Good morning, Mr. Davidson. This is Detective Gil Ramos. Would you mind if my partner and I came to your place to ask a few questions? It's a routine follow-up. We won't be a long."

They could hear Davidson's hesitation. "If you must, you can come now. You know where I live?"

"Marcus Worthington told us you have a condo on Park Ave. What's the address?" Gil wrote it on a pad and said, "Thanks. We'll be there shortly." He picked up car keys, and turned to Lex. "Let's go."

▲

Davidson's condo was located about seven blocks from Grand Central Station. The up-scale residence at the corner of Park Avenue and Thirty-Third was known as the Zagrin Building. The detectives went inside and were greeted by a concierge whose name, Artie, was sewn into his shirt.

"Mr. Davidson is expecting us," Lex said.

"He was here earlier to pick up his newspaper. Take the elevator, fourth floor, unit two."

On the wall adjacent to the elevator was a row of mailboxes and opposite was a small desk. A TV mounted on the wall above it was tuned to ESPN. The detectives got into the elevator and proceeded to Jerry Davidson's condo. He opened the door and welcomed his visitors into the living room. Lex thought it was nicely furnished with a cherry coffee table and matching end-tables, two contemporary upholstered chairs, and a four-cushioned couch. A plush aqua carpet stretched the length of the hallway leading to other rooms. At the rear of the living room, sliding glass doors opened to a balcony large enough for a couple of chairs, a table, and a grill.

The detectives sat on the comfortable couch while Davidson took a seat in a chair opposite them. Lex noticed a large painting leaning against the adjacent wall. "Is that a Cambourd?" she asked.

Davidson replied, "It is."

"Reminds me of Monet," Lex said.

"Yes, it really does. I haven't gotten around to hanging it yet."

Lex crossed her legs and was ready to take notes, while her partner was set to look for hesitations and eye movements; any telltale sign that could signify a lie. "We had a nice chat with Marcus

Worthington," she said. "He was very upset and told us you had gone to see him right after you left the studio. We thought you cancelled that appointment."

"I couldn't wait, I had to tell him about Fredrike."

She responded, "If I remember correctly, you stated you helped Mr. Cambourd sell his paintings at a gallery."

"That's correct. Heinrich Altman's."

Lex viewed the room again and saw a few wine bottles in a rack. Then she spotted something interesting on the fireplace mantle and nudged Gil. He silently acknowledged the subtle message to do some snooping. She asked their host for a glass of water, and Gil requested to use the bathroom. Davidson directed him down the hallway, and asked Lex if she would prefer Perrier. "That would be very nice. Thank you," she said. "I'm sure my partner would appreciate some too."

Gil headed toward the lavatory, and Davidson went into the kitchen. She thought, *Well that nice gesture is certainly out of character. Does he think he's going to get me to ease up by offering Perrier?* With both men out of the room, Lex got up to take a closer look at what she had seen and then returned to the couch.

Davidson placed a glass and a napkin on the table in front of the couch. Gil neared the kitchen on his way back to his partner, and Davidson said, "There's a glass of Perrier on the counter for you."

Gil fetched the drink that was sitting next to a coffee mug and what appeared to be spilt sugar on the counter. He took a sip and walked to the couch, setting the glass on a table napkin.

Lex picked up her glass and drank from it. She looked at Davidson, again sitting across from the detectives. Resuming her questioning, she asked, "Would you mind telling us again about arriving at the studio and finding Mr. Cambourd?"

"I got there about nine a.m., knocked on his door and when he didn't answer, I went inside and saw his body. I knew he was dead. I yelled for help, but no one came, so I called Nine-One-One. Then I puked my guts out."

Lex thought about what the man just said. *I don't recall him saying he yelled for help.*

Davidson continued. "I was careful not to touch anything and waited for help to arrive."

Lex was quick to note that unnatural response. *Why would he make it a point to say he touched nothing?*

She let him keep talking. "I was speechless and sick, especially after vomiting." He closed his eyes. "I couldn't stomach looking at all that blood, and the smell got to me. I walked to the back room. I wanted to leave and go to my appointment."

Lex stared at him. *I could swear the officer told us Davidson was dazed, and he escorted him to the back room. Now the guy says he walked into the back room by himself.* "You walked straight to the back room by yourself and stayed there? And you said you didn't touch anything."

"That's what I said."

"I was under the impression an EMT examined you."

"Oh, yeah. Took my vitals and asked about nausea. I said I just needed to sit here a little longer."

"It hadn't occurred to you that you might want to cancel your appointment?"

"I couldn't think straight." He cringed. "It was horrible."

"It was. I'm sure that's why you were so nervous when we questioned you." Lex had heard him again say he'd gotten to Cambourd's close to nine a.m. "Can you explain something?" she asked.

"Like what?"

"You told us you got there at nine, a few minutes one way or another, but the call for help came in at nine-eighteen. Why the delay?"

Lex saw the blank look on Davidson's face. He said, "I don't know. I guess I froze, became numb for a few minutes before I realized what to do."

She fired off the next question. "When was the last time you saw

Mr. Cambourd, prior to the morning of March 18?"

"It was a few days before."

"Do you remember what you discussed that day?"

"Not really. I only stopped to see how he was doing."

"Why do you suppose somebody would kill him?" Lex inquired.

"I already told you. I can't even think of anyone who disliked him."

She examined Davidson's face, and he began to sweat like he had when questioned at the murder scene. "We noticed there was no cell phone or computer in either of his places. Does that strike you as odd?"

Davidson furrowed his brow. "Not at all. He hated technology, but he did have a flip phone."

That answer coincided with what Worthington told them, except for the flip phone. That was new information. Lex continued, "You said he had few friends. Do you know any?"

"Just Marcus."

Lex had an idea and solicited, "Could you do me a favor? You have Cambourd's cell number, right?"

"Yes. Why?"

"May I have it?" She knew no one would answer the dead man's phone if she called, but if the artist's phone was somewhere in Davidson's place, she was hoping it might ring. It could be dead, but she had to take that shot.

Davidson recited the number, and Lex called. The phone rang, but no sound came from inside the condo, so she disconnected. "No answer and no voicemail." Lex paused and then turned up the heat. "Do you mind telling us exactly where you were on the evening of the seventeenth?"

Davidson wiped sweat from his forehead. "I was at Heinrich Altman's gallery until around eleven-thirty, came home, and went to bed," he snapped. "Woke up about eight, had breakfast, and went to Fredrike's studio. The rest you already know." Davidson's face was taut with anger. He stood and harshly said, "You still think I killed him, don't you?"

Lex made direct eye contact and noticed his were glassy. "I'm not making any accusations. I only want answers."

Agitated, he took a few steps back and forth before again sitting. "I walked straight home, and I got here a little after midnight and went to bed."

Lex uncrossed her legs and edged forward. "You said you were his closest friend, right?"

"Yes."

"How often did you drink wine with him?"

"Occasionally, but it was usually a special event like when he sold a painting."

Lex took a breath and firmly said, "Think. Who else was close enough to share a late-night bottle of wine with him?"

"I can't think of anyone except for maybe Marcus Worthington."

"How often did you make it up to the apartment?"

"Only a couple of times. It was a clutter box. He spent most of his time in the studio and only used his apartment to sleep and eat." Still sweating and glaring at Lex, he glanced at his Rolex and uttered, "I hate to cut our chat short, but I have another appointment."

Having heard that line before, Lex stared at him. This time she picked up her notepad and decided to end the discussion, but the sharp-eyed detective needed one more question answered. "Where's your gun, Mr. Davidson?"

"I already told you. I don't have one."

Lex moved close to him. Demanding an answer, she said, "Then how do you explain the certificate on your fireplace mantle from the American Gun Club? Why did you lie to us?"

"Jesus Christ. So I own a gun. I didn't tell you because I wanted to leave the studio and get you off my back."

"Do you mind if we see the weapon?" Lex challenged.

"I'll get the damned gun. It hasn't been fired in years."

Davidson stormed off to another room and came back with the

handgun. "Here, you happy now?"

Lex and Gil looked at the Smith and Wesson. "Not quite. Can we see your permit?" she asked.

"For God's sake. It's registered." He went to get the paperwork, reentered the room, and handed it to her. "Here. Are you satisfied?"

Lex scanned the paper. "Happy as a lark, sir. Thank you. One more thing. You said this weapon hasn't been fired in a while. Just how long ago did you shoot it? Would you mind telling us about that?"

Irked by that question, Davidson replied in a hostile voice, "I shot it at the range, maybe two, three years ago. Any more questions, or are we finally done?"

Lex smiled at him. "We're done...for now, sir. Thanks for your hospitality."

The interrogation was over, and Davidson opened the door to let his guests out. When the detectives reached the lobby, Lex stopped. "Wait a sec." She swung back and walked up to the concierge. "Artie, is there someone here all the time?"

"No. Me and Jensen work from six a.m. to six p.m. We alternate four and three."

Lex asked, "Is the entrance locked when you two are not working?"

Artie answered, "Yes. Residents have keys and they can buzz visitors in."

"Are there cameras in this lobby?" Lex asked.

"Yes, ma'am. The security company is Wintergreen Security. Their sticker is on the front door."

The detectives walked outside, and Gil wrote the name and number of the company on his pad. When they got into the squad car, Lex asked her partner, "What did you find in the bathroom?"

"Not much, it's very tidy. There were a couple of scrips in the medicine cabinet. Xanax was one; the other was Flomax. I use that myself." Lex stared at Gil, and he stared back. "It's not like Viagra. It controls your peeing," he said.

Lex laughed. "I know. Just checking to see if you had any problems at home. I want to get a look at the lobby video to see exactly what time Davidson got home from Altman's."

"What about the cell phone?" Gil asked?

"That's a mystery." Lex paused. "You know what really bothers me? Why did Davidson have to tell us he didn't touch anything? I never asked. He just threw it out there. I'm not buying it. I'm not sure I believe his explanation of the approximate fifteen minute gap in time from when he got there until he called for help. He's hiding something, and it might be murder." She then uttered, "It's obvious he doesn't like me. He's slick, offering Perrier. If he thought that was going to get me to back-off, I think he knows it didn't work."

CHAPTER 12

Lex paced the squad room. *Did Davidson get home when he says he did? He lied about the gun, so what else did he lie about? The Zagrin lobby video could be interesting.* She neared the designated snack area as Gil entered the room. "You're early today," he said while approaching the coffee pot.

Hutch was picking through the doughnuts. "She's been walking around ever since I got here."

"Save me one," Gil replied.

Lex approached her two comrades and tapped her partner on his shoulder. "How about giving the security company a call?"

"Can it wait until I get my coffee?"

"Make it quick and don't take one of those things."

Hutch said to Lex, "Wouldn't hurt if you had a doughnut every now and then."

She glared at him. "Wouldn't hurt if you had *only* one every now and then." Lex then redirected Gil, moving him away from the table. "Don't even think of it. Grab that cup and let's go."

"Okay, okay." He took his drink and followed his assertive partner to their cube. Setting the coffee down, he reached into the top drawer and took out the Wintergreen Security phone number. "I'm calling them."

"Wait. They might be willing to give it to us, or they may insist on a court order."

"I guess we'll find out what they will do," Gil said as he dialed the number.

Lex heard him talking and she saw his head shake. When the call ended, he turned to her. "No luck. Since there was no crime committed there, they insist on the paperwork."

"I'll get the boss on it," Lex replied. She strode into Pressley's office. "We need to get the video from the lobby of Jerry Davidson's condo, but the company won't release it without a court order."

"Do me a favor," Pressley said. "E-mail me the details of exactly what you need, and I'll take care of it."

She crossed her arms and stared at her boss. "E-mail? I'm right here."

Pressley stared back at her. "Don't give me that look."

Lex peered at the captain and curled her lip. Pressley nodded and shook his head. "Okay," he said, "I'll get the damned warrant."

"That's more like it, sir."

Pressley took the necessary information and when he was finished writing, Lex said, Thanks, sir."

"You're welcome, Miss Marple, and don't give me that phony 'sir' stuff." The captain smiled at her as she exited his office.

Lex tapped Gil's shoulder. "All set, he's on it. I'm going to the ladies' room."

"You go there a lot."

"Maybe I need to get away from all the testosterone in this room. Ever thought of that?"

"Hostile, are we?" Gil remarked.

"Grab a doughnut while I'm in there, and you'll see hostile."

"You sound an awful lot like my wife."

"Yeah, but I don't think she'd shoot you. I might."

She came back from the lavatory, picked up a pad, and opened to her notes. "Jerry Davidson said we could find Cambourd paintings at the Heinrich Altman gallery. We need to visit the place."

"That's what I was thinking. I'm one step ahead, Lex. His gallery is on Sixth Avenue near Bryant Park. We can walk there. Want me to call him?"

"I'll call," Lex said. Altman's assistant, Laura answered and summoned him to the phone. Lex's conversation with Altman was short and cordial. Minutes later, the detectives were on their way to the gallery.

▲

When they reached Altman's, Lex looked in the window, and viewed a couple of magnificent paintings. She also noticed that the gallery wasn't open to the public. It was appointments only. Gil pressed the doorbell, and a female appeared allowing the detectives to enter. "I'm Laura. Heinrich told me to expect you."

"Thank you," Lex said.

Inside the large showroom, track lighting illuminated paintings hung on the walls. A baby grand piano was in one corner of the large showroom.

The detectives followed Laura to Altman's office. The dark-suited, middle-aged man was waiting for them, and welcomed his visitors. "Please have a seat." He pointed. "Those chairs are quite comfortable."

Enclosed locked bookcases with shelves of Asian artifacts occupied an entire wall. In the center was an encased bronze vase that was no more than twelve inches high. On the desk was an expensive looking teak box, and a computer. Behind Altman's desk was a credenza. On top were a coffee maker, and a tray with liquor bottles and glasses. A file cabinet and safe were to the right of the credenza.

Lex said, "You have a lovely gallery. It almost feels like a museum."

Altman grinned. "That's kind of you. I've been in the business all my life. The funny thing is, I can't draw a stick figure."

"I hear you," Gil chuckled. "That's about the only thing I can draw."

Lex said, "We'd like to discuss Fredrike Cambourd."

66

Altman momentarily closed his eyes and shook his head. "Tragic. Fredrike was a talented artist. I've sold several of his paintings."

"How well did you know him?" Lex asked.

"I met him at the Met a few years back, but that was the only time I'd ever seen him."

Lex said, "As we understand it, Jerry Davidson had an arrangement with you and Mr. Cambourd."

"True. He brought the artists paintings here."

"What do you know about Jerry Davidson?"

"At one time he worked for Sutherland Auctions and then he decided to go on his own and become a broker. He also works for museums." Altman scratched his neatly trimmed goatee."

"Are there any Cambourd paintings in the gallery?" Lex asked.

"There are. Would you like to see them?"

"Yes," she said. "We saw one in Jerry Davidson's condo. Curiously, there were none in the artist's studio or his apartment. There was only a partially painted portrait in the studio that was severely damaged when he was murdered."

Gil asked, "How much are his paintings?"

Altman gently stroked his salt-and-pepper chin hair. "That's an interesting question because last week, I sold one for twelve thousand. If I had that same painting right now, I would be asking twenty-five. Death always increases the value of an artist's works."

Lex was curious to know the business arrangement. "Mind if I ask, what was your deal with Davidson and Cambourd?"

Altman flipped the lid on his teak cigar box, placed a wrapped stogie in his hand, and said, "It's a little complicated. Depends on size and market value. The paintings sold for between twelve and sixteen."

"What about the profits? How were they split?"

Altman unwrapped the cigar but didn't light it. "I normally don't have a middleman to deal with, so it's usually a fifty-fifty split with the artist. This time we each got one-third."

"Do you know how many of his paintings you have sold?"

"Nine or ten. I'm pretty sure it's ten."

Lex shifted the questioning. "Was Davidson here the evening of March seventeenth?"

"Yes, we had an exhibit for one of my new collections."

"Do you remember what time he left?"

"It was around eleven-thirty. I closed up and left shortly thereafter."

"Do you mind telling me where you went after leaving here?"

Altman held the unlit cigar. "Home. I live in Westchester. Got there about an hour later."

Lex asked. "Did you and he discuss Cambourd?"

"We briefly talked about him. I was concerned that he had not been painting as much."

"Did Davidson make any phone calls while he was here?"

"Not that I remember." He fiddled with the cigar. "Wait. I do remember him talking to someone before he left here, but I have no idea who that was."

Lex gave Gil a nod, and they thanked Altman. "May we see the artwork now?" she asked.

"Follow me," Altman said. They entered the gallery, and he pointed to the Cambourd paintings. "He loved the Impressionists."

Lex observed five pieces with Cambourd's signature. "These are similar to the one in Davidson's place. Very Monet-like. Thank you for showing them to us."

The detectives left the gallery and started walking. "At least Jerry Davidson's story checks out," Gil said.

Lex stopped. "Yes, but we still don't know what time he got home, and there's a new twist. We have another person of interest, and his name is Heinrich Altman. He has a motive...money. Cambourd died, and now the paintings are worth significantly more. That's a pretty good incentive to kill someone or have them killed. He said he drove right home. We don't know that to be true. The only thing we know is, up until midnight, Jerry Davidson has an ironclad alibi."

Heading back to the precinct, Lex's cell vibrated. She opened her purse, answered the call, and struggled to hear her lawyer's voice. "Creighton," she yelled into the phone, "I'm on Sixth and can barely hear you."

"I can tell," he shouted. "Those jackhammers are loud. Call me back."

As soon as the detectives got back, she promptly phoned Manning. "Hi, Creighton."

"We need to talk. Can you stop by here first thing tomorrow?"

"What's happening?"

"It's about Jon."

"What did you find out?"

"Be here at nine. I'll fill you in."

"Creighton," she said. "This sounds bad."

"Trust me. See you in the morning."

Placing the phone back into her purse, she told Gil, "I have to see him tomorrow morning." She paused. "He said not to worry. That's like a doctor saying you might experience a little discomfort. I need to tell Pressley I'll be late."

After informing the captain, she felt her heart beating fast, and her anxiety reaching a fevered pitch as she headed to her car. She took several deep breaths. *Keep it together, Alexis. Stay calm. I have to maintain my cool for Liz's sake.*

▲

She made it home and smiled at her daughter. "How was school?"

"Good. We need some more cat food."

Lex tried to keep her poise. She knew she had to take a walk. "You know what? I'm not hungry. Ate a late lunch. There should be enough chicken from last night for you. I'm going for a walk, and I'll pick up the cat food."

"I'll come."

"Not this time, sweetheart."

"Say hi to Grandpa. You're going there, aren't you?"

Lex hugged her daughter. "Yes, I have to."

Reaching the record store, she gazed into the window. *Something really bad is happening, Dad. That bastard Jon is playing games with me.*

Games? What is it, Alexis?

I should have listened to you. Somehow, you knew Jon was a womanizer. The bitter divorce was one thing, but now he's fighting for custody of Liz. My attorney is going to fight for me. Wish us luck, Dad. I'll stop by again soon.

Lex headed home and thought about the day of her wedding. Everything from the church ceremony to the reception was perfect, except for one thing she saw but chose to ignore. It was the look Jon had shared with one of her bridesmaids. The eye contact and his admiring of her figure, as if he'd seen it without the crimson gown. The fact was, he had not only seen it, he'd slept with her two nights before. Lex shook her head. *All the signs were there, but I was stupidly blind to them...and he's got the kahunas to sue me.*

Lex stayed awake most of the night imagining what Manning might say this time.

CHAPTER 13

Dressed in a gray pant suit and sleep deprived, Lex arrived at her attorney's office with a hot drink in hand. "Good morning, Ms. Stall," his secretary said.

Manning came out of his office, escorted Lex inside, and closed the door. She placed her latte on the corner of his desk. "How are you?" he asked.

Lex settled into a chair and sipped her drink. "I'm okay, at least I'm trying to be." She adjusted her position, waiting for him to speak.

"I met with Asino in his office." Manning passed an envelope to her. "Open it."

She opened the envelope and saw a certified check. "How about that? Five grand, back support."

"Yes," Manning said. "That's the good news. It's paid to clear the record. However, he's playing a game intended to make us think twice about going to court." Manning leaned toward his client. "I'm not about to let him and Jon make us back away from a good fight."

Lex had a blank look on her face. "What are you getting at?"

"Here it is. Asino has drawn up a list of allegations. If we go to court, he'll argue each one." Lex closed her eyes and shook her head while Manning opened a file. "I need your reaction to these accusations."

Lex curiously said, "Go ahead."

"Jon claims your job interferes with the ability to provide a stable home for Liz because you are often on call and sometimes leave her alone in the middle of the night."

Lex's agitation was apparent as she threw her hands up. "Never! I have a very good neighbor I can wake at a moment's notice, and she comes over to be with Liz. She even gets her off to school."

"Would that be Sheila Wyatt?"

"Yes."

Manning waited a beat. "Looks like they've done some checking on her. She may be a problem because apparently, she has an alcohol addiction, and she dropped out of AA. What do you know about her issue?"

Lex stared incredulously at her attorney. "When she moved in several years ago, Sheila had been through a rough time due to the sudden death of her husband. Her quick answer was liquor, but I knew she went regularly to AA. She said she was doing fine."

"Are you sure she doesn't drink anymore?"

"I'm not positive, but I haven't seen any signs of alcohol around her."

"How confident are you if she was called to testify that she'd say she's clean?"

Lex threw her arms up. "I don't know."

"We have a problem because according to Asino, Liz told Jon she sometimes smells liquor on Sheila's breath. We both know recovering alcoholics don't drink occasionally, so either she drinks or she doesn't. And what would Liz say under oath?"

"Are you saying they might subpoena her?"

"Asino could subpoena Sheila and Liz." Lex's face grew red. "What time do you usually get home from work?" Manning asked.

"Why? Is that an issue too? Liz and her friend Shannon are always together after school. If they're not at my house, they're at Shannon's. Her mother, Elaine, and I are friends."

Lex reached for her drink and her hand shook. "Lex, take it easy. I'm asking so I can prepare a defense. The allegation is that Elaine works too, and the two teens are left unsupervised until you or she gets home."

Lex had fire in her eyes as she took a healthy sip of coffee, and then muttered, "What's wrong with that? They're old enough to be alone during the day."

Manning hesitated. "I think you're right, but that's prime time for kids to be doing pot, drugs, and sex. The court may view it differently than you and me."

Clearly angry, Lex rose out of her chair and put her hands on her hips. "I can see where this is going. Do I have to quit my job, for God's sake?"

Manning stood as well. "I don't think that's necessary, but I wanted to tell you what we're up against. Now let's both take a breath." Begrudgingly, she glared at Manning. "One other thing. Do you leave a loaded gun on your nightstand?"

Lex was livid. "What? Yes, I have a gun, but it's in the nightstand, and it's not loaded. Do they think I'm stupid?"

"Listen, Lex. I'm merely setting the record straight. I don't want any surprises when we go to court. This needs to get personal. Do you ever drink, do drugs, or have men sleep over?"

Lex put her hands on the desk. "No. Never. That's ridiculous! Who came up with that one?" She was close to tears. Infuriated, she barked, "Is he serious? No. I haven't even dated since our divorce." She picked up her tepid latte and finished it. "I need to visit the ladies' room."

Lex looked into the mirror and took a few deep breaths. *This is worse than I could have imagined.* She calmed herself and trudged back into to the lawyer's office.

He waited until she was seated. "We need to talk about Jon. I want to know about his behavior since the divorce, including visitations with Liz."

Lex admitted Jon had never cancelled a visit. "Hate to say it, but he's been a good father."

"What about his wife, Julie?"

Lex's voice rose. "That slut? I guess the only saving grace is that he married her. Now that she's a stay-at-home, it wouldn't surprise me if Jon was banging some other teacher whore."

Manning shook his head. "Hold it, Lex. We know about his past."

Lex felt her blood pressure rising. "This is ridiculous. I'm a damn good mother. That bastard has no right to do this! I pack a gun, you know. I might shoot his head off or something lower! And that bastard better not subpoena Liz."

Manning held back and tolerated Lex's rant before once again attempting to calm her. "No, I don't think they would subpoena Liz, but it could happen. Look, Lex, I know how upset you are. I can play games too. I'm going to check out Jon, and I have a few connections in the judicial system. I can get us in front of Judge Charlotte Fleming. She's a divorced, single mother with custody of her two teenaged girls." Manning leaned in. "She'll be able to relate to you." He glanced at his watch. "Lex, trust me. You need to let me do my job."

Lex got up and left her cup on the desk. "Great. Call me." She walked out of his office. *Is this all I have to gamble on, a judge who may be on my side? I don't like those odds. And if they think Liz is going to testify, well, over my dead body.*

Lex had to hold herself together in order to survive the day, so she made her second Starbucks stop on the way to the precinct.

⚊

She forced a smile but couldn't hide her sadness as she whisked past Starsky and Hutch.

Gil asked, "What happened with Manning? You look like you could kill someone."

Pressley entered their cubicle. "What's wrong?" he asked. "Bad question. In my office now!"

Gil escorted her into the captain's office and closed the door. With tears in her eyes, she said, "I think I threatened to shoot him."

"Manning?" Pressley questioned.

"No, Jon. Well, I don't know. Maybe I threatened Manning too."

Pressley suggested, "You need some time off?"

Lex gritted her teeth. "No, I need to be a cop now."

"Good. I have something for you." The captain reached into the tray to his left. "This is Rusty's report. Interesting reading. One set of fingerprints on the wine glasses were Cambourd's. The other set was an unidentified person who left traces of lipstick on her glass. Those prints aren't on file. Take a look at this, though." Lex and Gil leaned in while the captain continued. "There were two sets of prints on the wallet. Cambourd's were all over it, but there was a second set of partials that were undefinable. The desk prints were checked. IAFIS matched them to Jerry Davidson."

Lex took the report from Pressley. "Jerry Davidson. Doesn't surprise me. I wonder if he had a friend with him. The other prints obviously don't belong to Lorena Tufts. They would have matched her gun permit. Great, now we have an unidentified female."

The detectives went back to their workspace. Lex read the lab report. "Not what we were hoping for."

Benzinger rapped on Lex and Gil's half-wall. "Hey, this just came." He handed her a FedEx package.

"The video," she said. "Thanks."

"What exactly is it?" Benzinger inquired.

"The lobby of Jerry Davidson's building," Lex replied. Opening the envelope, she removed the disc. "Let's see what we have."

"Mind if I watch?" Benzinger asked.

"Sure." Lex said as she turned to her computer and inserted the disc. "Let's skip to around eleven-thirty and run it from there. Davidson said he arrived about twelve."

They kept watching. "Where the hell is he?" Lex wondered.

"Fast-forward it," Gil said.

She advanced the footage and Davidson appeared and 1:37 a.m. Lex paused the disc. "I knew it. He said he got home around midnight and went to bed. There goes his alibi." She restarted the footage. "I want to see what time he left the building in the morning."

Gil said, "There. Davidson's leaving at 8:26 a.m. Walked right past Artie."

Lex had hoped to see something, perhaps a glimpse of a gun from their suspect's jacket, but nothing was visible. However, the timeline was off. She blurted, "That son of a bitch has some explaining to do. Where did he go after leaving Altman's? We know when he left the gallery, and we now know when he actually got home, but he needs to explain that roughly two-hour gap in time."

"Sounds like a good one," Benzinger said as Lex removed the disc.

"He's a prime suspect for sure. Now we have to nail him," Gil said.

"That's exactly what I plan to do," Lex replied.

Benzinger walked over to his partner, while Gil and Lex went to the captain's office to tell him what they'd seen. "I'm looking forward to grilling Davidson again. I wonder how much I can make him sweat," Lex said.

"I'm sure you'll test him," Pressley said.

Lex heard her desk phone and the detectives returned to their cube. She answered, "Hello, Mr. Worthington."

"Yes, Detective Stall, I'm sorry for the late notice. I meant to call you earlier. Anyhow, I wanted to let you know, Jerry Davidson and I arranged a funeral for Mr. Cambourd."

"I didn't know the body had been released."

"Yes. A couple of days ago. The funeral is tomorrow morning in West Babylon, Long Island at Water's Edge Cemetery. Ten a.m."

"We'll be there. Thank you."

"What was that all about?" Gil asked.

"Worthington said Cambourd's body had been released. Davidson signed for it and there's going to be a funeral tomorrow morning."

"Where?"

"A cemetery in West Babylon. I said we'd be there. Better get here bright and early because we have about an hour drive."

"Isn't that awfully fast for a corpse to be released?" Gil asked.

Lex said, "Depends on the pathologist. I'm pretty sure a body can be released forty-eight hours after the autopsy."

CHAPTER 14

Water's Edge Cemetery was high on a hill overlooking Long Island Sound. The morning sun whispered in and out from behind gray clouds while gusts of wind slithered through the tree-lined burial ground.

Lex and Gil stood beside Jerry Davidson, Marcus Worthington, Heinrich Altman, and a few museum employees whom the detectives did not know.

A hearse was parked fifty feet from the grave site. Four men dressed in black suits carried Fredrike Cambourd's casket to its final resting place, while the clergyman waited for them to place the pine box on the belts that would lower it into the ground.

The men retreated and the pastor opened a prayer book to begin the service. The small crowd bowed their heads and the clergyman recited his first selection.

Lex looked up and saw something interesting. She nudged Gil. "Look straight ahead by that tree in the distance."

"I see her."

A tall woman wearing a black dress with a white sweater and a black hat was observing the rite. Nearby was a silver car. "Keep an eye on her," Lex said.

Gil did, but before he could get out his cell phone to snap a picture, she was gone. He nudged his partner. "She's gone. Someone else was with her. She got into that silver sedan that's leaving."

A few minutes later, the service ended, and the slain artist was laid to rest. Worthington paid the pastor and headed back to the Met with his staff. Altman drove off in his Mercedes with his passenger, Jerry Davidson.

"Who was she?" Gil wondered.

"Could she be the visitor who had wine with Cambourd?" Lex replied. She thought for a second. "If it's a friend's car, we're out of luck, but if it was an Uber or Lyft we can find out."

▲

An hour later, they were in their workspace. Lex said, "I'm calling Davidson. We need to see what he has to say about the video. How about checking Uber and Lyft?" she said to her partner.

While Gil was making his calls, Lex phoned Davidson. His cell rang three times before he answered. "Nice funeral wasn't it, Detective Stall?"

"It was. Gil and I need to talk with you again as soon as possible. Can we swing by later?"

Davidson laughed. "Later? How much later? Hear that noise in the background? I'm at LaGuardia at a TSA checkpoint. I'm headed to London."

Stunned, Lex questioned, "When will you be back?"

"Can't say for sure. I haven't booked my return flight. Could be a few days, maybe a week, or two. I'm sure you'll keep Manhattan safe until I get home."

"How about calling me when you get back?"

Lex was sure she heard the man chuckling. "Sure thing."

"Have a nice trip," she said before ending the call.

She turned to Gil who had just spoken with an Uber manager. "She didn't take Uber,"

"Guess what?" Davidson is at LaGuardia. He's on his way to London for a while."

"How long?"

"He wouldn't say. Could be a couple of weeks." His words

79

gnawed at her. *Keep Manhattan safe? That son of a bitch. I'll get him.*

"Let me try Lyft," Gil said.

Lex listened and a few minutes later, he turned to her. "No luck." She replied. "Then it had to be her car, or a friend's car."

Lex's phone rang. "Hi Sedona, any news?"

"Lorena hasn't called, and I'm holding her paycheck. I'm worried."

"We're still trying to locate her. We've got the Hartford police checking too. Let me ask you something. I believe you said she worked the evening of March seventeenth."

Sedona replied, "She did."

Lex asked, "If I remember right, you said her shift ended at midnight."

"That's correct."

"Thanks, Sedona. I'll keep you posted." Lex began pacing the squad room. *Interesting. Could I be wrong? Could she have killed Cambourd and vanished? She could easily have walked into the studio without anyone hearing or seeing her.* Lex pulled up her chair and moved it next to Gil. "Sedona just called me. Lorena finished her shift at midnight the night Cambourd was killed, and I'm sure she knew he would be in his studio."

Gil shrugged. "What are you saying? You think she could have killed him?"

"It's possible." Lex got up and placed her hands on his shoulders. "It's also possible she saw someone. Maybe she saw the killer."

"That makes more sense, but why would she up and leave before the crack of dawn?"

"I don't know, but there was nothing on her calendar beyond her last workday. It's also possible, she may never have gone back to her apartment."

CHAPTER 15

Entering her home, Lex took off her shoes and headed to the kitchen. Van Gogh was in Shannon's arms. "She's so cute," Liz's friend said. "I asked my mom, but she's not ready to adopt one." Van Gogh leapt onto the floor, and the cat rushed off to her litter box.

"Can I eat at Shannon's?" Liz inquired. "We have a test tomorrow, and we need to study."

"If it's okay with Elaine, it's okay with me."

"I already asked my mom," Shannon said.

"Fine," Lex responded. "I'll be going for a walk, and I'll stop by after. Tell your mom."

Liz and Shannon picked up their backpacks and left the house. Lex changed her clothes and then took that walk. She had one place in mind. Staring into the record shop window, she whispered. *Hi, Dad. Remember everything I told you? I'm a wreck inside, and I'm afraid I won't handle it well if Liz is gone.*

She was silent, then heard, *I love you. Be patient. Things have a way of working out.*

Thanks, Dad.

Lex stopped at a nearby café and had a bite. She opened her purse intending to call Liz, but there was no phone inside. Realizing she'd left it on the kitchen counter, she shut the purse.

Leaving the café, she walked to Elaine's house before returning home with Liz.

Entering the kitchen, Lex picked up her phone and noticed a message from her attorney, so she returned the call. "Hi Creighton,"

"How are you doing?" he asked.

"I'm okay."

"I heard from Asino earlier. He's pushing for a mediator. I told him we'd discuss it, but I'm not entertaining his request. I don't think he knows I have an in with Fleming and will be holding out for her. She's checking her schedule."

"Are you sure she's the right judge?"

"Look, she's divorced with two kids, so if she isn't the right judge, then there is no right judge. Trust me."

"Okay. Call me when you hear something."

After Liz went to bed, Lex remained awake until nearly midnight. She heard her father's voice again telling her to be patient. Finally, she went upstairs and fell asleep.

CHAPTER 16

L ex's anger toward Jerry Davidson was magnified by his sudden dash to London. She thought, *What if he doesn't return?*

She said to Gil, "I want to talk to Altman again. Davidson is gone, but Altman may be able to tell us who the mystery lady is."

"Good idea. I'll call him."

Lex peeked at the wall clock that read 8:30 a.m. "It's early. If he's not there, leave a message."

Thirty minutes later, Gil's phone rang. Heinrich Altman said, "I got your message. I'll be here all day."

"Great," Gil replied. "We'll be there soon."

As they headed out, Hutch leaned over and whispered to Gil, "You two going to a motel again?"

Gil replied, "Better, the Roosevelt."

Lex was a few steps ahead of her partner. "What kind of smart-ass comment did he make?"

"He said how lucky I am to have you for my partner."

"It's a nice day, so let's walk."

▲

Arriving at the gallery, Laura escorted the detectives into Altman's office. "What can I do for you?" he inquired.

Gil glanced at the encased twelve-inch vase. "You know, for some reason, that little artifact intrigues me," he said.

Altman grinned. "It's quite old. I paid a lot for it. It's a Chinese beaker, sometimes called a Ku. Very rare."

Sitting on a chair with pen in hand, Lex was ready to ask questions when Gil asked, "Would you mind if I used the bathroom?"

Altman pointed. "Across the hall."

A few minutes later, Gil came back. Lex tapped her pen and looked at Altman. "We know Jerry Davidson went to London after the funeral. I take it he asked you for a ride?"

"Yes. He told me he'd be leaving after the funeral, and he asked if I could drive him to the cemetery and then drop him off at the airport."

"When did you find out about the funeral?"

"Only a day before. Jerry was here, and I told him I would come. That's when he asked for the ride."

"Tell me," Lex requested, "when he left here after your exhibition, when was the next time you heard from him?"

"He called me the following afternoon to tell me about Fredrike."

"What did he say?"

Altman leaned back in his chair. "He said Cambourd was dead. Shot and killed in his studio."

"Did he say anything else about that morning?" Lex asked.

As was his habit, the gallery owner removed a stogie from his teak box. "Not really," he answered. "He sounded very upset and didn't want to talk about it. He said he went to see Worthington."

Lex switched gears. "Did you notice a female standing in the distance at the funeral?"

"No. Why?"

"We saw a woman observing the proceedings and then she vanished in a silver car."

"I did see the car."

Lex glanced at the artwork on Altman's wall. "I'm curious about something you had told us. You said as soon as you found out

Cambourd was dead you upped the prices on his paintings."

Altman's palms were suddenly facing out in front of him. "Whoa. I also stated it's not unusual after an artist dies. What's wrong with raising the ask?"

"I noticed none of the paintings in your gallery have price tags," Lex said.

He nodded. "Ah, you also notice this is a high-end gallery. My clients are wealthy. They don't need to be shown numbers. If they're interested in a piece, then we negotiate a fair offer."

"I recall, you said the Cambourd paintings were sold between twelve and sixteen thousand, and the proceeds were split evenly. Is that correct?"

"They were. Why are you asking?"

Lex continued, "I'm the curious type. Did you pay the artist directly?"

"I paid Jerry, and he gave Cambourd his share. I had no contact with the artist. Actually, Jerry wanted it that way."

"Let me ask you this," Lex said. "Can you say for sure if Cambourd actually received his money?"

Altman unwrapped the cigar. "I assume so. Are you saying Jerry undercut him?"

"We can't say that. It's a possibility." Lex leaned toward him. "Did you go straight home after you closed up after the March seventeenth exhibit?"

A red-faced Altman responded, "I don't know what you're getting at. Are you accusing me of something?"

"Relax. It's a routine question, so would you mind answering it?" Lex replied.

Altman leaned forward. "I already told you I did, but I can't prove it, if that's what you mean. I'm single and live alone."

Lex sensed she may have struck a nerve and assured him that he wasn't a suspect...even though he might be one. "We believe you," she said. Giving Gil the familiar, I'm done look, they rose and said goodbye.

"Anything up with the bathroom?" Lex asked outside of the gallery.

"Nothing, it's clean." Gil faced his partner. "And why is it that I'm the one who usually inspects the bathrooms when you're the one who usually has to pee?"

Lex tugged his arm. "Because I'm a lady, and we don't snoop around bathrooms."

Gil smugly asked, "Really? You don't check your dates out when you're in their bathrooms?"

Lex rolled her eyes. "Maybe once or twice, but when was the last time you heard me talk about a date? Haven't had one in a while, and unless you have some friends I don't know about, it's going to stay that way." Lex's gait picked up speed. "Come on, let's go for a long walk. It's the timeline. I want to see how much time Davidson had to walk from here to Cambourd's and back home. Note the time," Lex said. "Let's go."

They started walking to the artist's studio and made it in twenty-nine minutes. Then from there, it took them twenty-six minutes to get to Davidson's condo.

Gil peeked at his phone. "About an hour. That's plenty of time to have done the job. Wish we had the gun. Marg Helgenberger would have solved this case in that short time span."

Lex shook her head at Gil. "Aha, that's why you watch *CSI?* You have a thing for good-looking redheads."

Gil smirked. "Hey, don't be so harsh. It's a good show." He paused before adding. "Ever think about red hair?"

Lex gazed derisively at her partner. "Something you don't like about mine? I suppose you're obsessed with those housewives shows too?" She nudged him.

Without responding to Lex's comment, Gil said, "You want to take the train back?"

"Are you tired? All those doughnuts are weighing you down. It's still nice out, and it won't kill you to keep walking."

"Hey, I walk my dog every morning and night."

"Good to hear. Maybe he should be my partner."

"Funny, Lex. Funny." They headed back to the precinct. "How's the cat doing?" Gil asked.

"Great. Liz loves it, but Van Gogh is a she."

Gil raised his eyebrows. "What did you do, take it to the vet?"

"I am a detective, right?" Lex said with a huge grin. "I picked it up, and do I have to tell you what I didn't find?"

"Okay. Good work, another case solved."

They entered the squad room a half-hour later, and Lex's phone rang. Dan Shields said, "Lex, I have some interesting information for you. I tracked Lorena Tufts to a hotel in Farmington. She registered as Lorena Standish. Paid cash. She checked out this morning. The concierge said she took a cab. I'm checking the taxi companies to see where she might have gone. I'm getting close."

"Thanks," Lex replied.

"Talk to you soon," Shields said.

CHAPTER 17

The captain was standing by his desk and Lex saw him grimace. At first she thought he was having an ocular migraine. Then she saw the phone to his ear, and he glanced toward her and Gil. He waved at them and they hurried into his office.

She heard Pressley say, "Lex was right." There was a pause, and he pivoted toward his detectives. "Tufts is dead," he said. He spoke into the phone. "Thanks, Harold, talk to you soon." The captain sank into his chair.

"I knew it. Suicide?" Lex asked.

Staring at his encased bullet, Pressley said, "It's a little more than suicide. "That was Captain Syms in Hartford. He's back from his surgery. Dan Shields was too late. It seems Lorena's mother's name was Standish, and she'd been transferred from a nursing home in Florida to a hospice in Hartford. The old woman died last night. Lorena was there. The home confirmed her presence. This morning, Lorena walked into the Woodland Medical Center to see her surgeon, Doctor Anson Lavery." Pressley took a breath and swallowed. "Witnesses said she checked in with the receptionist. Said it was an emergency and Lavery took her into his office. Seconds later, there were two shots, and they were both dead."

"Great," Lex grumbled. "I had a bad feeling if she was thinking suicide, she was going to take someone with her...and she did. We need to tell Stillwell."

The detectives exited Pressley's office and Gil called to inform the landlord of his tenant's death.

Lex then said, "I want to talk to Shields." She phoned him. "Hi, Dan."

"One more day and I may have been able to prevent this," the Hartford detective said.

Lex sighed. "Sometimes it just goes that way. We're one step behind. Thanks for your help, Dan."

"Anytime," he replied. "Next time I come to the city, I'll try to stop by the precinct."

"Please do so." Lex paused. "By the way, we heard you have a reputation. Are you really a detective who breaks all the rules?"

"I'm just a detective doing what I have to do," Dan laughed.

Lex grinned. "Between you and me, I've broken a few myself," she wryly quipped. "Take care."

Sedona had to be told of the tragedy, and Lex suggested to Gil, "I think we should break the news to her in person. Let's go to Mid-Manhattan."

▲

They entered the hospital and went directly to the head nurse's office. Sedona looked up. "I'm afraid we have bad news," Lex said. "Lorena Tufts is dead."

Sedona gasped. "Oh my goodness. What happened?"

Lex told her everything they knew. "All the signs were there. We were fearful she'd do something worse. At least she had no vendetta with her coworkers."

"She hated herself that badly," Sedona wiped tears from her face. "You know, she did talk about her doctor. Lavery, I remember the name."

Lex said, "We're sorry to have had to tell you the bad news, but now she'll rest in peace. It's another story for the doctor and his family."

"I don't know what I'm going to tell my staff."

"The truth. We need to get back. Let us know if there's anything you need."

⚔

Lex and Gil were outside the precinct about to enter when Hutch and Starsky whisked past them. "Hey, not so fast," Gil yelled. "What's up?"

"Gotta go make an arrest," Starsky loudly replied. "Sollie Briggs."

Lex and Gil went inside, straight to the captain's office. "How'd they nail him?" Gil asked.

"They found Arnetta's sister. She and Dray are living with her in the Bronx. Late yesterday, Hutch and Starsky went out there and got a confession from Dray and a signed statement from the mother. I got on the warrant, and they know where Sollie's located. How'd it go at the hospital?"

"As well as could be expected," Lex said. "It's never easy."

CHAPTER 18

Lex rarely stepped into Hutch's space. She neared him and looked at Starsky. "Good job, guys. I knew you'd actually solve a case someday."

"Thanks," Hutch replied. "And you look lovely today. You have a hot date last night?"

A half-eaten doughnut was on his desk. "Eat up, don't want you to starve."

She approached Gil. "Just got an interesting call from Kelly," he said. "They're moving stuff into the new property room and re-logging. She recounted the money that was in Cambourd's box, and discovered a false bottom. There were two keys taped inside another envelope."

"What kind of keys?"

"One looks like an ordinary padlock. The other may be a locker or safe-deposit box."

"Really? Let's go get them."

Entering their official home base, they headed to the new main floor property room, and went in. "Hi, Kelly," Lex said.

"You have something for us?" Gil asked.

Kelly retrieved the keys. "Here they are." She said while handing them to Gil.

"Interesting," Lex said. "This guy had a few secrets."

Gil glanced at the keys. "Small one looks like a locker key. The other one could be for a padlock. A little noisy here isn't it?" he said.

"It doesn't bother us. The second floor is almost done. They should be moving up to the third in a day or so. Go take a look."

"Thanks, Kelly," Lex said as she and Gil walked up one flight and peeked at their eventual digs. "Nice," she said. "I'm kind of getting used to the park."

Gil grinned at her. "You're just having a love affair with Butterscotch."

When they returned to the Central Park precinct, Gil studied the metal objects. "Looks like the man had a skeleton or two in his closet," he said. "All we have to do is find the closet."

"These certainly aren't keys to his apartment or studio. The smaller looks like a safe-deposit box key."

"You know what?" Gil said. "The studio occupied the basement front, but I'll bet there are storage bins in the back half of the cellar."

"Good thought. Let's check it out." After conversing with the landlord, Lex said to Gil, "You were right. There are storage units down there, and Cambourd has one. We need to take a look."

▲

Stillwell was waiting for the detectives. "You got some kind of key for a storage bin?" he asked.

"We do. It could be for Cambourd's," Lex replied as Stillwell lowered the TV volume.

"Come on, follow me."

He led Lex and Gil to the back stairs and they proceeded down to the storage area. A musty odor assaulted their nostrils. "Watch out for mouse droppings," Stillwell warned as he opened the door, reached up, and yanked on a chain. "Damn bulb is out."

"You got a flashlight?" Gil asked.

"Yeah, in my kitchen. Wait here. I may have a spare bulb too."

"You creeped out?" Gil asked Lex.

"Being with you? All the time."

Stillwell returned with a bulb and a flashlight. He handed Gil the flashlight, then reached up, removed the dead bulb, and replace it. He pulled on the chain and the room was still dark. "Damn, this one's crapped out too."

Gil aimed the flashlight the length of the room where there was an old coal converted furnace and a row of storage bins. Lex spotted cobwebs on the only window casing.

"Second one is Cambourd's," Stillwell said.

Lex took the flashlight from her partner, and they approached the storage unit. She stepped back. "I think a mouse just scooted past me."

Stillwell nodded. "Just a little fellow."

Gil commented, "It's not even locked." He opened the bin's door. For good measure, he tried the keys. "These surely don't fit that lock."

Lex and Gil stood in the center of the roughly six by eight unit. "All I see are a few wooden easels, several blank canvases, used drop cloths, brushes. Nothing to kill for," Lex said. "Takes care of that." She spun toward Stillwell. "I want to take another look inside his apartment to make sure nothing was missed."

"You gonna clean it out soon? I finally found a new tenant for the empty. Now I have to find another renter."

"We'll let you know, but it shouldn't be long before you can have it cleaned," Lex assured.

They went back to the dead man's place. Gil flicked the light switch on, and the detectives began poking around again. Not finding anything new in the kitchen, except for a dead roach, Lex joined her partner in the main living area. "I don't think we missed anything important," Gil said.

They moved to the bedroom where Lex removed the dresser's sparsely filled drawers, but there was nothing behind them. She saw Stillwell, now standing at the door, and asked, "Mind if we check the studio again?"

"Gotta get that ready too," he commented.

"That could take a little longer," she said. "The studio is a crime scene."

The building owner traipsed downstairs and let them inside. "I got stuff to do. Tell me when you're done."

"Will do," Gil said. "I still smell the bleach in here."

Lex hit the lights, and they proceeded into the back room again where the wine and cheese had been. She spotted a cork that was wedged under a small refrigerator and bent to pick up the object. As she pried it loose, she noticed something shiny that was tucked under the refrigerator and grabbed the object. "A female was definitely here. This is no man's earring. This one is heart-shaped with a ruby. The backing must be here too." She checked under the fridge again, and there it was near the wall. "Got it."

"The mystery woman," Gil stated.

Lex placed the earring and stud in her purse. "We have to find out who she is. Let's close up and get back to the precinct."

"I'll let Stillwell know we're leaving," Gil said.

▲

Once they got back to their office, Gil placed the keys on his desk. Lex said, "That key looks like a safe deposit box key. We have Cambourd's papers. If we get lucky, we'll find a bank name."

Gil placed the cardboard carton that contained the dead artist's items on the table, and the detectives began sifting through it. "Bingo," Gil remarked. "A letter from First Europe Bank. It references a box number and says the bank is discontinuing safe-deposit box rentals."

Lex took a look at the letter. "It says he has to clean out his box by year's end. The number is 2978. He obviously hadn't done so if this is indeed that key. If he had, the bank would have kept it. I know there's a branch not far from his apartment. I'll get Pressley to obtain a warrant so we can open the box."

94

CHAPTER 19

Jerry Davidson was back from London and a subsequent visit to Boston. He had no intention of calling the detective whom he'd loathed. Lex was nothing but a pain his ass, but there was someone else he needed to see.

Entering his condo, he dashed to the kitchen and opened a canister that was next to the toaster. The white powder inside the tin was almost gone and had to be replaced as soon as possible. He went to the bedroom to unpack and change into casual clothes, then he emptied the canister and finished the last of his cocaine supply before settling into his reclining chair.

With his stash depleted, Jerry called his dealer. "Money," he said. "Two hours. Meet me. Same place."

"Two hours? No can do. I'm busy. Tomorrow morning."

Hearing a female's voice in the background, Jerry asked, "Is she a customer or some street whore? Meet me at eight a.m. sharp."

"Whoa, Jerry. She's fine like wine. You mean nine. I'll be up a while tonight. Don't forget the bread. And bring some extra. Tomorrow's my day off."

"Day off, my ass, and don't you be late."

Hungry, Jerry picked up a menu from a nearby Chinese restaurant and ordered food that was delivered thirty minutes later. After eating, he watched TV, became sleepy, and went to bed.

His alarm went off at 7:15 a.m., and he knew he didn't have to rush. After showering and donning his gray Calvin Klein suit, he fidgeted, not able to eat. He kept eyeing his Rolex; time seemed to stand still. Finally, he picked up his briefcase and rode the elevator to the lobby.

"Morning, Mr. Davidson," Artie said. "Newspaper?"

"Thanks." Jerry took a copy from the concierge and exited the building.

He walked onto Park Avenue and headed toward Grand Central Station, making a brief stop at an ATM to withdraw cash before arriving at his destination. His dealer liked the huge terminal to conduct business because it was easy to blend in with the crowd.

Entering the train station though the Lexington Avenue door, Jerry was surrounded by hundreds of commuters. After walking downstairs, he passed a men's room, sat at a table across from the bakery, and scrutinized the area. His briefcase was on the table, and he began reading the newspaper and glanced at his Rolex. Money was late. Trying to sort through the crowd, he didn't see the smart-assed dealer. Finally, from his left, a scrawny male with dreadlocks appeared with a Tootsie Pop hanging from his mouth. Money pulled up a chair, set himself down across from his client and swiveled his blue and white Giant's cap around. After taking a quick look at the crowd, he opened the pouch strapped to his belt.

"You're late," Jerry said.

"Traffic. I'm here now. Got the greens?" Discretely, Jerry slipped an envelope containing cash to the dealer. Money did a quick count. "Where's the rest?"

"What do you mean?"

"You know our deal."

"Yeah, but since my friend is dead, I'm only buying for myself now."

"Can't do that, man. We got a deal. You need to keep buying like before, or you can find yourself another sucker. I gotta make a living, and I ain't selling small stuff."

Jerry opened his wallet and handed him the extra cash. Money then unzipped the pouch and gave his client two bags containing cocaine. Jerry quickly put them inside his attaché. "Now, about my tip?" Money hinted.

"Tip, my ass."

Getting up to leave, Money placed his hand on Jerry's shoulder. "See that cop in the corner? He's a friend, and I can have him open your briefcase in a flash."

"You son of a bitch," Jerry said.

Money held out his hand, and Jerry opened his wallet again and shoved a twenty into the dealer's palm. "There. Now get lost."

"Hey, no hard feelings. Have a good one, Jerry."

With a new supply stashed inside his briefcase, he went outside and hailed a cab to the Met.

When he entered the huge museum, Jerry headed to the bathroom, took a hit, and then made his way to Marcus Worthington's office. The director said, "I got your e-mails. You did a great job getting those collectors to commit to the exhibition."

"It wasn't easy, especially the old geezer in Boston. I had to get Maxine Simmons from the Museum of Fine Arts to help me. She's the one to thank for his contribution."

Marcus picked up his phone. "I think it's time to get Edward Gastone in and bring him up-to-date."

Edward Gastone, whose obsessive-compulsive disorder didn't interfere with his work, entered Worthington's office. He drew his hand back when Jerry reached out to shake it. "Good to see you," Gastone said to the businessman.

"I just got in from my trip and have good news," Jerry replied. "We have commitments from several collectors, and Maxine Simmons spoke highly of you."

Gastone had been a conservation technician at the Museum of Fine Arts in Boston for five years before coming to New York to work with Cambourd. He smiled. "My staff and I will be very busy uncrating and examining all the artwork."

"Maxine said she hated to see you leave Boston."

"She treated me well," Gastone responded. "I have work to do, so if you don't mind, I need to get back to my office."

Marcus waved at him. "Go. I wanted you to hear the news."

The meeting adjourned, Jerry picked up his briefcase, and Marcus said, "Good job. Have a nice day."

Upon exiting the building, Jerry hailed a cab. This time, he headed home.

CHAPTER 20

Gil was at his desk with the Daily News sports section in his hands, while Epstein and Benzinger gathered around him. Lex entered the crowded space and tapped Gil's shoulder. "Yankees win?" she asked, placing her hot cup on her worktop.

"Nice one. The Mets won, but take a look at this article," he said.

She glanced at the third column. "That's terrific!"

Gil grinned proudly. His twin sons, Darryl and Dwight, each hit home runs, powering their high school team to their third straight victory. "They both want to go to Florida State next year. A recruiter visited us, and the boys might get scholarships."

"Congrats," Benzinger said before turning toward the coffee maker as his partner headed into the captain's office."

Lex sipped her coffee. "I'm going to check on the warrant."

"Gil said, "Looks like you'll have to wait. Epstein's in there."

Ten minutes later, Epstein exited and Lex stepped into Pressley's office. "Were you able to get a warrant for the safe-deposit box?" she asked.

The captain reached into his tray and gave her the court order. "Thanks. What's up with Epstein?" she asked.

Pressley shook his head. "He's got a real problem. His parents moved to Florida six years ago. They're in their eighties. His father has Alzheimer's and needs to be placed in a home. His mother isn't coping well. Epstein is taking a leave to go down and take care of her. Can't say how long."

"I'm so sorry to hear about that. I'll keep it quiet."

"That's not necessary. Benzinger knows, and Epstein was going to tell everyone else, so you can tell Gil."

With the paperwork in her hand, she went back to Gil, and informed him of Epstein's family issue. She showed Gil the warrant. "Let's hit the bank as soon as it opens."

"I'll drive," Gil said.

A

The detectives entered First Europe Bank. ATM machines were on both sides of the area between the outside door and inside entrance. Five tellers were straight ahead, and three cubicles and an office occupied most of the floor space. A coffee station was in one corner; to the left of the teller stations was a door that led to the vault and safe-deposit box area. The detectives walked to the manager's office, and they stood at the open door.

"May I help you?" Gayle Munson asked.

"Yes," Lex replied while presenting her badge to the manager. "We'd like to ask a few questions about a customer."

Gil showed Gayle the warrant. "We have the key to a safe-deposit box that we need to get into. It belonged to Fredrike Cambourd. He died recently, and we found a letter in his apartment stating that he had to empty the box because you are discontinuing that service." Gil produced the document and the key. "He still had this key, so it appears he hadn't come to empty it."

Gayle said, "We are phasing out safe-deposit boxes, but our customers legally have a year to empty theirs before we can pursue probate."

"May we access the box to see what's inside?" Lex asked.

"Follow me," the manager said, leading them to the safe-deposit box area. "She inserted her master key and Gil slid Cambourd's into the lock. The door opened. "You can use one of the tables behind these curtains, if you wish. Call me if you need anything." Gayle headed back to her office.

Gil pulled out a long metal container, placed it on a table, and opened the lid. "Here we go."

Lex removed the top item. "A passport. Looks like he went to Paris several times."

A black tattered address book was under the passport. "Wonder how old this thing is?" Gil said.

Lex leafed through it. "Looks like friends in Paris; all these names and addresses are French. Chandelle, Bergeron."

Gil removed a half-dozen envelopes from the box. "Francs and Euros and more cash. You any good at foreign currency?"

"No. I should ask Liz. She takes French."

Gil counted the cash. "Don't know how much the foreign currency amounts to but by my count, there's another twenty-five grand in good old dollars in here."

"That makes a hundred with what was in his apartment," Lex said. "Here's a will. Everything goes to the museum. I wonder if Marcus Worthington is aware of this."

Gil placed a bankbook on the table and opened it. His eyes lit up. "Holy moly! Get a load of this," he remarked.

Lex eyed the passbook. "Are you serious? A little over a million and several deposits. Fifty, sixty, a hundred grand. We know his salary didn't amount to this much. Where'd he get all this money? I'll ask one of the tellers for a bag."

Gil slid the empty box back into its slot. Lex caught the attention of a teller, and she gave the detective a green tote. "Thanks," Lex said, placing the contents into the bag. "We need to see Gayle."

The detectives entered the bank manager's office again. "How did it go?" Gayle asked.

Lex queried, "Did you ever observe Fredrike Cambourd here?"

The manager replied, "No. Actually, I've only been in this branch about five months."

"Can you tell when he was last here to access the box?"

"He would have signed in. I can look, if you'd like." Gayle faced her computer and accessed the register. "Last time he signed in was three weeks ago. Before that, six months back."

"I'm puzzled," Lex said. "I wonder why he didn't empty the box then."

Gil handed Gayle the key. He said, "I don't think he knew he was going to die, and he probably thought he had more time to take his belongings."

"True," Lex said. She thanked Gayle and the detectives exited the bank.

After stopping to drop off their new found money with Kelly they went back to the Central Park precinct. Gil headed to his desk while Lex abandoned him and began pacing the room. *Davidson is sly. If he really did know about the money, he may well have wanted it.* She sat beside her partner. "Davidson knew Cambourd better than anyone else, so it's quite possible he was aware of his friend's fortune."

Gil said, "He implied the artist was a pauper but obviously, that wasn't true. Gil shook his head. "But why would he kill Cambourd? Davidson has money."

"Some people never have enough," Lex replied.

CHAPTER 21

Lex realized they didn't know much about their main suspect. She addressed her partner. "We haven't investigated Jerry Davidson. We need to know more about his background. We can start with checking the criminal database and his work history."

Hearing heavy footsteps, Lex saw an angry Hutch marching toward Pressley's office. Starsky was right behind. "What happened?" she asked.

Hutch stopped and pounded his fist on Epstein's desk. "Bastard, Sollie Briggs is out. He posted bail. We're gonna keep an eye on him and the next dime bag he sells, we're gonna drop his ass back in jail."

"Great system isn't it?" Gil lamented.

"Damn right," Hutch angrily said as he and Starsky walked into the captain's quarters.

Turning back to Gil, Lex said, "Altman told us Davidson once worked for an auction house. Sutherland, as I recall. Why did he leave? Was he fired?"

Gil said, "I'll log into the criminal database." He found several Davidsons, but none matched their suspect. "I don't see a Jerry or a Gerald for that matter," he said.

Lex retrieved her notes. "I was right. Sutherland Auctions. I'm pretty sure they have an office here." She googled the company and came up with a New York City address and phone number. "Here we go. They're on Madison. I'm going to give them a call."

Lex spoke with the executive director, Douglas Helmsworth, She stated they wanted to speak with him about Jerry Davidson, but never told the man specifically why."

Helmsworth cordially invited the detectives to his office.

▲

A large awning outside the building had the company name imprinted on it in bold blue letters. Lex and Gil were greeted at the front desk by a receptionist and were directed to Douglas Helmsworth's office. Tall, dark haired and wearing a blue suit, he appeared to be in his mid to late forties, and welcomed the detectives.

Plush carpeting, fresh flowers, expensive looking artifacts, chairs, a large wall-mounted TV, a long bar, and a mahogany desk: everything inside this office smelled of money.

Taking a seat behind his desk, Helmsworth invited his guests to sit on the chairs opposite him. Lex crossed her legs, her pen and pad in hand, and she said, "Thank you for meeting with us. As I mentioned, we want to ask you about Jerry Davidson."

Helmsworth picked up a file and opened it. "Very interesting scammer. For starters, his real name is Jeffrey Danielson."

Lex side-glanced Gil. "What?"

"Oh, yes," Helmsworth said. "He was hired by us as Jerry Davidson, and his resume stated he'd been employed by Sotheby's in London. One day, almost two years after his hiring, I was in London and saw Simon Gilbert of Sotheby's. Simon had never heard of Jerry Davidson, so when I got back here, I did some investigating and confronted Davidson. After a lot of stumbling around, he confessed his name was really Jeffrey Danielson. Turns out he'd actually lived in London for a while and worked as an independent consultant."

"Did he say why he changed his name and lied?" Lex asked.

"He said he'd spent a few weeks in an Ohio jail for petty theft.

He assured me it was a mistake that he regretted and wanted to work for us so badly, he thought it best to hide his identity." Helmsworth paused. "The crazy thing is, we always do a background check, but Davidson was so convincing, we never did one on him. That glitch was on us. Never again."

"Very interesting," Lex noted.

"I had to let him go right on the spot; had him escorted out. That's the last I'd heard of him until you called."

Lex was nearly speechless. "Obviously, he's still using Davidson, and he's working as a freelance art consultant," she said.

"May I ask?" Helmsworth said. "Is he in trouble?"

"Were not quite sure," Lex said. "We're investigating an incident that may have involved him. Is there anything else we should know? Any other reason to believe he couldn't be trusted?"

"No. That's it. His phony identity. It's one strike and you're out here."

"Thanks again," Lex said as the detectives headed for the elevator.

The surprising information Lex and Gil just received gave them a disturbing insight into their prime suspect.

⁂

Once they got back to the precinct, Gil wasted no time and logged back into the criminal database. He quickly got a hit. "Jeffrey Danielson. It's here. Take a look, Lex."

She read the file. "He spent more than a few weeks in that prison. Two years for embezzling from a Cleveland art dealer. We need to tell Pressley."

The detectives entered the captain's office, and he handed Lex a three-page document. "Read this."

Before sitting, she read the medical examiner's report and was stunned when she came to the second page. "Cocaine? There was cocaine in Cambourd's body? How's that for a kicker? The old artist was on coke."

"You can sit now," Pressley said.

Seated, she commented, "But there was no evidence of it at his studio or his apartment." Lex eyed the report again.

"Damn it," Gil growled. "I thought Davidson was high when we talked with him. How'd we miss that? He had time to clean up the art studio before police arrived."

Lex suggested, "He emptied the wallet to throw us off. And the cane. He had to move it for some reason. Maybe to get at the cocaine that was inside the desk drawer."

"Wait a minute," Gil said. "Remember when we were at his condo, and I said there was what appeared to be spilt sugar on his kitchen counter? That wasn't sugar. It was cocaine. I searched his briefcase, and it was empty, except for papers and a laptop."

"The cocaine wasn't in his briefcase. He knew we'd search it. He stashed the drugs in his suit pocket."

Pressley reclined back. "Nice theory. Go prove it."

"Captain, there's something you need to hear about Jerry Davidson." Lex filled him in, and the detectives exited the office. She picked up her desk phone. "He better answer."

Jerry Davidson did answer his phone. "Hello, Detective Stall. How are you today?" he asked. "I've been meaning to call you. I got home a couple of days ago."

Lex felt her blood boil. "I thought I made it perfectly clear you were to call me as soon as you got back. You know damned well I did!"

"I apologize. Something came up."

"We need to see you right now," she asserted. "We'd love to hear about your trip, and we may have something interesting to share with you."

"I'm busy today, but if you want to come tomorrow morning, say ten a.m., I'll be here."

Lex sighed. "You better be there, or we'll have you picked up and brought here. Do you understand me?" Not waiting for a response, she said, "Have a wonderful day."

"What was that all about?" Gil asked.

"He's been home for a couple of days. Thinks he's playing with me. I'd really like to get him here to grill him, but I feel he'll tell us more in his comfort zone. We're going to see him tomorrow morning at his place."

Lex's cell rang. It was Manning. "Lex, I know it's short notice, but Fleming put us on the docket for Monday. Asino is agreeable."

Her hand shook while she held her phone. "Are you sure about this?"

"We have to do it now. Fleming is doing me a favor. She's moving up to appellate in a couple of months. Are you okay?"

"I don't know. I guess so."

"We're first up on the docket."

Lex saw Gil's concerned look. "You're pale as a ghost," he said.

"We're going to court Monday. I'll be right back. I need to tell Pressley and then I'm leaving."

"What about tomorrow? Jerry Davidson."

"Tomorrow's Friday, don't worry. I wouldn't miss that visit for the world. I need to get out of here. I have to talk to my neighbor, Sheila."

Butterscotch was always a calming presence to Lex, so before she got into her car, she paid the horse a visit. "You have a good day?" Lex asked. "I know, they're all the same to you. Wish I was so lucky. See you."

Lex got into her Corolla, popped in her Fleetwood Mac disc, and headed home. The one thing she was sure about was that Liz would not be in court. There was no subpoena for her, and she knew Jon wouldn't stoop low enough to drag his daughter into the fray, even though it was about her.

When Lex got home, she called Sheila Wyatt. "Hi, how are you doing?"

Meekly, Sheila answered, "Okay." Silence followed and Lex knew her friend would be in court to testify about the drinking habit.

107

"Listen," Lex said. "It's fine, Sheila. I know you've been summoned. You have to tell the truth." Sheila was silent. "I said it's okay. I'll be right over."

Lex spent the next hour at Sheila's convincing her that nothing would stand in the way of their friendship. Sheila was chewing gum, and Lex became suspicious. She checked the kitchen cabinets and found a bottle of Vodka. *I knew it, the gum chewing.*

She confronted her friend. "Are you still going to meetings?"

Sheila began sobbing. "You don't understand."

Lex stared harshly at her. "I do understand. If you don't stop, you'll kill yourself with this stuff. It's poison. You have to get back on track. Promise me."

Sheila nodded.

"I'll see you in court," Lex said before leaving for home.

▲

She opened the front door, and heard Liz talking to Van Gogh. Seeing her daughter, she asked, "How was school? Have much homework?"

The student's backpack was on a kitchen chair. "I finished it in study period."

"I need to discuss something with you," Lex said. "Let's sit in the den."

Van Gogh followed them. Lex explained the court proceedings and thirty minutes later, Liz hugged her mother. "Can we get pizza?" she asked.

Lex smiled. "That's my girl."

"Can Shannon come?"

"Good idea. I need to talk to Elaine. We'll all go."

The four dined together. Afterward, they all went back to Elaine's house, and Lex brought her friend up-to-date on the court appearance. Although she'd had the urge to stop at the record shop, Lex didn't. Elaine had her ear on this night.

Chapter 22

One workday and one weekend away from the courtroom, Lex and Gil headed to the Zagrin Building. Artie greeted them and asked, "Did you get the lobby video?"

Gil replied, "We did, thanks. Mr. Davidson is expecting us. We know the way."

Exiting the elevator, Lex saw Davidson standing at his door waiting for his guests. "Artie buzzed me. Said you were on your way up. Nice to see you again."

Lex didn't expect the warm reception. Stepping into the condo, she glanced toward the kitchen and noticed a canister on the counter. *I'm sure if we opened it, we'd find cocaine.*

The detectives positioned themselves on the couch while Davidson sat in his chair. "Here we are. What have you got to tell me?" he asked.

Lex made eye contact with him and saw the glazed look. "Did I tell you how much I adore this condo?"

"No, but thank you. I'm sure that's not what you came to chat about."

Gil said, "Sorry, I have a weak bladder. Can I use the bathroom again?" A couple of minutes later, having walked through the kitchen on his way back, he commented, "Lex is right. Terrific place."

"Okay. So, what is it?" Davidson asked.

Lex was still staring at him. "It's the truth, Mr. Davidson, or perhaps I should say Danielson."

That reveal made her prey begin to sweat. He shook his head, and glared at the brash detective. "How did you know?"

"We're detectives. Did you forget?" Lex said. "Two years in jail. What else are you not telling us?"

"Oh, Christ. You don't know anything about what happened in Cleveland. That dealer set me up. The bastard gave me fake artwork. I sold it to a gallery for twenty-five grand. When the purchaser found out the paintings weren't real, he demanded his money back. I'd already given the proceeds, less my commission, to the dealer who consigned me the paintings. He denied the entire transaction, but it was the guy I sold the artwork to that sent me to jail."

"So you decided to change your name when you went to Sutherland," Lex said.

"When I got out, I knew I had to change my name and fudge a resume. It worked until Helmsworth ran into Gilbert. Then the shit hit the fan, and I left."

"You mean you were fired," Lex stated. "Now, tell us about your glazed eyes and the cocaine habit."

"Damn it. I can't seem to kick it. It started in that damn jail, and there were worse things there."

Lex leaned forward. "I'm sure there were. When did you get Cambourd hooked on the stuff?"

Davidson bowed his head and put his clammy hands together. "How'd you know he was doing coke too?"

Gil pointed at him. "She already told you, we're detectives. The medical examiner's report showed it in his system. We added two and two and came up with Davidson."

Lex kept her eyes on his. "Why don't you go back and start at the beginning. You entered the studio and then what?"

Davidson huffed. "I found him dead. I panicked and knew I had a small supply for him inside my briefcase. I also knew he had some in his desk, so I took what he had, stuffed it into my baggie, and placed it in my inside suit pocket. I moved what I had in my briefcase to the pocket as well."

She nodded. "So that explains the gap in time before you phoned for help. You knew someone would be searching your briefcase."

"I figured there was a good chance of that happening."

"You moved the cane, didn't you?" Lex asked.

"It was leaning on the desk, and I had to open the drawer. I know you think I killed him."

"We never said that," Lex replied. "Did you?"

Davidson protested, "How many damned times do I have to tell you? No!"

Lex eased off. "Then help us out. We're sure he and a female were together that night. Who was she?"

"I honestly don't know. He did tell me a younger woman had friended him."

Lex asked, "Friended? Like Facebook?"

"No. He'd met her a few times. All he said was that she was a family friend."

"I thought you said he didn't have family."

"As far as I knew, he didn't."

"Why do you suppose he kept her a secret?"

"How do I know? Fredrike was a very private person."

Lex asked, "Did you notice the woman peeking out from behind a tree at the funeral?"

"No. What woman?"

"A woman in a black dress. She disappeared in a silver car before the funeral was over."

Davidson checked his Rolex. "I told Worthington I'd see him this morning. I have to go."

"Not yet," Lex replied. "We visited Heinrich Altman, and he verified your story about being at the gallery until around eleven-thirty." She noticed Davidson's mock grin, and continued, "Tell me something. It's obvious you lied about what time you got home. As I recall, you stated you were here in bed at around midnight." She paused and again stared directly at him. "We know that's not true.

This building's lobby video shows you entering around one-thirty a.m. How about explaining that gap in time?"

He walked toward the patio, then walked back toward the detectives. "Okay, okay. You know about my addiction. I met my dealer at Grand Central. That's it. That's the truth. I need to call Marcus." Davidson took a few deep breaths and phoned the museum director to delay their meeting.

Lex pressed on. "Sit down, Mr. Davidson. Let's talk about Altman. He said you provided him Cambourd paintings. There are still five in his gallery. What was your agreement with regards to commission and the artist's cut?"

"We split one-third."

"And you each got between three and five thousand for every painting sold?"

"Sounds about right. Why?"

That information verified what Altman said. "Did Altman ever show you the sale prices or receipts?"

Davidson shrugged. "What? Are you saying he was cheating us?"

Lex shook her head. "No, but he did tell us that he is doubling the prices on the remaining pieces in his gallery. You do realize there are no price tags on any of the items there."

"I do, but that's not unusual for a high-end gallery."

"Tell me one more thing," Lex said. "You implied you knew Cambourd didn't have a lot of money. How do you know that?"

"You saw his place. Did that look like he could afford a better one?"

"Good point," she replied. "Then would it surprise you if I told you the man wasn't the pauper you thought he was?"

"What are you saying? He was a miser."

"He may have been that," Lex asserted. "But his bankbook says he stashed away a lot of money."

"Well, he didn't get rich on the paintings Altman sold. How much are you talking about?"

Lex hesitated. "Let's just say it's a hefty sum."

Davidson was speechless, and the detectives rose from the couch. Lex said. "We can get you help for the drugs. Think about it."

"Thanks. I will." Davidson got up and opened the door for his visitors to leave.

The detectives got back into the squad car, and Gil drove toward headquarters. "He was pretty convincing that he had no idea of Cambourd's wealth," Gil suggested.

"I agree."

"You planted quite a seed with him. You think he'll confront Altman on the actual sales prices?"

Lex smiled. "I'm betting he will. And next time we go back to Altman's, I'm planning to ask the same question. To me, something's not quite right with Altman. Don't know what it is, but there's more to him than meets the eye."

Once they reached the precinct lot, they exited the vehicle. "I'm going home," Lex said. "This is Jon's normal weekend to have Liz, and I want to see her before he picks her up."

▲

It wasn't long after Lex got home that she had to say goodbye to her daughter. Liz was packed and ready to go to her father's house. "I'll see you Sunday night," Lex said when she saw his car stop. Before walking downstairs, Liz said, "Love you."

Lex's best friend, Elaine, a phlebotomist employed by a local lab, was also divorced. Her ex had alternating weekend custody of Shannon. Lex called Elaine. "Hi. Liz just left."

"Shannon was picked up a half-hour ago. You want to get a bite?"

"Sure. I'll be right over."

The two women went to their favorite bistro and then went back to Lex's.

113

Sitting in the parlor, Lex said, "I've never been so nervous, and Sheila was summoned."

"I'm sure everything will be fine."

"I'm going to make tea."

A few minutes later, Lex returned with two cups and set them on a table. She sipped her drink and asked, "What do you think I should wear to court?"

Elaine cracked a grin. "How about a pink teddy?"

Lex laughed. "I don't even know where my red one is. Haven't had it on…or off in a long time."

Elaine laughed too. "Me neither. Mine is in the bottom dresser drawer. The only balls it's seen are moth balls."

"We're pathetic," Lex said. "We're gonna have to get out sometime."

Elaine drank her tea. "I can just see us in a bar with a bunch of perverts."

"Not to worry. I always pack my weapon," Lex grinned.

Elaine chuckled. "Seriously. We should go out sometime." It was getting late, and she yawned. "I better go get some sleep."

"Me too. Thanks," Lex said. "I needed a few laughs."

CHAPTER 23

Liz returned home after spending the weekend with her father; the reality of Monday morning came early. Lex saw her daughter leave for school and then got ready for court.

Dressed in a black suit with a white blouse, Lex put her shoulder-length hair into a bun. She limited her makeup to mascara and lipstick and then noticed the darkness under her eyes, which she hid with a concealer. It was 9:30 a.m. when Lex arrived at the Lafayette Street courthouse. *Okay, Alexis, be calm and be confident.*

Inside the building, she opened her purse for inspection, sans her weapon, before going through a metal detector. Having passed the test, she took the elevator up one floor. At the end of the corridor was the courtroom where her marriage had ended. Unpleasant memories filled her head when she stepped into the room.

Creighton Manning was sitting at the table furthest from the door. She walked past Asino and Jon before joining her attorney. His open briefcase and a couple of folders were on top of the table. He rose and slid a chair out for Lex. "Thanks," she said. "Do you remember what happened in this room?"

"I remember." He poured Lex a glass of water, and she glanced to her left at her ex and stumpy Anthony J. Asino. Appropriately named, she thought, because in Italian, his name translated to jackass. Several law students were seated in the gallery with their laptops. Sheila Wyatt was there too. The bailiff positioned himself beside the vacant judge's bench. Flanking the wall in back of her chair were the American and New York State flags.

At precisely 10.00 a.m., black robed, Judge Charlotte Fleming approached the bench. All rose while the bailiff announced her presence. She slammed the gavel and announced that court was in session. Everyone sat and she directed her first question to Asino. He got up and addressed the judge. While twirling a pen in his hand, the brassy lawyer vigorously rehashed his client's complaints, including the accusation of a loaded gun on Lex's nightstand. He even tossed in a lie about her being promiscuous and demanded that Jon Stall be named the primary custodial parent of Elizabeth Stall.

While Lex saw Jon smiling at the antics of his attorney, Creighton Manning had to restrain his client who could barely control her anger. She clutched her fists and muttered obscenities under her breath. *Lying bastards.*

When Asino finished his presentation, he took his seat, and she saw Jon gave him a nod of approval.

Manning stood. "Your Honor, Mr. Asino has put on a good show. One big circus act to camouflage the real reason Mr. Stall wishes to be the primary custodial parent, the status Alexis Stall was awarded at the divorce hearing."

At the mention of his name, Asino poured himself a glass of water. Manning continued, "Jon Stall's motives are strictly financial. He's only seeking to remove the burden of child support and alimony. Alexis Stall is an exemplary mother, always has her daughter's interest at heart, and Liz is not wanting for anything." He paused to point at Jon and then at Asino. "Your Honor, I can assure you any accusation that Detective Alexis Stall keeps a loaded handgun by her bedside is preposterous. She's a trained police officer and would never do such a thing."

Lex sat forward with her palms on top of the table while Manning continued. "My client is a hardworking woman. Any supposition of Alexis Stall being promiscuous are absurd and an outright fabrication. Further, if you check Mr. Stall's background, you will find it filled with infidelity, hardly a good environment for a young impressionable girl."

Asino jumped up and objected. "Irrelevant, Your Honor. That was argued in the divorce hearing."

"Overruled," Fleming said. "Mr. Asino, please sit. You'll have another chance to speak."

Manning asserted, "There is one other recent matter. It's the fact that Mr. Stall was accused of striking a student."

Asino immediately popped up again and vociferously interrupted, "Objection, Your Honor. That student later admitted it didn't happen."

"Sustained," Fleming said.

Manning moved closer to the bench. "Your Honor, Alexis Stall is and always has been a dedicated role model to her daughter, Elizabeth. I'm asking you to throw out the plaintiff's request for primary custody and leave things as they currently exist. Thank you, Your Honor." Manning returned to his seat, and Lex took a pack of tissues from her purse.

Judge Fleming allowed a rebuttal from Asino. "You can see by his sworn statement that Jon Stall is in a happy marriage and is a loving husband, father, and stepfather. He is a deserving man desiring to be the rightful primary custodial parent."

Lex saw Asino casting his sights on Sheila Wyatt. "He's not going to call her, is he?" she asked Manning. Her answer came a few seconds later when Sheila was sworn to testify. After admitting to using alcohol, including daily drinking and withdrawing from AA, the judge dismissed the witness.

Fleming left the room to mull her decision.

Lex drank a cup of water, although a shot of bourbon would have been more suitable. Manning closed his file and sat back. Twenty minutes passed, and it seemed like an eternity to Lex. Then Judge Fleming returned to the bench, picked up her gavel, and announced the court was back in session. Manning held Lex's hand as they braced themselves for the ruling.

Fleming glanced at each of the parties. "Mr. Manning, Ms. Stall,

Mr. Asino, and Mr. Stall. I have made a decision, and it was a very difficult one, but I had to consider all of the factors." She stopped to address Lex. "I find several things disturbing about Elizabeth Stall's current living conditions. I don't like the fact that you are on call and, at times, leave your daughter with an admitted alcoholic. I also don't like the unsupervised after-school activity. You admit to having a weapon in your nightstand. Whether it is loaded or not, I can't be sure."

The judge then addressed Jon and Asino. "Certain facts are undeniable. Jon Stall is an exemplary educator, having twice been awarded 'Teacher of the Year' honors at his school. His wife, Julie, is a stay-at-home mother with her son and would be able to provide afternoon supervision for Elizabeth. Therefore, I believe the more stable environment for Elizabeth Stall is with her father, Jon Stall."

Before she could continue, Lex stood and yelled at Fleming, "Are you kidding me? What kind of mother are you?"

Manning quickly grabbed his client. "Sit now and shut up, Lex, or you'll be in contempt, and I'll be bailing you out of here!" She sat with tears streaming down her face.

Fleming gave her a cold stare. "You better control yourself in my courtroom," she said harshly. "You're close to contempt. My decision is final." Fleming then read the new conditions of custody. The only positives for Lex were that Jon Stall and Asino had waived child support and granted liberal visitations. Fleming said she would deliver the court documents to each lawyer within the next forty-eight hours. It would only be a week before Liz would have to take up residence with her father.

Manning and a teary-eyed Lex left the courtroom. Her hands trembling, she wiped her eyes, took a deep breath, and wondered how she would break the news to Liz.

▲

Lex drove home with tears trickling down her face. When she

arrived, she immediately went to Liz's room and hugged an armful of stuffed animals that were on the bed. While most of these little critters would be staying, Liz would soon have to pack up and move to Brooklyn.

Lex notified Pressley and Gil that she would be taking a few days off. Empty and disillusioned, she wondered if she could she ever get herself back together again. *Was being a detective worth it?* Lex felt like a knife had pierced her heart.

That afternoon after Liz got home from school, Lex had a long talk with her. The teenager was devastated, didn't return to school, spent most of her days in her room with Van Gogh, and evenings clinging to her mother.

Meanwhile, during the week away from work, Lex spent most afternoons aimlessly walking around Washington Square. At times she just sat on a park bench observing the pigeons, and trying to make sense of it all, while pondering her future. The one thing she couldn't do was stand at the record store window and talk to her father.

Saturday came and Jon picked up his daughter.

That Sunday afternoon, Lex looked in Liz's empty room where Van Gogh was on the bed. "Don't worry, you're not going anywhere," she said to the sleeping cat.

Lex grabbed a sweater and walked toward Washington Square again, this time she didn't sit on a bench. She continued walking and neared the NYU campus where she stopped and thought about Corey. She wondered what her life would have been like had her college boyfriend not walked into Linton's Drugstore that night.

To this day, those murders have never been solved.

Somehow, Cory gave her strength and she finally stopped to talk to her father. She wished he could hold her now and with that thought, she could feel his arms around her. Even if it was her imagination, Lex heard her father's voice. *Alexis, you have a wonderful daughter, and so do I. Liz will be alright. She's only a few miles away.*

It was what Lex needed to hear. *Thanks, Dad. I love you.*

Lex walked back through the park, aware of the many positive things in her life and headed home.

Chapter 24

It was Monday morning. Lex had called Pressley and Gil last evening to tell them she'd be back today.

She calmly entered the squad room with a cinnamon latte in her hand after having spent a few minutes with Butterscotch. Pressley rushed to greet her. "Good to see you."

"Thanks."

The rest of the detectives welcomed her back. Hutch said, "I've missed you."

She responded, "Hutch, that's the nicest thing you've ever said to me. Keep it up, and I may actually hug you someday."

"She's back." Gil laughed.

"Enough," Lex demanded. "This is a police station isn't it?"

"I get the message," Pressley said. "Welcome back."

Proceeding to her desk, she asked Gil, "What have you been up to?"

"I've been digging through Cambourd's stuff. He kept records of all his paintings that were at Altman's, but he also has a blank page with the heading 'Stefan.'"

Lex took a look at it. "Interesting."

Gil opened another ledger. "This appears to be a list of museum paintings that he restored. There are over fifty here: less than half have asterisks, and there's a notation written in French. 'Je suis le meilleur.' And there's another strange note on the bottom of the page."

He pointed to it, and Lex read, "ISG 180390 KU-EGG." She sipped her latte. "Did you look up the meaning of the French notation?" she asked.

Gil grinned. "As a matter of fact, I googled it. It means, 'I am the greatest.'"

Lex smiled at him, "Very good." She hesitated for a second. "Listen, there's something on my conscience. It's Corey. I've been thinking about him, and you know his murder is still unsolved. I want to dig into that cold case to see what I can find. Let's do it."

He jerked back. "What? It's been how long…fifteen years?"

Lex stared into her partner's eyes. "Almost eighteen, and it's time to take a fresh look."

Gil said, "You're serious about this?"

"Very."

He nodded. "You gonna run it by the captain?"

"Right now."

Pressley smiled at his favorite employee. "It's really great to have you back. You look good."

"Watch it, there could be cause for sexual harassment."

The captain grinned. "Now I know you're back. Besides, if there ever is cause for a harassment case, you know it will be Hutch."

Lex nodded. "That windbag is harmless." She knew Pressley might not like what she was about to say. "I did some thinking while I was off. You remember why I joined the force?" After a moment, she announced, "I want to reopen a cold case."

Pressley's face grew taut, and he moved forward. "Corey? There's an entire unit downtown in charge of cold cases."

"Right, sir, but if anyone reopens it, it has to be me. It's been eighteen years, and Corey's killer has not been found. No one cares."

"I don't like it, Lex. If you want to reopen the case, you'll need new evidence." Pressley crossed his arms.

"Right, and that's exactly what I expect to find. DNA testing is a lot better now than it was back then. And I'll go through the case file with a fine-tooth comb. I'll find something."

"I can't let you, Lex. Unless you want to transfer out of here."

She stared at her boss and leaned on his desk. "Remember the sexual harassment thing?"

"Don't give me that crap," the captain harshly said.

Lex stared hard at her boss. "Look, sir. I'm serious about this, and I'm going to dig into it. If that means transferring downtown, then get the paperwork ready."

Pressley sighed and rocked back. "You know something? For a female, you have a lot of balls. Go, but keep me informed."

Lex smiled at him. "I knew you'd understand, thanks."

She tapped Gil on the shoulder. "He's in. Let's go to headquarters at Park Plaza."

Gil leaned back and held up his hands. "Wait. We can go there anytime. Let's tie up a few loose ends before taking on Corey. Okay?"

Lex took a deep breath. "Okay, but we're going there soon. Altman. Let's talk to him again. I want to see exactly what he knows about Jerry Davidson and probe the sales."

⟡

Two hours later, the detectives were standing outside the gallery, and Gil rang the bell. Altman came to the door to let them inside. "Laura's off today. Come on back," he said.

Altman sat in his leather chair, and Lex saw Gil staring at the Chinese vase again. "I'm fascinated by it.," he said.

"Altman stated, "It's two hundred years old." He took a cigar from his box and addressed Lex. "What would you like to talk about?"

Lex prepared to take notes and spoke, "Jerry Davidson. Did you know he was fired from Sutherland?"

Altman raised his brow. "He was? He told me he left there because he decided to become a consultant. What happened?"

"It's a long story," Lex replied. "I bet you didn't know his name is really Jeffrey Danielson."

"Huh? Why the name change?"

"Because he did time in an Ohio jail."

"For what?"

Lex explained.

"Are you serious? Do you suspect he's conning me somehow?"

"I don't want to imply that. I only want you to be aware of his past, in case you get suspicious. I am curious about something else. You stated Cambourd's paintings routinely sold for about twelve to fifteen grand."

"That's right, but Jerry thought they should have been priced higher. Now they are, and you know why."

"I realize why, but we also know there were never any posted prices on any of his pieces, so couldn't you have sold them for any amount?"

"What are you saying? You think I may have sold paintings for more than what I told Jerry?"

"I don't want to imply that, but would you be able to show us your sales records, who you sold the Cambourds to, and at what prices?"

Altman's voice intensified. "My records are private, between me and my clients...like a doctor and a patient."

Gil nodded at Lex. "He's right."

She backed off and asked, "Does the name Stefan mean anything to you?"

Altman replied, "Stefan Martine has a gallery near Herald Square. Why do you ask?"

Lex interjected, "Cambourd had written that name on a ledger page."

Altman checked his watch. "I have a client coming soon. We need to wrap this up."

"No problem. Thanks for your time," she said.

"I'll see you out," Altman offered as they headed for the front door.

When the detectives got outside, Lex immediately commented, "Interesting. He's very protective of his sales records. What he might not understand is that we can obtain them with a warrant, should we decide to do so."

"I get the impression we'll be doing that," Gil said.

CHAPTER 25

Entering her quiet home, Lex kicked off her shoes and stared at Liz's most recent school picture that was atop the parlor bookshelf. Van Gogh was eagerly awaiting her supper, so Lex headed to the kitchen and opened a can of food for the hungry kitty.

Sirens caught Lex's attention, and she walked to the front window. Glancing down the street, she saw an ambulance double-parked in front of Sheila Wyatt's home. Two black and whites were in back of the emergency vehicle. Stunned, Lex put on her shoes and rushed to Sheila's brownstone.

A team of paramedics had gone inside, along with uniformed cops. Lex hurried up the front steps, and an officer stopped her. Lex said, "I'm a police officer and neighbor. What happened?"

"Not sure. Looks like she had too much to drink."

Lex went inside, observing a broken lamp, an empty bottle of vodka next to Sheila's prone body, and some blood on the floor. "Is she okay?" Lex asked a paramedic.

"She's coming around. Pulse and vitals are okay. The cut on her leg from the broken glass isn't serious."

"Who called you?" Lex questioned.

"She did. Must have passed out after calling the helpline. Her cell was still in her hand."

Sheila began to realize what was happening. "Sit still," Lex said. "You've got a leg cut. Let the EMTs take care of you. Do you remember what happened?"

Groggily, Sheila slurred, "I must have had a drink and fallen asleep."

"Yeah, that's it." Lex moved toward the paramedic. "You don't need to take her to the hospital, do you?"

"No. The cut on her leg was free of glass and we bandaged it. She'll sober up."

"I'll stay here with her tonight. Let me get a few things. I live close by. I'll be right back."

"Okay."

Sheila was on her couch when Lex got back. The police officers had left the scene and the EMT's departed soon after Lex entered the room.

While Sheila slept off the drunken stupor, Lex cleaned up the shards of glass from the lamp and threw the vodka bottle in the trash. Opening the cabinet above the refrigerator, she found two bottles of liquor, grabbed a kitchen chair to stand on, and placed the vodka containers on the counter. After pouring the liquids down the sink drain, she found a shopping bag and put the empties in it. Lex then made a pot of coffee and waited for Sheila to awaken.

A few hours later, Sheila began to stir. She struggled to sit up, and Lex said, "Don't stand. Are you okay?"

"I gotta pee. What are you doing here? My leg hurts."

"I'm making sure you're okay. Let me give you a hand. You've got a cut on your leg."

They made it to the bathroom, and Lex then escorted her to the couch. "Do you remember anything?" she asked.

"A lamp. I think I broke a lamp. Ouch," she said as she moved her leg.

"Do you have any pain killers?"

"Motrin is in the drawer."

Lex retrieved the pills and filled a glass with water. "Take both of these."

Sheila downed the tablets. "Did I call the cops?"

"Somehow you did."

"Yeah. I had a drink or two."

"How about a whole bottle of vodka," Lex said. "Have some coffee. I made a pot earlier."

"What time is it?"

"What difference does it make?"

Lex took her by the arm and marched her into the lighted kitchen. "Sit, Sheila. We need to talk. What are you doing?" Lex pointed to the empty cabinet.

"It's so bright in here," Sheila said.

Lex directed Sheila's attention to the empty cabinet. "That's how it should be, no liquor. You have to stop now. You're going back to AA."

Sheila broke down in tears. "I'm really sorry I hurt you and Liz. I couldn't deal with it. I thought you'd never talk to me again."

Lex put her arms around her friend. "Don't worry about it. I'm here. You did what you had to do. You were subpoenaed and testified under oath. It's okay."

"You're a good friend, Lex."

"You are, too, and you'll be a better friend when you quit drinking."

"I've tried before. I'm willing to try again."

"You get some sleep. Let's get you in bed. I have to go to work in a few hours, so I'm going home." Lex pulled the covers over her. "I'll call you later."

Chapter 26

It had been a long night. Lex managed two hours of sleep before she showered, dressed, and ate a small breakfast. She called Sheila, who sounded sober, and then the detective headed to work.

Arriving at the precinct after a stop at Starbucks she set her hot drink on her desk. Gil said, "You look beat."

"I am. What a night. It's my neighbor Sheila." Lex explained what had happened, and drank from her cup. "I need this. Do I look that bad?"

"No, just a little tired."

"I'll be right back."

A few minutes later, she was at her desk. "How do I look?" she asked.

"Beautiful, fresh as a daisy."

"Thanks, handsome. Eat your doughnut."

A strange noise made Gil and Lex look into the squad room where Hutch and Starsky were wheeling in a red boys' bike. Hutch exclaimed, "Look what we got."

"Cool," Benzinger said.

Hutch brushed his hand on the leather seat. "Picked it out myself. Well, Starsky helped. We felt bad for Dray because his reward from Sollie for setting the fire was going to be a new bike."

"What's the latest on him?" Gil asked.

Hutch threw his hands up. "Son of a bitch is gone. According to Arnetta, he has relatives in Mexico. Her guess is that's where he is.

Probably won't be back." Hutch and his partner exited with the bike and set out to deliver it to the boy.

Lex finished her coffee. "How about checking out Stefan Martine?" she said to Gil.

"Sounds like a plan."

She called him and a couple of hours later, Lex and Gil took a squad car to the gallery. From the outside, the place appeared smaller and less ornate than Altman's. Next door to the gallery was Martine's picture framing business. They entered the gallery and Lex saw a tall, handsome man approaching. He extended his hand to the detectives. "I'm Stefan Martine."

Lex shook his hand. "Mr. Martine, I spoke with you earlier. This is my partner, Gil Ramos."

"My pleasure," the business owner said.

Lex glanced at the quaint room that was indeed half the size of Altman's. "Very nice. I like your display of art. I see you also have a frame shop."

"Yes. That's how I started my career. Now I devote my time to the art world. My employees take care of the shop. Let's go to my office."

Lex took him to be close to her age and noticed his quick glance at her tight skirt and upper torso. He wore a tailored dark suit with a paisley tie and pocket hanky. She thought he had a striking resemblance to John F. Kennedy Junior. He sat behind his desk, and the detectives placed themselves on a gray couch. The wall behind the man displayed portraits of women in various stages of undress, and Gil observed a signature that appeared to be Martine's. "Did you paint those?" he asked.

Lex saw Martine's face beginning to blush as he glanced at her. "I hope you aren't offended. My younger brother paints, and he gave them to me. I chose to hang them in here rather than in the gallery. To be honest, he's never worked a day in his life. Forty-three years of sponging off our father." Stefan paused. "Sorry for the family saga."

Lex said, "Actually I find the art quite nice, Mr. Martine." She crossed her legs and noticed his blue eyes staring at them. "I'm not offended. I appreciate art."

"Please, call me Stefan."

Lex smiled. "Do you have a ladies' room?"

"Of course." He pointed down the short corridor. Lex felt his eyes following her as she walked away. She hoped she looked as good as Gil had said.

When she returned a few minutes later, Lex fetched her pad and pen from her purse. "I mentioned Heinrich Altman to you. We're interested in knowing what you can tell us about him, Jerry Davidson, and Fredrike Cambourd."

Stefan leaned back in his executive chair. "Where do I start?" He paused. "First, I never met Fredrike Cambourd. I had been to Heinrich Altman's for an event and noticed the artist's paintings. I thought they were exceptional." Stefan made eye contact with Lex. "Would either of you like something to drink? Water, Perrier?"

Lex thought. *Perrier? Davidson slyly offered it to me, but I'm sure Stefan's motive is sincere.* "No, thank you. We appreciate the offer, she said while glancing at his unwrinkled suit

He continued, "From what I know about Heinrich, he can be a Jekyll and Hyde kind of person."

Intrigued by that remark, Lex asked, "Really? How so?"

"Davidson told me, a while back, Altman had an exclusive. Often, an artist will assign a territory to a gallery. No other place can sell their paintings within a certain mile radius. A gallery in Norwalk, forty-eight miles from Altman's, was selling this particular artist's paintings. Altman had a fifty-mile exclusive, and somehow he found out, so he sued the other gallery owner and got proceeds from a couple of paintings sold at the competitor's business."

"Pretty cold," Gil said.

"Here's another interesting story. Davidson also said Altman had once shot a would-be robber at his gallery. One night, he heard an intruder in the showroom. Altman was in his office and had a gun in his top drawer. He shot the guy in the leg. But here's the strange part. Altman was arrested for having an unregistered weapon."

Lex uttered, "Interesting. Tell us about Jerry Davidson."

"He came to me not too long ago. This is not common knowledge. He was going to sever ties with Altman and offer me a contract to sell Cambourd paintings."

"Why?" Lex asked.

"I told him I was expanding, in fact merging with Candlelight Gallery. The owner is Adrienne Chandelle; came here from France a couple of years ago. Very knowledgeable."

That name rang a bell with Lex. She remembered seeing it in the artist's address book. "Do you know if she knew Cambourd?"

"Adrienne said she remembered him from Paris."

Lex asked, "Did you know about the funeral? You weren't there."

"I knew about it, but I was away. I know Adrienne was there."

"She told you she was there?"

"Yes. She got a ride."

"Do you know who took her?"

"She didn't say."

Lex closed her pad, opened her purse to put the notebook and pen inside, and said, "Thank you, Stefan. We might be back."

He escorted the attractive detective and her partner out. Lex momentarily glanced back and saw him staring at her. She and Gil got into their vehicle, and he started the engine. "We may have found our mystery lady. Adrienne Chandelle," Lex declared. "How about Altman? I think we need to check a little deeper into his past."

"And Martine?" Gil quizzed.

"Nice guy, isn't he?"

Gil glanced at his partner. "He studied you up and down. The whole time, I think he was picturing you up on his wall, naked, with all those other women."

Knowing Stefan had a younger brother, she realized the gallery owner was probably five to seven years older than her. "He is handsome. Charming too."

Gil shook his head. "Are you saying you'd date him?"

Lex grinned. "I didn't notice a ring. If he were to ask, I'd think about it. But he'll get a background check for sure." Lex's cell vibrated. It was Elaine. "I'm at Sheila's. I left work early. She's shaking like a leaf and keeps asking for a drink. What should I do?"

"Hang on. I'm on my way back to the precinct. Can be home in about an hour." Lex put the phone back inside her purse. "I have to get to Sheila's. Elaine's with her. Apparently, Sheila's in withdrawal."

▲

An hour and ten minutes later, Lex walked into Sheila's house. Elaine said, "She's hyper. I helped her change the bandage."

"She really had a lot to drink last night. I'll try to calm her," Lex offered.

"I need to go," Elaine said. "Shannon will be home soon, and we have to get to the orthodontist. You're lucky Liz doesn't have braces."

"I guess. That's one genetic blessing. My parents had great teeth."

Sheila complained, "I have the shakes. I need a drink."

"No, you don't." Lex put her arm around her friend. "You need coffee and food. Just make it through today." Sheila was unsteady when she tried to stand. "Hey, it's going to be okay," Lex assured her. "The first day is always the hardest. Sit."

"I've had a few first days," Sheila said. "It's the rest I'm worried about."

"I hear you. I'll get you into AA again tomorrow."

Sheila straightened up and smiled at her friend. "I know what I have to do. Go home. You must still be tired from last night. I'll be okay."

"You call me if you need me."

Sheila seemed calmer and stopped shaking, so Lex headed home. Van Gogh hopped off the couch and followed her to the kitchen, sidling up to her servant's leg as Lex fed the hungry pet fresh water and cat food.

This had been a long tiring day, and Lex was ready to relax. Before eating dinner, she made her daily call to Liz. Afterward, Lex took a bath and went to bed.

CHAPTER 27

The file Pressley had placed on Lex's desk caught her attention. She opened the manila folder, and began to read it while still standing. Gil entered the cube and asked, "What are you reading?"

"The ballistics report. It's interesting. They couldn't find fingerprints on the casings. Not even a trace or a smudge. Totally clean."

"Really?" Gil said. "You think Davidson was smart enough to load the gun while wearing gloves?"

"That's a heck of a question." Lex stepped out and began pacing. *Cambourd's killing was certainly premeditated. We know Davidson has that gun club award on his mantle. Wiping ammo?*

She nudged Gil. "What are you thinking?" he asked.

"Davidson has that certificate on his mantle. Is it possible he's so smart that he'd make sure prints weren't left on the casings?"

Gil leaned back. "I don't know, but why then would he leave his prints on the desk? Besides his Smith and Wesson is a forty caliber. You think he has another gun?"

"I don't know, but we know Altman has one. Let's check him out."

Gil faced the computer and accessed the gun registry. "Wow. He owns a few handguns, a hunting rifle, and an AK-47."

"What the hell does he need an AK for?" Lex asked.

"Rats. There are big ones in this city."

"Speaking of rats, we know Davidson wasn't who he said he

was, and he spent time in jail. What about Altman? Maybe he has a skeleton or two in his closet."

Gil turned to the computer again. "I'm tapping into the arrest records."

Lex watched over her partner's shoulder as he searched the database.

"Bingo. Here it is. Martine was right. Altman was arrested for having an unregistered Sig Sauer. I did see one registered. He must have paid a fine and subsequently registered it."

"Keep going. Can you print the record?" Gil hit print, and Lex retrieved the report. "Sounds pretty much like Martine described it. The robber was shot in the leg, arrested, and taken to Mid-Manhattan. Altman had reason to shoot, so the only crime he committed was not registering the gun. Do a background check."

It wasn't long before the detectives learned Heinrich Altman had been honorably discharged from the army, and he had served time in Iraq. He'd earned a Medal of Honor in addition to a sharpshooter award. "How interesting," Lex said. "He could be savvy enough to wear gloves. No prints."

"Wow," Gil said. "He was also assigned to munitions."

Hutch leaned in. "You guys got a minute?"

"For you," Lex chided with a smile, "anytime."

"I'll remember that, sunshine. Remember that wine bottle you guys found at the artist's pad?"

"What about it?"

"That was no ordinary bottle. It was a bottle of Chateau Petrus Pomerol, an expensive vintage."

"You know that for a fact?" Lex asked.

"Yeah. We were at the lab. Rusty had it in his office. I looked it up."

"Since when are you a wine connoisseur?" she challenged.

"I subscribe to *Wine Spectator*. I know my wines. That bottle goes for around two grand. I asked Rusty if I could have it when he releases it."

"Thanks for the info," Lex said.

Hutch started toward his cube, and Lex heard Starsky slam the phone. "We gotta go," he yelled. "It's Arnetta Briggs. She's been beaten and stabbed. She's at Mid-Manhattan."

"What about Dray?" Hutch pressed.

"Sollie took him."

Pressley rushed out of his office. "What happened?"

Hutch said, "Briggs. Sollie beat her, and he has the kid. Arnetta is hospitalized. Next time we nab that bastard, we'll lock him away for good. Gotta get to the hospital."

Lex glanced at the ballistics report again. "Altman. I want to talk to him again. That incident with the robber wasn't the first time he fired a gun, and now it's easy to understand why he shot the guy in the leg. Most people would have shot to kill, but Altman knew what he was doing firing that gun. I'll give him a call."

"Mr. Altman," Lex said, "something's come up, and we'd like to come see you."

"Like what?"

"It's important. We won't be there long." After a reluctant assent, Lex hung up. "He's not the happiest camper, but he'll see us."

▲

When they arrived at the gallery, Laura opened the door and pointed to Altman's office. He addressed them. "This better be as important as you say it is. I'm a busy man."

Lex focused on him for a few seconds before saying, "If it wasn't important, we wouldn't be here. Would you rather be dragged to the precinct?"

"I detect some sarcasm," Altman replied.

Lex got straight to the point. "How about telling us about the burglar you shot?"

"You're kidding. Who told you about that?"

Lex didn't want to reveal the true source of that information, Stefan Martine. "We did a background check and that incident popped up."

"Nothing to tell. The guy was lurking in the gallery and I shot him in the leg."

"With an unregistered weapon," Lex said.

"I paid the fine and it's registered now."

"And so is your AK-47 and other guns. Why the AK?"

"They're legal and I have a right to own one."

Lex pressed on. "We saw that you served in Iraq, received a Medal of Honor, are a sharpshooter, and munitions squad member."

She saw Altman's face tighten. "You want to know about the Medal of Honor?" He angled forward. "I'll leave out the blood and guts. I saved two of my platoon buddies. Four others died." He stopped. "You know what? That's all you need to know."

"That is enough. I'm sorry," Lex said.

Altman took a deep breath and let it out.

"Would it surprise you to know the shell casings from the gun that killed Cambourd had no fingerprints on them?" Lex asked.

"What are you saying?" Altman squinted and shrugged.

"I'm saying that's very unusual. Someone with a lot of experience with guns and knowledge of ballistics might have worn gloves to load the gun."

Altman raised his voice. "Jesus, you think because of my experience in munitions and my shooting ability that I did it? Are you accusing me?"

Gil chimed in, "I don't think we're accusing anyone. Those are just interesting facts."

He took out a cigar and put it in his mouth. "I think you two have overstayed you're welcome." He lit the cigar and pointed to the door. "Laura can see you out."

Once the detectives were outside the gallery, Lex said, "He got a little uncomfortable, don't you think?"

"That he did," Gil said. "If you haven't noticed, you seem to have a knack of making people feel that way."

Lex smirked. "I know you get antsy at times."

Gil broke a grin. "So, you can tell?"

Lex took out her cell phone. "Who are you calling?"

"Jerry Davidson. We have time to drop in on him."

He answered his phone. "You know, detective, you have a habit of calling me at inopportune times."

"We need to see you."

"Well, you'll have to wait. I'm in Chicago."

Lex rolled her eyes. "How soon do you think you'll be back?"

"When I finish my business here. Have a good day."

"Hold on. I want an answer. Is it a day, two, a week?" Lex asked.

"A few days."

"You call me this time as soon as you get back here." Lex shook her head. "He's in Chicago and will probably be back in a few days. He better call me."

CHAPTER 28

With Davidson unavailable and Altman rattled, Lex opened her drawer and removed the earring she had found. "Time to meet Adrienne Chandelle. I have a hunch she'll recognize this. Let's go drop in at the Candlelight Gallery. I hope she likes surprises."

▲

The detectives entered the establishment. Thin, model-like, dark-haired, and appearing to be about fifty, Adrienne Chandelle greeted the detectives. "Come in," she politely said, her French accent adding to her charm. "May I help you?"

"Thank you." Lex showed her badge. "This is my partner, Detective Gil Ramos. May we talk?"

Adrienne led the detectives to her office. Two chairs were opposite her glass-top desk that held a metal sculpture of the Eiffel Tower. The gallery owner sat in a modern-style chair. There was a small wine rack on the floor behind her and a few wine glasses on the wooden credenza, also behind her.

Lex opened her pad, and said, "Stefan Martine told us you came here from France."

"I was raised in Paris but always wanted to come to New York. The opportunity arose when I found this gallery. I bought it and renamed it."

"Did you study art in Paris?"

"Oh, yes," she said. "My father owned a gallery, and I grew up around the art world."

"Mr. Martine said you and he are merging your businesses, planning to compete with Heinrich Altman," Lex stated.

"That is our plan."

"Do you know Mr. Altman well?"

"No. I've actually never met him. Stefan has told me about him."

"What about Jerry Davidson?"

"I haven't met him yet. Stefan was going to introduce us."

Gil noted, "I see you have a few bottles of wine."

"It's the drink of choice where I come from. Would you enjoy sharing some with me?"

Lex said, "That's nice of you to offer, but we can't drink while we're working." She was done with the niceties. "Why were you at Fredrike Cambourd's funeral?" Adrienne's eyes opened wide, and she blushed. Before she could speak, Lex said, "We noticed you behind a tree and then you were gone. We saw the car leave and wondered who you were and why the secrecy."

Adrienne reached for the box of Kleenex on her desk. Holding back tears, she said, "I was there, but I wanted to remain at a distance. Stefan told me about the funeral, but since he had to be out of town and couldn't make it, I had my sister Brigitte take me there."

"But why the secrecy?" Lex challenged. "You obviously knew him."

"I always admired his paintings. He had been friends with my father many years ago. I was maybe ten or eleven and the talented Fredrike Cambourd was in his early twenties. I was told he'd come to New York and I had to find him. For some reason, he asked me not to tell anyone."

Lex knew there had to be more to that story. "Why were you in his studio the night he was murdered?"

"He invited me so he could show me the portrait he was painting."

"The woman in the painting was you?"

"It was. He was planning to work on it after I left."

Lex continued, "Tell me something. Do you always bring thousand-dollar wines to guests' homes?"

"He asked me to bring it. He said the shop he goes to doesn't carry expensive vintages."

Lex opened her purse and placed the earring in front of Adrienne. "And how is it that you lost this?"

"I don't know. We drank and reminisced about my father. When I got home, I realized the earring was missing."

"So, it just fell from your ear? Were you intimate?"

Adrienne gasped, "God no. I can't explain how the earring fell."

"What time did you leave the studio?"

"It was a little after nine, and it seemed unusually dark outside. I hailed a taxi."

"You realize he was hooked on cocaine, right?" Lex watched her closely.

Adrienne sighed. "Yes, but he said he was quitting."

"Do you use drugs?"

"No. I have never."

Lex knew the next question might unnerve Adrienne. "Do you own a gun?"

Shocked by the question, Adrienne winced. "Why are you asking me that? No. I don't own a gun."

Lex backed off. "It's just a routine question. We have a murder on our hands, and a killer is still out there."

"I understand. Please find him."

"We're doing our best. When you were with Cambourd, did he ever mention anyone who he may have had a problem with?"

"No. He was a humble man."

Lex closed her pad. "Thank you. I appreciate your honesty."

Adrienne walked with them to the door, opened it, and let the detectives out.

"Do you think Adrienne had anything to do with killing him?" Gil asked.

"No. I believe her…at least most of what she said. But I'm feeling like they may well have been intimate."

"I admit she's an attractive woman. You really think they were having sex?'

"Anything is possible with a two-thousand dollar bottle of wine."

Gil stopped and gave Lex a strange look. "Aha, so you would do it for two grand?"

Lex glared at him. "You know the only reason I don't shoot you is because I don't want RayAnn to be a widow."

Getting into their vehicle, Gil asked, "Where to now?"

"Police Plaza. I wrote Corey's case number on my pad. Let's get that file."

Arriving at headquarters, Lex and Gil approached the semicircular station on the main floor, and she recognized the officer at the console. "Hi, Chelsea."

"Well, what brings you here?"

Lex stated, "We need to get into the dead file room."

"You working on a cold one?"

"We will be as soon as I retrieve a case file," Lex said.

"Gotta ask you guys to sign in. Go see Val."

A couple of minutes later, Lex and Gil were downstairs. Val greeted them. "Been a while. What are you up to?" she asked.

"We need a cold case file labeled Linton-Randall. I have the case number. Here it is."

"How old is this case?"

"Eighteen years," Lex said.

"Wow. That file is in Death Valley. Most of that stuff is digitized, you know."

Lex responded, "We need to examine the physical evidence."

"It should be next door. That room has a mountain of stuff. Follow me."

They entered the larger storage area and Val hit the light switch. "There's a ladder in the corner if you need it. See me before you leave. You'll have to sign it out. Shut off the lights."

Lex looked around the huge room and saw rows of metal storage racks lining the aisles. She moved to her left. "The numbers run this way." Eleven rows down, she said, "It should be in here."

Boxes were stacked on shelves. Two rows from the back, Lex saw the number she was seeking. "That's it, fourth from the top. It says Linton-Randall."

"I can reach it," Gil said. He grabbed the box and set it on the floor.

Lex removed the cover and slid out a few pictures from a manila envelope. She was speechless for a few seconds and welled up. "This is Corey." She took a deep breath and sighed.

"You okay?" Gil asked.

"I will be in a minute. This hurts."

"Put it back, Lex. Let's sign it out."

Placing the pictures back inside the envelope, she then closed the box. Gil picked it up and carried it to Val. "Looks like you got it," she observed.

"I'll sign for it," Lex said.

"Good luck."

"Thanks. We're going to figure this one out."

"Why is this one so special?" Val asked.

Lex nodded. "It's personal. One of the victims was my college boyfriend."

Gil placed the box in the back seat of their car. When they got to the precinct, Lex set it on her desk.

Hutch and Starsky were in Pressley's office. The captain waved for Lex and Gil to join them. "Bastard Sollie is in custody," Hutch said. "Arnetta will be okay. She's got bruises and shoulder lacerations. He was high as a kite, came to her place, beat her, and took off with Dray. They caught the mother—sorry Lex—fucker at Port Authority. He was trying to buy bus tickets to Texas."

"Where's Dray?" Lex asked.

"He's okay. He's staying with Arnetta's sister. Time to head out.

Been a long day," Hutch said.

"Amen," Gil agreed. "I'm out of here. Let's go, Lex."

Their day was done, but Lex had another job to do. Once she got home, she called Elaine. "Hi. You hear from Sheila?"

"I stopped there after work. She might need a push, but I think she's ready for AA."

"I'll get her there."

Lex kept her promise and later escorted Sheila to a meeting.

CHAPTER 29

L ex had gotten to the precinct ahead of Pressley and everyone else, except Benzinger. The young detective stepped into her workspace and said, "You're early."

"You are too. What's your story?"

"I'm an early riser. Caught a local."

Lex said, "I'm doing a little research on an old case."

The young detective pointed to the box on the table. "Is that a cold one?"

"It is. What made you become a detective?"

He clasped his hands together. "It was predestined. Third generation. My grandfather and my father were both cops."

"Really? Where did they work?"

"My grandfather was a lieutenant in New Hampshire. Dad moved us to Bridgeport. He retired, and now my parents live in North Carolina. What about you? What made you become a cop?"

Lex pointed to the box. "This. It's a long story."

Gil joined them. "How's it going? You two having fun?"

"Just getting to know each other," Benzinger said.

Gil commented, "You guys beat me today."

"Got here about an hour ago," Lex replied as Benzinger walked away. "I had to dig into this stuff. There's several crime scene pics. The detective on this case was named O'Rourke, and I want to find him. I remember him. He interviewed me, and I'm sure my statements are on one of these pads."

Pressley entered the squad room, briskly headed toward his office, and slammed the door shut. "Wonder what's got him?" Gil questioned.

"Only one way to find out," Lex said.

"No, Lex. He looks like he shot someone."

She saw him pick up his phone and slam it back down, before he sat with his back to the door. The curious detective got up and opened the captain's door. "Hey," she said. "What's going on? You're awfully agitated."

He swung his chair around. "Close the door. My idiot son, Bernard got into a car accident last night in White Plains. He's okay. The car's not."

"You should be happy he wasn't hurt."

"I am. It only happened a few blocks from his house. No one was hurt, but he was cited for causing the crash. He was on his cell. The car is pretty damaged and was towed, but the jerk's insurance lapsed, and he has no coverage. He got cited for that, too, and I'm sure the other guy's insurance company will litigate. Uninsured. How many times have I told those kids of mine to not be stupid?"

"Take a deep breath," Lex said. "There's nothing you can do now."

Pressley breathed deep and let it out. He grinned. "I can shoot him. Don't worry about me and not a word to your partner or anyone else."

Lex returned to her chair. "What was that all about?" Gil asked.

"Nothing. He's annoyed because he had to take his dog to the vet, and it set him back over three hundred."

"Yeah, tell me about it. I took mine for shots and that ran almost two."

Lex placed a few crime scene photos on her desk. "That's Linton on the floor behind the counter. Corey's in front. Blood all over the place." Lex opened the crime scene report and began to read it. She found O'Rourke's notes too.

Victim one – Linton. Shot once in the chest. Appeared to have been forced to open register, which was empty, and then shot point-blank. Shelves in back appeared to have been rifled. Drugs likely taken.

Victim two – Randall. Wearing green hooded jacket with a cigarette box by his side. Jacket ripped. Appeared to be a struggle before he was shot in stomach.

"Witnesses?" Gil asked.

"Not really. The person who called it in said he saw two men running from the store. They were wearing ski masks." Lex was silent as she studied a photo.

"I know it's tough," Gil sympathized.

Lex sighed and held back a tear. "If I hadn't stayed in his dorm room that late, he would have walked me home earlier, and he wouldn't have been killed."

"Hey, it wasn't your fault," Gil said. "Let's find the killer."

"O'Rourke came to our house and talked with me. He was heavyset, had a mustache, and spoke with a slight lisp. He appeared to be in his late fifties, maybe older. I hope he's still around. We need to talk to him. Paramedics and fire were there, as were a half-dozen uniforms. It had snowed, and the store floor was a mess."

"Who was first on the scene?"

"Officers named Parks and Ryder. Maybe they're around too. Maybe Pressley will recognize these names."

Lex approached the still agitated captain. "Got a minute?"

"Since when do you ask? What's the scoop?"

"Corey. I've been digging through the files with Gil. Do you know the names O'Rourke, Parks, or Ryder? O'Rourke was the detective at the scene, and the other two were the first officers there."

"That was a long time ago. They don't ring a bell. Check with Captain Hernandez at the sixth. I saw him a couple of weeks ago." Pressley looked at his contact list and wrote Hernandez's number on a sticky note. "Here, call him."

"Thanks." Lex left the office and returned her partner. She tapped Gil on the shoulder. "Captain Hernandez at the sixth. His number is on this sticky note." Picking up her desk phone, she called. "Captain," she said, "this is Detective Lex Stall. Captain Pressley suggested I contact you."

"How can I help you?"

"I'm calling because I'm working on a cold case that dates back eighteen years."

"That's before my time. What have you got?"

"Linton's Drug Store was robbed, and two people were shot and killed, including Mr. Linton. A detective named O'Rourke and officers named Parks and Ryder were there. Are you familiar with any of them?"

"Vaguely. I know the name O'Rourke. One of my guys has been here a lot longer than me, and I remember him talking about the detective. I think it's Kevin O'Rourke."

"That's correct," Lex said. "Any idea what happened to him?"

"I think he retired about a year before I got here. That would be seven years ago."

"Any idea where he is?"

"I might be able to find out. Let me check with my guys."

"I appreciate that. Please call me later. You have the precinct number. I'll give you my cell too."

"Fine. I'll get back to you."

Lex placed the photos and documents back into the case file box. "It's a start. Hernandez remembers the name O'Rourke, and he's going to try to get me information on him."

CHAPTER 30

Jerry Davidson walked into Marcus Worthington's office, and the director asked, "How are you? How was Chicago?"

"I'm fine. It was a successful trip. While I was on the plane coming home, I had a thought, and I think you'll like this idea."

Worthington stepped to his liquor supply. "Would you like a drink?"

"No, thank you. Listen, the exhibit. What would you say if I could bring a few Cambourd paintings here to display?"

"You mean to put into the exhibit?"

"Yes."

"I have to think about that. Cambourd with Monet, Renoir, Degas, Cassatt, Manet, Seurat, Pissarro? I don't know. How would we make him fit?"

"How about including him as a disciple. A gifted protégé deserving to be recognized as a colleague of the masters."

The director thought for a minute. "I like it. Let me consider it."

"I have a Cambourd at my place and I plan to get back a few from Altman."

Worthington rested his glasses on his desk. "I want to consult Mr. Gastone. He will have to find an appropriate space to hang them in relation to the other paintings."

"That means you agree?"

Worthington nodded. "I do."

"I'll be in touch," Jerry said.

"Wait. I'll get Gastone here and we can discuss it."

Jerry said, "I'm tired, Marcus. I'll let you two decide. I'm actually not feeling too well. I have to go."

"Okay. Hope you feel better."

Before getting outside, in a corner of the main entrance, Jerry made a phone call. He had unfinished business with Altman and had to settle things. Exiting the building, he walked onto Fifth Avenue, waving at a cab.

He arrived at Altman's fifteen minutes later and rang the bell. Altman came to the door. "I know you're here for the Cambourds, but let's talk first."

"What's to talk about, Heinrich? Where's Laura?"

"Not here. I'm sure we can work this out."

"So you admit you're a thief?"

"Be reasonable. Let's start over."

Jerry shrugged and followed Altman to his office. Seated across from each other, Jerry leaned in and raised his fist. "You dirty bastard, you stole from Cambourd, and you stole from me. There's no starting over."

Altman sneered at his accuser. "Me? What about you? You're an imposter. Working for Sutherland? I guess that was a joke. I know you were fired, Jeffrey. And how did you like the prison food?"

"How the hell did you find out?"

"None of your business. You're a fake."

Jerry yelled back, "You son of a bitch! I never stole anything from Sutherland, and I was framed; should never have gone to jail. But you fucked your friends. Martine and Chandelle won't rip me off. Cambourd agreed to paint exclusively for them, but that's obviously off the table."

Altman grew irate. "You bastard."

"Me?" Jerry shouted. "You never told me the actual sale prices, so you stole from me and him. The cops are onto you. I know they suspect you were skimming profits."

"How do you know that?"

"Because they implied it to me. They were fishing, but I clammed up. I want to settle this now."

"What do you mean settle?"

"I mean you owe me money. I'm guessing at least ten grand, maybe fifteen. I'm taking the remaining consigned paintings. My guys are on their way with a truck."

"Hold it. Let me open your ears a little before you stomp out of here. Those detectives have you in their sights. You better be prepared to answer to them again."

"I'm not worried about that bitch and her partner. I want my money now!"

Altman's face was red as he squirmed. "How much do you want?"

"Show me the receipts."

"Five grand. I'll write you a check right now."

"I'll bet you will. I want the receipts."

Altman snarled. "Six. That's it. Take it or leave it."

"You fucking shyster."

Altman was bursting with anger when he opened his drawer, pulled out his Sig Sauer, and aimed it at Jerry. "Get the hell out of here and take those damned paintings with you."

Jerry stood. "You want to shoot me too? Is that the gun you shot that robber with, or is that the one you used to shoot Cambourd?"

At that moment, the doorbell rang, and Jerry heard his men outside. "Guess I'm saved by the bell. It's my guys. The sooner you let them in, the sooner we'll all be out of here."

Altman shoved the gun back into his drawer and let the men in. Jerry led them to the artwork and a few minutes later, the Cambourd paintings were wrapped and loaded into a van. Altman slammed the gallery door shut, and watched the truck drive away.

▲

The men had hauled the Cambourd's into Jerry's living room. He unwrapped them and took a close look at his friend's paintings, noticing how the artist's more recent works differed from his earlier efforts. The dominant colors were more muted, and his palette seemed to change, much like Monet's did as he aged.

Jerry swore he was kicking the cocaine habit, but he had made that pledge before. Gazing at his briefcase that was on the table next to his chair, he called his supplier.

"Jerry, what's up?" Money asked.

"Meet me, you know where, in one hour."

"You all out so soon?"

"I'm out alright. Cash, lots of it."

"What's that mean? You sound hostile."

"I'm a little edgy. Be there with a new batch."

Forty-five minutes later, Jerry walked to Grand Central, entered the train station, and proceeded downstairs. He muttered to himself that he should be quitting but knew that demon would win out, and he couldn't stop. Looking around at the horde of people surrounding him, he wondered how many were hooked on drugs.

He waited near the bakery, saw the time on his Rolex, and began fidgeting. The anxious addict paced the area, turning in every direction but couldn't spot his cocky dealer. Jerry's phone rang, and he answered it. "Where the hell are you? I'm waiting."

Money's voice was distorted by crowd noise all around him. "I'm comin'. Be there in five."

Those minutes seemed like forever to Jerry, and he finally spotted the drug dealer heading toward him with his familiar Tootsie Pop hanging from his mouth. Money sat across from his customer and took a bite of the candy. Jerry glared at him. "You better give me the good stuff this time, because the last batch was crap. I want a refund. This shit you gave me is in my briefcase. You're taking it back, and I don't care what you do with it, but it's real cheap shit."

Money stared back. "Hey, you know me. I only deal in high quality."

Jerry pointed his finger at his supplier. "High quality, my ass. As long as you get your cash, you don't give a damn what you sell."

"Hey, I got a reputation."

Seething, Jerry said, "I'm telling you this stuff is no good."

"Don't point at me." Money kept licking his Tootsie Pop. "I'm an honest businessman like you. Only thing is, we dress different."

Jerry leaned in. "Don't give me that shit. You know the last batch was inferior."

The dealer said, "Listen, I get what I get. If my boy tells me it's good, I take it."

"Who the fuck are you kidding? I know you sample this shit before you hand over your bread, and so help me, if the stuff you have with you is crap, too, I won't be alone for the next purchase. You hear me?"

Money took another bite of his candy. "Damn, back off. Everyone slips up now and then, but I guarantee this batch is high quality."

"It better be, and I'll know it later because the last hit made me hyper. And stop eating that piece of Tootsie turd while we're talking."

Money frowned. "Take it easy. I'm addicted to this stuff. You should try it sometime. I can get you a whole box of Tootsie's real cheap." The dealer took out a bag of cocaine as a uniformed cop passed by.

"Put that away," Jerry said. "That cop is staring at us."

Money glanced to his left. "Him? No prob. That's Trotter. He's a regular." Jerry opened his briefcase, and Money said, "Keep that shit and take this. We even now?"

Ending the meeting, they went their separate ways. Jerry strolled up Park Avenue, reaching his building in fifteen minutes. Once inside his condo, he opened the briefcase, filled the kitchen canister with the new supply, and took a hit. It wasn't long before the addict knew this batch was good.

CHAPTER 31

A detective named LaCosta contacted Lex. The Sixth Precinct officer said he had known O'Rourke. The bad news was Kevin O'Rourke died a few years ago.

"Damn," she said to Gil. "That's one down. There should be records of officers named Parks and Ryder. Human services should be able to find them." Lex began pacing the room. *What if they're dead too? What if we can't find them?* Nearing her desk, she heard her cell, rushed to open her purse, and answered the phone. "Hi," she responded to Jerry Davidson. "I appreciate you calling."

"You did ask me to call when I got back from Chicago, and I have something to tell you."

"We have a couple of things to discuss with you as well. May we come to your condo?"

"I don't think so. If you want to meet with me, there's a diner across from Grand Central, under the bridge at the beginning of Park and Lexington. Meet me there in an hour."

"I know the place. We'll be there." Lex glanced at her partner. "He wants us to meet him at the diner across from Grand Central in an hour."

Sixty minutes later, the detectives entered the crowded eatery. Lex saw Davidson, casually dressed and seated at a table in the rear corner. A plate with a slice of apple pie and a cup of coffee were in front of him. "They have the best pie," he said.

Lex nodded. "I've been here. Go ahead and finish it."

The detectives took their seats. Lex observed the man's pupils and had no doubt he was high. "We had a conversation with Heinrich Altman. He's got an interesting military background."

Davidson rested his fork. "Go arrest him if you think he killed my friend."

"Not yet. We need hard evidence." Lex said. "However, we do know he was cheating you both, and we intend to obtain his sales records."

"Damn right, he was. I saw him yesterday, and he offered to pay me off." Jerry ate a piece of pie and then continued. "I severed my relationship with him and took back the remaining Cambourds. That thief, Altman wanted to write me a check for five grand, then six, to walk away and call it even. My guys showed up to haul the paintings back to my place, and I said goodbye to him. Never took the money."

"Like I told you, we intend to get his records, and I'm sure we'll see discrepancies. We'll probably go after him for embezzlement."

"How about attempted murder? That son of a bitch pulled a gun on me."

"He what?"

"He was acting like a madman just before my guys came in. They may have saved my life."

"Did any of your men see or hear Altman threaten you?" Gil asked.

"No, but I told them about it. I was glad to be out of there." He finished the pie and drank his coffee.

"Pressing charges would only be your word against his," Lex said. "What about Laura? Was she there?"

"No."

"If he contacts you, let us know," Lex requested.

"He won't." Davidson stood. "Can't wait to see him jailed."

"We'll be chatting with him again," Gil replied.

"Wish I could be there," Davidson said. Directing his attention to Lex, he said, "Good to see you again,"

Lex replied, "Same here. I'm sure we'll see you again too."
The detectives exited the diner. "He was high," Lex remarked.
Gil nodded. "I noticed."

▲

Upon getting back to her desk, Lex placed the cold case crime scene report in front of her. "I want to see what Parks and Ryder saw. There should be statements here. I want to look at O'Rourke's observations again." She re-read what the detective had written. "Know what's odd? He noted a gold chain near Corey. Corey didn't wear a chain. That jewelry had to have been ripped from the shooter when Corey tried to fight him off." Lex opened the envelope containing the crime scene photos and placed them across the back table.

"I didn't think you wanted to see any more of those," Gil said.

"I have to." She scanned them from left to right. "Look at this."

Gil examined the photos. "What are you seeing?"

"It's what I'm not seeing. Tell me what you see in these first six shots that you don't see in the last two."

Gil scratched his head. "The chain. What happened to it?"

"Someone at the scene picked up the gold chain. They stole it. It's not in this box of evidence. What happened to it? The only people inside the store were the victims, the killers, EMTs, and police. One of them made off with it."

"Why?"

"Maybe someone recognized it and knew the killer," Lex surmised.

"Maybe someone wanted it to pawn," Gil said. "This isn't the first or last case where evidence was compromised. That chain could mean nothing."

Lex took a deep breath. "Anything's possible. Call it what you like, but I have a funny feeling about it being mysteriously missing. Besides, it's the only straw we have right now. It's worth exploring."

She put the photos back in the box. "We know the names of everyone at the crime scene. Let's start with Parks and Ryder. They should be in the resource database."

Gil searched and a few seconds later, he got a hit on an officer named Parks. "Donnell Parks," he said.

"Interesting," Lex replied. "He'd be forty-two now. He was new to the force at the time of the murders." She paused. "Look at this. He was suspended three months after Corey was killed. And he didn't just quit…his badge was taken. He was fired. I don't like it. He's a possibility.

Gil then found Gavin Ryder's file. "Worked in Manhattan for thirty-nine years. Retired ten years ago. Married. Last address was Westchester."

"If we're lucky, he's still around."

Gil did a search. "Gavin Ryder. Westchester doesn't come up. Orlando…this is it. Previous address is Westchester. Looks like he retired to Florida. Landline is listed. I'll print it."

Lex retrieved the info. "I'm calling him right now." She heard Ryder's phone ring, but it went to voicemail so she left a detailed message, along with her office and cell numbers. "I hope he calls back."

Gil checked to see if he could locate Donnell Parks. "Nothing in the area. A bunch of addresses in and near Los Angeles. Last one is in Garden Grove. No phone listed."

"If Ryder gets back to me, he may be able to tell us something meaningful." Lex remembered she had a call to make. "I have to get in touch with Sheila to make sure she's going to AA."

Sheila didn't answer her phone, so Lex called Elaine. "Hey, are you home yet?"

"I'll be leaving work in about an hour, why?"

"Sheila isn't answering her phone."

"Oh no."

Lex said to her partner, "I need to go check on Sheila."

She drove toward the Village. *I hope I'm not too late.* Lex called

158

again and still no answer.

Twenty minutes later, arriving at Sheila's, Lex rang the bell. No one came to the door, so she knocked on it and shouted, "Sheila! Are you there?"

Lex heard sounds coming from inside the house and finally, the door opened. "Are you okay?"

Sheila rubbed her eyes. "I think so."

"You didn't answer your phone."

Sheila shook her head. "I took a sleeping pill. I shouldn't do that during the day.

Lex said, "You have an AA meeting tonight. You had me worried. I need to call Elaine." Lex called her friend. "Sheila's fine. I'm with her. She took a sleeping pill. False alarm. She's going to AA later."

"Thanks. I'm glad."

Relieved, Lex went home. Van Gogh was spread out on the couch when she entered the parlor. "Wish I could be as unstressed as you."

CHAPTER 32

Lex saw Hutch staring at her. "Something smells good," he said. "What are you wearing?"

With a hot latte in her hand, she said, "Starbucks number five. You got a splash of Old Spice again?"

"Tried and true, lady."

"Tried, maybe. The truth is, it's what my father wore." She continued walking. Gil was nowhere in sight, and Pressley followed Lex, stopping her. "Listen. Something interesting happened late yesterday afternoon. I got a call from an attorney named Alfred Toberman. He was Cambourd's lawyer. It seems he spoke with Toberman a few weeks ago. The subject was his will. Cambourd asked the lawyer to change the beneficiary from the museum to Adrienne Chandelle."

Thoughts began to swirl in Lex's head. *Now that expensive wine makes sense. She knew. She said she had no idea he had money. She lied. Why?*

"The thing is," Pressley said. "He never signed the new will. It's not valid."

"What? You mean she may think she's getting an inheritance?"

"Maybe." Pressley gave Lex the lawyer's number. "I told him you'd be contacting him."

The captain retreated to his office as Gil approached Lex. "What happened with Sheila?"

"Nothing, she's okay. Listen, Pressley got a call after we left

160

from Cambourd's lawyer." She relayed what the captain had said.

"Are you serious? Can she fight it? You know...probate court?"

"I don't know. I'll ask the lawyer." Lex set her drink on her desk.

"Let me fill my cup."

"I'll wait so you can listen."

Gil placed his coffee next to her latte and she dialed the attorney's number, putting the call on speaker. "Hi, Mr. Toberman, this is Detective Lex Stall. Captain Pressley gave me your number. May I ask you a few questions?"

"Yes, detective."

"Thanks. When exactly did Mr. Cambourd contact you?"

"Which time?"

"How many were there?"

"Three. I prepared a will for him soon after he retired. He came back to sign it and get a copy before I filed it. I hadn't heard from him since then until about six weeks ago."

"You said, heard from him. He called you?"

"Yes. Mr. Cambourd said he'd located a close relative by the name of Adrienne Chandelle, and he wanted his will amended to have her as the primary beneficiary."

"And the museum?" Lex asked.

"The Metropolitan Museum of Art instead of being the only beneficiary was now going to inherit whatever paintings Cambourd had left."

"As I understand it, the revised will was never signed, making it invalid."

"That's correct."

"Assuming Miss Chandelle knew about the change in the will, could she contest it?"

"Anything can be contested. I could represent her, but even then, it could take years in probate before a judgement is made."

"If I wanted a copy of it, could I get one?"

"The existing will is public record. The revised one is just a piece of paper."

"I doubt we'll need it. Thank you for your time."

"Looks like we have another potential suspect," Gil said.

"Guess we do, but we haven't ruled out Altman as the killer. I still want to check out his sales records. He wasn't going to let us look at them without a warrant. And I still think there's something about Jerry Davidson that isn't right. And I might want to chat with Marcus Worthington too. I'm curious to see if he knows the museum is the benefactor."

Lex was about to go to the ladies' room when her office phone lit up. She answered and heard, "Detective Stall, this is Gavin Ryder. I got your message. What can I do for you?"

"Thanks for returning my call. It's about a case you worked eighteen years ago. Linton's Drug Store."

"I remember it well. The druggist and a student were shot and killed."

"That's correct. I'm reopening the case."

"Really? What new evidence have you found?"

"Honestly, I'm still working on that. There's something you need to know. At the time, I was Corey Randall's girlfriend. I remember talking with Detective O'Rourke, and I was sadly informed he passed a few years ago."

"He was a good guy. I was at his funeral."

Lex said, "I became a law officer because of that homicide."

Gil pointed to the phone, and Lex put the call on speaker. "I want to ask you about what you remember from the time you got to the drug store to the time you left. According to the incident report, you and an officer named Donnell Parks were first on the scene."

"We arrived just prior to the EMTs. As I recall, it had snowed, and there were no real witnesses."

"Did you and Parks arrive together?"

"Kind of. We were in separate vehicles, but we got there within

162

minutes of each other. O'Rourke was right behind us."

"What do you remember seeing?"

"I recall the male victim, a student, and the store owner both being shot and killed."

"Do you remember seeing a chain, a gold chain, on the floor near Corey's body?"

"I do remember a chain."

"That's my problem," Lex said. "There are crime scene photos clearly showing the chain. Then there are a couple of photos where the chain is mysteriously missing."

"Maybe the lab guys took it."

"There's no indication that they took it. No notation of evidence, and it's not in the box we have. It appears to have been stolen by someone at the scene." Lex moved to a different angle. "How well did you know Parks?"

"He was kind of rough around the edges. Suspended if I remember right."

"Parks was asked to turn in his badge a few months after the robbery-homicide. What do you mean when you say he was rough around the edges?"

"I know he was in a gang once, and he had a twin brother doing time. A long time, as I remember."

"Any idea where Parks may have gone?"

"No, but his brother might still be locked up. Try the prison records. If you're lucky, you might get a hit on him."

Gil nodded and Lex said, "Thanks for the chat. Hope you're enjoying retirement."

"Thanks. And let me know what you find out."

The call ended. "We may be on the right track," Gil cautioned. "Let's not get our hopes up too high."

"Donnell Parks has a twin. I bet his name is similar. It shouldn't be too hard to find an inmate with a name similar to Donnell."

Gil went to the computer and searched New York state prison

records. "Parks." He scrolled the list. "This might be it. Dexter Parks. He's at Attica."

"Interesting," Lex said. "Dexter Parks has a long list of robberies. He's serving life for killing a security guard at an all-night pharmacy in the Bronx. Wow, it happened seven months after Linton's. He sounds like a possible suspect. I wonder if Pressley knows the warden's name." She got up. "I'm going to the ladies' room and then I'll ask him."

"Want me to check with him?" Gil asked.

"He'd rather see my face than yours. I'll be right back."

Returning from the lavatory, she entered the captain's office. "Yes, my ace detective. What can I do for you now?"

"Question: do you know the warden at Attica?"

"No. Why?"

Lex explained what she and Gil learned about the cold case. "We need to contact him."

"I'll find out and get back to you."

"Thanks."

CHAPTER 33

What began as a routine morning quickly changed after Lex purchased her latte. She left the coffee shop with her drink in her hand and heard her phone. Stopping to set her cup on a bench, she answered the call. It was Creighton Manning; he had intriguing information that she had to see and asked her to come to his office as soon as possible. Lex picked up the drink, got into her Corolla, and phoned Gil. "Hi, I just got a call from my lawyer. I don't know what it's about yet, but he wants to see me immediately. Tell Pressley where I am."

"He's not here. What's going on?"

"I told you, I don't know yet. I'll see you later."

Lex arrived at Manning's building and set foot into the lobby. She gripped her purse while waiting for the elevator. It seemed to take forever for the doors to open. Finally, they did, and three people exited the car before she got in and rode to floor eleven. When the doors opened, she eagerly walked to Manning's office. His secretary said, "He's waiting for you, go ahead in."

"Good morning, Lex. Please have a seat." As he opened a file, her heart pounded anxiously, waiting to hear what he had to say. "My staff has been checking on Jon. We've come up with revealing information." Lex's eyes grew wide as Manning continued. "Let me get some things straight. You and Jon have been separated for four years."

Lex nodded. "Nearly five."

"Jon has been remarried for three years, right?"

Lex again nodded and wondered where this was going.

"Jon's wife has a five-year-old son, right?"

It was another yes from Lex.

"That makes Jon the stepfather, right?"

"Right, but what's that got to do with anything?"

Manning showed her copies of Jon Stall's federal tax returns for the two years after their divorce and before he remarried. "See anything wrong here?"

Lex slowly read the documents. "Not really, why?"

"Look a little closer. See the dependents Jon listed?" Manning ran his finger to that line. "This is troublesome. Jon listed Elizabeth Stall, which was correct since he paid child support, but he also listed Adam Baxter."

Lex didn't know what to make of it. "Why would he claim Adam? He wasn't his stepson back then," she said.

"That's right. Jon wasn't married to Adam's mother until two years later, so why would he claim the boy on his income tax?"

"What? I don't get it."

Manning came around to Lex's side. "I believe Adam is Jon's son, not his stepson."

Lex's jaw dropped in disbelief. "What? I thought Adam was from Julie's first marriage."

"Afraid not. Her husband died more than a year before Adam was born."

Lex was nearly speechless, looked at Manning and uttered, "That means Julie and Jon had him while that bastard was still married to me?"

"That appears to be true, but it also means Jon and his lawyer, Anthony Asino, lied to Judge Fleming when they said the boy was Jon's stepson. They have some explaining to do, because if Jon says he didn't lie to the judge, then he lied to the government by claiming Adam as his son. So, you see, he's either guilty of perjury or income tax fraud."

Lex was stunned. "What are you saying?"

Manning placed the file in his tray. "I'm saying we're going to court again to get Liz back. I'm going to file a petition with Judge Fleming, visit her, explain the situation, and demand a paternity test. I may have misjudged Fleming before because I thought she'd be on your side, a single mother to single mother," he said. "Now I think our chances are a lock because the one thing judges loathe is lying, and one way or the other, Asino and Jon lied to her."

Lex stood with tears in her eyes and threw her arms around the lawyer. "Thank you very much, Creighton."

As she was leaving, he stopped her. "Lex, there's one more thing. We're also suing for all the attorney's fees, so you won't owe a dime."

Exiting the office, filled with joy, she made it to her car and drove out of the garage. Lex slipped in her Fleetwood Mac CD, and when she heard Stevie Nicks singing "Silver Lining," she knew Liz was going to be back home in the village.

▲

Smiling as she entered her workspace, Gil said "You look happy. What did Manning tell you?"

"He said I'm getting Liz back. What did you tell the captain?"

"Pressley got here a half-hour ago. He was late because he had one of those migraines. He's better. I said you had an appointment with your attorney."

"I'll be right back to fill you in."

Pressley stood when she entered his office. "What's up?" he asked.

"What about you?" Lex replied.

"Just a headache."

"I have good news." Lex reiterated what Manning had told her.

The captain raised his thumbs. "Go get him," Pressley said. "Wait. Warden's name is Cho. Henry Cho. Here's a number."

"Thanks. I'm going to call him."

Getting back to her cube, she tapped Gil. "I have the warden's name. It's Cho. I'm calling him."

"You're leaving me hanging! What happened with Manning?"

Lex explained the details about her deceitful ex-husband before contacting the warden. She made sure the phone was on speaker. Cho answered, and Lex stated why she called. "Dexter Parks is a tough one. Been here a long time," the warden said. "I can have him brought here, but there's no guarantee he'll talk."

"That's good enough. We'll see if we can crack him, "Lex said. "How soon can you have him in your office for a video chat?"

"Give me an hour? What's the number you want me to call?"

Lex recited it and then repeated it. "Got it," Cho said.

An hour later, Gil and Lex were in the conference room when the call came. Cho appeared on the TV screen. "Warden Cho," Lex said. "Thank you. This is my partner, Detective Gil Ramos."

In back of the warden was a muscular prison guard. To his right was another strong guard, and seated beside the warden was an inmate dressed in orange and black. The prisoner sat silently with his arms crossed. His dreadlocks hung below his shoulders and he appeared to be about two-hundred-fifty pounds. Lex took him to be over six feet tall. She saw his hostile look, and wondered if she could soften him with a polite opening. "Mr. Parks. How are you today?"

When he opened his mouth, he revealed two gold teeth. "What's this about?"

"May I ask you a few questions?"

"Depends."

Lex stared at him. "Do you have a twin brother named Donnell, a police officer?"

He didn't say a word.

"Donnell is your brother, isn't he?"

Dexter glared at Lex. "Maybe he is and maybe he isn't. Why?"

Lex knew she had a fight on her hands knowing this thug wasn't going to open up easily. Switching to hard tactics, she sternly said,

168

"Okay, Dexter. Let's cut to the chase. We know Donnell is your brother, and we know he was a crooked cop. Were you a gang banger too? Both of you cold-blooded killers."

"Fuck you, little lady."

Lex pressed on. "Tell us about the security guard you killed."

"What about him?"

"Why'd you shoot him?"

"What difference does that make? I'm doing life."

"Right," Lex said. "You ever shoot and kill anyone else?"

"Maybe…maybe not. Why?"

"Where is Donnell?"

Dexter was reluctant to answer and Lex sensed she might lose him. She pushed harder. "Come on Dexter. You know where your dirty killer brother is."

Dexter's eyes grew larger. "Bullshit. He's no killer. Last I knew, he was on the West Coast. Haven't heard from him in years."

"Do you remember a place called Linton's Drug Store?"

Dexter was stone-faced. "I don't have to talk to you no more." He attempted to rise from his chair and a both guards forced him back down. The inmate icily stared at Lex.

The gutsy detective kept going. She had picked up on Dexter's protecting his brother, Donnell, and she was hoping to strike a nerve. "After Donnell shot that drug store owner and that college student, he gave you that chain. Didn't he?'

Lex saw she'd indeed gotten to him, and the prisoner gritted his teeth. Without hesitation, he said, "No. God damn it. Donnell was on duty and showed up. That fucking kid shoulda never grabbed my chain."

At that moment, Lex realized he might confess to the killings if she pushed one more time, so she took another bold shot at him. "It was you, Dexter. It was you who shot them, wasn't it. Like you said, you're already serving life. You can't get more time than that."

Lex felt Dexter's hostile stare. "You're pretty hot for a cop. Damn right I did."

169

Lex's innards were churning as she lashed out. "You're nothing but a low-life killer. You're a gutless coward. Go back to your cell and rot."

Dexter barked out, "Go get fucked, you bitch."

Lex closed her eyes momentarily, and then opened them. "Warden, you can send him back."

Cho ordered his guards out of the room with Dexter. "You're a hell of an interrogator. I didn't think he'd talk. Great job, detective."

Lex took a deep breath. "Thank you, sir."

After the screen went blank, tears streamed down Lex's face. Gil drew close to her and placed his arm around her shoulder. "I've never been prouder of you, Lex."

"We did it," she said.

"You did it."

Lex breathed hard. "Of all the times to be out of Kleenex," she complained, wiping tears on her sleeves. "I'm fine. Let's wrap this up, document everything, and mark the case closed. I'm also going to let Gavin Ryder know."

She'd finally seen Corey's killer. The sight of Dexter Parks twisted her stomach, but knowing he'd never be back on the street gave her some satisfaction. However, nothing she could do would bring Corey back.

The good news was that Dexter had been locked up for years. The bad news was Dexter Parks hadn't been apprehended before he had killed again, and ex-police officer Donnell Parks was nowhere to be found.

CHAPTER 34

Lex was beyond thrilled to have Manning working to get Liz back. She browsed the mail and checked her home phone for messages. There were none. She went upstairs to change and came back wearing purple sweats. Her cell was on the counter, and she called Liz. Lex suppressed the urge to tell her daughter she would likely be returning to the Village. "Hi, Liz, how's it going?"

"I'm so excited! Dad's taking me to see *Cats*."

Lex's head spun. "How nice," she replied.

"There's a birthday party for Adam tomorrow, and I bought him a horn for his bike."

Lex didn't let Liz know the truth that Adam was likely her half-brother. Manning would have to prove that first. "Sounds like a fun weekend. Have a good time. I don't really have plans yet, but maybe Elaine and I will do something. Shannon is at her dad's."

"I know."

"Okay, love you."

Lex called Elaine and her friend asked, "Do you want to go get something to eat?"

"Sure. Let me put on a pair of jeans," Lex said. "How about going to that little bistro on Seventh? I'll be over in ten."

Before leaving, Lex fed Van Gogh.

Wearing her blue denims and a sweatshirt she rarely wore, she walked to Elaine's and went inside. Lex saw her friend's look. "Haven't seen that sweatshirt in a while."

171

Lex smiled. "I've kept this NYU shirt in pristine condition all these years and it still fits. I'll tell you a hell of a story while we eat."

"Okay. How's the cat? Shannon keeps asking me for one. Her birthday is coming. I might get her one. She likes Van Gogh."

The two women walked to the neighborhood bistro, found the last empty table, and ordered dinner. "This has been a crazy day," Lex marveled. She spared some details but told her friend how she'd solved Corey's murder. Then Lex explained how Manning had done his homework and was about to drop the hammer on Jon and his attorney. "I'm sure Liz will be back home very soon. Manning will do his best to expedite things with the judge."

Elaine said, "You deserve a treat. Let me buy this one. I'm incredibly happy for you."

Lex lifted her wine glass. "Good friends," she toasted.

They finished their casual dinner and headed to Lex's place. "You know what?" Elaine asked. "I think it's time we start dating again before we shrivel up and forget what it's like."

"Lex said, "I've thought about it."

"Anyone in mind?"

Lex said, "Maybe. There's an art gallery owner named Stefan Martine, handsome and charming, but he'd get a thorough check, for sure. That is, if he were to ask me out. Know what? I think I'll go shopping tomorrow for a new dress just in case."

"That sounds great. I wouldn't mind a new outfit myself. We can both shop. Want to go to a nice restaurant, like Scalia, after?"

"Love to."

"I'll make a dinner reservation. How's seven?"

"Book it."

CHAPTER 35

Lex and Elaine looked forward to their day of shopping and fine dining. They rode the subway to Herald Square and went into Macy's. Both women looked at several dresses. Lex couldn't decide between a low-cut, dark-blue one and a more mid-length red one. After trying on the dresses, she decided to buy them both. Elaine was partial to green, the color of her eyes and she bought a dress to match them.

The shopping spree continued to the shoe department and then to lingerie to complete the buying binge.

Stepping outside with their packages, Lex said, "Stefan Martine's gallery is a few blocks from here. I'd show you, but with these bags, I think we'd better take a taxi back home."

The women returned to their homes with their purchases, and a few hours later were ready to venture out to Scalia's. Lex wore the blue dress, new shoes, and her new undergarments. It had been a warm day, and Lex checked the forecast before completing her ensemble by throwing a white sweater over her shoulders. She went to Elaine's and complimented her on her outfit. "You look hot. Love the green on you."

"You're gorgeous," Elaine commented.

They entered Scalia's and enjoyed a gourmet meal, along with a bottle of wine. It was dark outside when they exited the restaurant. "It's a nice night," Lex said. "Let's take a walk."

They approached a bar that Lex and Corey had often frequented, and Lex peered inside. "This is almost surreal. I want to go in and have a drink for old times."

Elaine said, "You realize we'll be the oldest people in there? And we're dressed way too formal for that crowd."

"So what? It will be a rush."

The establishment's exterior was the same, but when they went inside, Lex didn't recognize the place. The dance floor was gone, there were more tables and TVs, and the bar was now extended in an L-shape. The two women squeezed through the tightly packed crowd to the bar. The music was loud and there were no empty stools. Lex noticed glances they were getting, and Elaine said, "I'm a little uncomfortable in here with these college boys. You really want to get a drink here?"

"Corey and I came here all the time. We'll have a quick one and go."

"Okay, but there's more eyes on your breasts than I can count."

"Relax and don't forget: my weapon is in my purse."

They stepped up, and the bartender approached them. "Look to your right," Elaine said. "That young guy in the corner is drooling over you. Must be all of twenty-one."

"What would you like?" the bartender asked.

"A tequila sunrise," Lex requested.

Elaine's cell phone rang, but the music was too loud for her to hear. She stepped outside and then came back in to find Lex. "I have to go. Shannon is sick and wants to come home from her dad's."

Lex thought about leaving but couldn't shake the memories of her and Corey sitting at this bar. "Go ahead. I'm going to have that drink for Corey."

Elaine exited, and an inebriated man immediately got off his stool and offered Lex his seat. "How about me buying you that drink," he slurred.

She sat. "No, thanks. I'm waiting for someone, but thanks for the seat."

After the bartender set her cocktail on the counter, she couldn't help noticing the young guy Elaine mentioned. He smiled at Lex, but she shied away. While sipping her tequila sunrise, the bartender placed another one in front of her. "Excuse me," she said. "Is there a two-drink minimum?"

The bartender pointed to his left. "No, miss. He paid for this one."

She glanced at the handsome stud, and Lex wondered how old he was. *Nice looking and so young.* She nodded a thank-you to him. He walked toward her. Lex guessed he was around six-one, his sandy hair was short, and he was clean-shaven. The confident young man wore a pin-striped dress shirt, navy blue sweater, and dark slacks. She smelled his cologne, and it reminded her of Corey. "I'm Aaron," he said, standing beside her.

"I'm Lex. So, what's your story?"

"I don't have a story, but I'm always looking for one," he said. "I'm a journalist. I enjoy talking with people, and you look interesting."

Lex sipped her drink. "Interesting, as in a news story, a woman, or something else?"

He drank from his glass. "Definitely, a woman. Let's keep it light because I don't want you getting the wrong idea."

Lex took another sip. "And what is the wrong idea?"

He gazed into her eyes. "I'm gay."

Lex stared at him. "Me too."

He laughed. "Right, guess that line didn't work."

Lex laughed. "Had me for a second…not really."

"Okay. Now that we've got that straight, your turn. What's your story?"

"What makes you think I have one?"

"You CIA?"

Lex laughed. "No. I'm a city caseworker, and you look like you could use some therapy."

He chuckled. "Where'd you go to college?"

"Right down the street; NYU," Lex answered.

He lifted his glass. "Let's toast. Me too. Did you know Professor Cricket?"

She touched her glass to his. "How can you forget that annoying voice? When did you graduate?" Lex noticed his hesitation.

"Two years ago, almost three."

Lex sensed he was still in school. "Really? When did you say you graduated?"

He grinned. "You're sharp. Soon."

She started feeling the effects from the wine she'd consumed at Scalia's as well as the drink she was having now. Lex stared at Aaron and she knew what was on his mind. He was charmingly seductive and actually resembled Corey. She finished her second drink, excused herself, and went to the ladies' room. Returning to her stool, she saw another tequila sunrise sitting on the bar. "Really?" she asked. "Are you trying to get me drunk?"

He lifted his glass of gin and tonic, touched hers, and peered into her hazy brown eyes. "Maybe. You trying to get me drunk?"

Lex was enjoying the banter, and slid her hand through her hair. "I don't think I'd have to try hard." Feeling young and enjoying herself for the first time in years, she imagined Corey standing there. "I think I've had enough," she slurred. "Two is plenty."

She left the untouched third Tequila Sunrise on the counter, and Aaron took her arm. "Are you okay?"

"I think so." Lex held onto his arm to steady herself. "I'm a little woozy," she said. "I should hail a cab."

Aaron placed his arm around her. "How about some air and a walk?"

Lex took another step and didn't resist his assistance. Once they got outside, Lex turned left. "Whoa," he said. "My place isn't far from here. You can sober up there." He spun her in the other direction and a few minutes later, they were inside Aaron's apartment.

Lex was a little tipsy, but she was aware of where she was, and not refusing his guidance to the bedroom, she let him undress her.

They slid into his bed, but Lex kept seeing Corey, as if it were he who she was about to have sex with.

Waking at 5:30 a.m. with Aaron's bare body beside hers, she got out of bed, picked up her underwear, and went into the bathroom. A stall shower was to her left and she quickly cleansed herself, toweled off and put on her bra and panties. She stared into the mirror, knowing the gratifying night of sex she'd had with Aaron was a mistake. Still in her mind, it was Corey who had pleasured her. Toothpaste was on the counter, so she put some on her fingertip and smeared it across her teeth, then swished the paste away before sweeping her fingers through her mussed hair. Wiping her hands on a towel, she noticed a pair of pink panties that were hanging on the hook of the door.

Exiting the bathroom, wearing only her underwear, she took her dress off a chair and put the garment on. Aaron was sitting on the edge of his bed. He reached for her hand, and she pulled it back. "I have to go home."

"Please don't. Not yet."

Lex said, "I really need to leave. You don't understand."

He jumped out of bed and put on his briefs. "Please stay. I'll make breakfast, and we can talk. Tell me more about your job."

Lex picked up her purse, opened it, and took out her card for him. Aaron's mouth dropped wide-open. "A detective? You're a cop? You said you were a caseworker."

"I am, but not the kind of cases you were thinking of."

"I'm not in trouble, am I?"

Lex laughed. "No. I may have been a little inebriated, but what we did was consensual."

"Can I call you? Have another drink sometime?"

She smirked. "I don't think so. Judging by the pink panties hanging on your bathroom door, it looks to me like you don't have any problem getting laid. You're quite charming. I'm going to leave now."

Lex retrieved her sweater and saw herself out. She briskly

walked toward home in the early morning chilly air as the sun began to rise. When she got to her street, she saw an ambulance and two police cars that appeared to be parked in front of Sheila's place, and hurried to her friend's house. A uniformed officer was standing at the entrance. Lex opened her purse and flashed her badge. Rushing inside, she saw an open vodka bottle. But it was the bloodstained floor and the body bag that startled her. She approached an officer standing near an EMT. "I'm a detective. She was my friend. What happened?"

"You have to look at this," he said. The uniform handed her a note.

Lex read it in disbelief.

So many times, so much alcohol. It got me. I can't think about anything but drinking. I'm so alone. I'm so desperate. I've been called. I'm out of here.

Lex collapsed to her knees. "How'd she do it?"

"Wrists. She slit them with a razor." He pointed to a table. "It's in that baggie. Probably had one last drink before she blacked out."

"Who called?"

"The lady in the kitchen. She's pretty upset."

Lex walked into the room and saw Elaine. The shocked woman's head was bowed, and she was breathing into a bag. Lex put her arm around Elaine. "Breathe easy. I'll get you home." Elaine nodded, released the bag, and sat up. "How is Shannon?"

"She's got a fever. I've been up with her half the night."

Lex was wearing her blue dress and white sweater. "You're still wearing your dress. You didn't, did you?"

"I sure did."

"You had sex with him?"

"I'll tell you about it later. Let's get you home. How'd you happen to be here?"

"It was strange. Since I was up anyway, I knew I needed Tylenol and decided to go to the all night drugstore. I was walking by here, and I saw the lights on. The curtains were open. I went to see if she

178

was okay. It was horrible. I called for help."

Lex escorted her friend home, left Elaine's, and headed back to Sheila's place. The EMTs and police officers were just leaving. "I have a key. I'll lock up."

"She got any next of kin?" the officer asked.

"No. I'm sort of it."

"It's all yours. If you want the report, I suppose you know where to get it."

Sheila's covered corpse was removed, and the uniforms exited the premises. Lex picked up the suicide note that had been left behind.

Her weekend had gone from something incredibly nostalgic to disastrous in a matter of minutes. Lex entered her residence, changed into a pair of sweats, and went downstairs. She fed Van Gogh and cleaned the litter box before making coffee and eating breakfast. Trying to make sense of the past twenty-four hours, Lex only came up with the fact that she had sex with a college student, and Sheila was dead.

CHAPTER 36

Dark clouds filled the sky, and the threatening weather matched Lex's mood as she headed to her workplace. She saw Gil with his hand in the doughnut box. "What are you doing?" she gruffly asked.

"Hi. No latte?"

"Not today. And you don't need that crap."

Hutch appeared. "Morning, mother Lex."

"Not now, Hutch."

"Testy today," he said.

Lex stopped in her tracks and stared at him. "You haven't seen testy yet."

Gil chimed in. "Hey, Lex, what is it? You're in a snit."

She sighed. "It's Sheila. She committed suicide yesterday."

"How?" Gil asked.

Hutch respectfully said, "I'm sorry."

Gil followed her to their cube, a cup of coffee in his hand.

Seated beside her partner, she took the suicide note from her purse and handed it to him. Gil read it. "Sad, Lex."

"I have to get her estate together. Elaine will help."

Pressley came around the corner. "Did I hear suicide?"

Gil passed the note to him. "Not a nice way to go," Pressley said. "Sorry, Lex."

Summoning up her detective exterior, she said to her boss, "With all that's been going on we neglected to ask for a warrant to obtain sales records from Heinrich Altman."

Pressley stepped toward his office. "I'll get on it."

Lex turned to Gil. "How about getting Roly-Poly Foley to come with us when we go to Altman's?"

Gil sipped his coffee. "The computer nerd?"

"Yup. He might be an insurance policy. I'm betting Altman has two sets of books. He might hand over his paper file, but I want to see what's on his computer, and Foley can get into any file that exists."

Gil smiled at his partner. "I like your brain. You going to call him?"

"I am."

Two hours later, the computer geek appeared at Lex's desk. "Foley. Long time since we've seen you," she stated.

"You're lucky it's lightened up outside or I may not have agreed to take a field trip today."

Pressley was standing at his office door. "Wow! Look at you. How'd you lose all that weight?"

Grinning, he answered, "A hundred pounds. Have a few more to go. All it took was the right woman. I'm getting married this summer."

"Congratulations. That's great," Lex said. "What's her name?"

"Cara. Met her at a laundromat. She lives around the corner from me. Works for a vet."

"You dog," Gil wryly said.

Foley shook his head. "Good one. Nice to see you too. Where are we going?"

Lex responded, "We're going to an art gallery to obtain sales records. We suspect the owner, Heinrich Altman, will likely hand us a cooked set. We're betting he has the real records on his computer."

"What about the warrant? We don't have it yet," Gil said.

"I'm not sure we'll need it." Lex retrieved an unrelated, expired warrant from her drawer. "Here. Shove this in your pocket. He'll never know the difference."

"You want to call Altman?"

"No. Let's surprise him."

Gil shook his finger at Lex. "He was surprised once before, remember? That time, he shot the intruder, and he didn't exactly enjoy our last visit."

▲

Standing outside the gallery door, Gil rang the bell, and Laura opened it. "Is Mr. Altman expecting you? He's waiting for a client."

"No," Lex said. "I apologize, but we have to see him. Now."

"I'll inform him you're here."

Seconds later, Altman came into the gallery. "What are you doing here? I've got a very important gentleman coming in."

Lex assured, "We can be out of here in ten minutes. Can we go back to your office?"

"You know where it is."

"By the way, this is Officer Foley. He's assisting us," Lex said.

Once inside the office, Gil said to Foley, "See that vase? That's called a beaker. It's Chinese and valuable."

"It's a Ku. So, what is it?" Altman asked.

Lex said, "We happened to hear a story about you aiming a gun at Jerry Davidson."

"He told you that? He robbed me by having his crew come in and take back the paintings he'd left here. Yes, I was pissed."

"Mad enough to shoot him like that robber you shot?"

Altman pitched forward. "That's pretty low, Detective."

The doorbell rang, and Altman said, "My client is here. You need to wrap this up fast. I have to ask him to wait. Laura can chat with him." Altman exited his office and a couple of minutes later rejoined the detectives.

Lex said, "Last time we were here, we asked to see your sales records regarding Cambourd's paintings. For some reason, you were

182

combative and wouldn't let us look at them. We want to see those files now!"

"I told you. They're private, and you're not the IRS."

"Okay. Let's not play any more games." She nudged Gil.

Her partner waved the invalid paper. "This warrant says we have a right to obtain those records. It also gives us the right to search this place for them should you refuse to give them to us."

Altman snapped, "This is outrageous!"

Making that unenforceable threat, Lex sternly said, "If you resist, we could take you to jail."

"Keep it down. I can't have my client hearing this. I'll be right back."

He engaged the man and asked him to come back at a later time. Altman also told Laura to take the rest of the day off before he returned to his office.

Altman moved to a file cabinet, reluctantly opened the top drawer, and pulled out his sales ledger. "Here. You gonna cut me some slack now?"

Lex said, "Thank you, but we're not quite finished, Mr. Altman. That warrant gives us the right to search your computer. Officer Foley is a computer analyst, so he will be checking your stored data."

"What?" a stunned Altman questioned. Foley took a step toward the desk where the computer was located, and asked "Are there any passwords I need to know?"

"No," Altman answered.

"Are you sure?" Foley challenged. "I can sit here all day and decipher anything that's here. You can save us a lot of time by telling me."

"You want me to log in?" Altman offered.

He did so and immediately Foley said, "Cambourd is here."

"Great. Print the details," Lex said.

"Just the one artist?" Foley asked.

"Yes," Lex answered.

He hit the print button. "I brought a flash with me and can download it," Foley suggested.

"Great," Lex replied. "Do it." She stepped to the printer and took the paper trail. "Should we compare these with the ledger Gil is holding?" she pressed Altman.

The gallery owner angrily said, "I have nothing to say. You'll be talking to my lawyer."

Lex retorted, "I suspect we will. Thanks for your time."

Foley, Gil, and Lex got into their vehicle. "I'd say we have what we need to file embezzlement charges. We'll know for sure once we compare the records."

▲

When they got back to the precinct, Pressley approached with a warrant in his hand. "I thought you wanted this," he said.

Lex took it from him. "I do. Thank you, sir." She gave it to Gil. "Hang onto this and ditch the other warrant."

"What are you talking about?" Pressley asked.

Gil showed the captain the paper he'd flashed Altman.

Pressley browsed it. "Are you serious? He thought this was a real warrant?"

Lex nodded. "Worked like a charm."

Pressley rolled up the paper and murmured, "Amazing, just plain amazing. You realize if his attorney hears about this, you're gonna be in trouble."

Lex held up the real warrant Pressley handed her. "Not as long as I keep this."

He went back to his office, shaking his head.

Foley rolled his eyes. "I have to get back. Had a blast. Call me if you need me."

Lex's cell vibrated, and she answered it. "Hi, Creighton."

"We're all set. Fleming reviewed my petition. She's advising Asino and checking her calendar."

184

"That's great. Thanks. Let me know."

"What's up?" Gil asked.

"We'll be back in court soon."

Gil took Cambourd's records from the box on the floor and placed them on his desk. In addition, he set Altman's ledger and computer printout next to the victim's papers. They studied each document. Gil said, "I'd say we were right on. The difference between these records is about a twenty thousand dollar discrepancy."

"That's called embezzlement. I'd like to get him on murder and save this stuff for later."

"Where do we go with Adrienne Chandelle?"

"Good question. We don't know for sure if she knew about the money. She said she remembered Cambourd from when she was a young girl. No way did it sound like they were related. She would have said that. Somehow, she got into the will."

CHAPTER 37

Sheila's estate needed to be taken care of, not to mention the burial. "We have to clean out her place and go through her papers," Lex said while sitting at Elaine's kitchen table.

"I know. I don't remember her talking about relatives," Elaine said.

"She had an older sister, a Nun, who passed several years ago. I'm sure there are no nieces or nephews. Everything she has will end up in probate, unless we find a valid will."

"Where is her body?" Elaine asked.

"County morgue. Actually, an autopsy has to be done. Suicides are technically crimes. It's illegal to kill yourself. I don't think she'd mind being cremated. It's the easiest way. I can look into that."

"You want to go to that bistro again? Shannon is with her dad. I want to stop by the pet shop and look at cats. I decided to get her one."

The two friends walked to the restaurant. Elaine waited until they were finished eating to ask about what happened at the bar they visited after dining at Scalia's. "So tell me, Lex."

"Tell you what?"

"You know. The young stud, the bar, the blue dress. That night."

Lex grinned. "Okay. If you must know, I stayed to have that one drink after you left the bar. That young student you saw staring at me is named Aaron. He is very charming and admitted he was a student at NYU. Anyway, before I knew it, I had a couple of drinks.

Add those to the wine we had at Scalia's and I was having a good time, not to mention I never could hold my liquor. It was almost surreal because I kept seeing Corey, and in a way, Aaron was Corey. I was ready to leave and was a little tipsy, so Aaron walked with me outside. I was intending to get a cab."

"And he took you to his place?"

Lex drank water from her glass. "His apartment wasn't far from the bar, and he convinced me to take a walk."

"He must have been some smooth talker to seduce you."

"I'm not too sure who seduced who. I wasn't drunk enough not to resist." Lex took a deep breath. "The truth was I wanted him. But when I woke up in his bed, I knew I'd made a huge mistake. Sleeping with a twenty-one-year-old!"

Elaine nodded. "Was it great?"

Lex smugly answered, "I have to admit, it was."

Elaine looked into Lex's sparkling eyes. "So—."

Lex cut her off. "No, it was one time." Blushing, she uttered, "Actually twice but it was just a one-nighter. You should have seen his face when I got dressed and left. I gave him my card, and he wanted to know if he was in trouble for sleeping with a cop." Lex picked up the bill. "My treat this time." She paid the tab, and they headed to the pet store where Elaine saw a few kittens and put a deposit on a black and white one.

When Lex got home, she changed into her pajamas and curled up with a book. Van Gogh took her place on the couch, and Lex's cell rang. She answered, "Hello?"

"Hi, I'm looking for a caseworker."

She closed her eyes, realizing it was him. "Aaron?"

"You're a heck of a detective," he said. "I hope you don't mind me calling."

"It's okay."

"Can I tell you something?" he asked.

"Sure."

"Listen, if I did anything wrong, I apologize. I can't stop

187

thinking about you."

Lex sighed. "Look, you did nothing wrong."

"But I want to see you again."

"Aaron, I'm almost twice your age. I have a teenaged daughter nearer in age to you than me. You and I had sex. An unexpected casual happening."

"I understand, but you're not like any other woman I've ever known."

Lex breathed deep. "I appreciate that, I think. Let's be honest here. I saw those panties in your bathroom. You can't tell me they were yours. I'm sure that box of condoms on your nightstand won't last long. Leave it at that."

"But you're different."

"Keep it real, there is no different. I think I've said enough."

"I guess I've made a fool of myself."

"You haven't made a fool of anyone. If I were your age, I'd be all in. You're a charming young man."

"You know what? You're a hell of a caseworker and a beautiful woman."

"Thank you, Aaron. You have to move on."

"I guess so. I'll never forget you, Lex."

"In a way, I'll never forget you either. Take care."

CHAPTER 38

Lex had a latte in her hand and she saw Gil rummaging through Cambourd's papers. "There's a few things that are puzzling," he said. "Take his bankbook and passport. He went to Paris eight times in a four-year time span but his last trip was two years ago. Here's the interesting part: it appears each time he flew back from Paris, a significant deposit was wired into his bank account."

Lex put her cup on the desk and studied the documents. "What was he doing when he went to Paris? Selling his paintings?"

"Here's something else," Gil said. "Receipts from FedEx. It appears he had packages delivered to him at the museum. Art supplies. You think Marcus Worthington would know why? I mean there's a ton of supply shops here. Why have supplies shipped from Paris? And that address book. Chandelle's name is in it."

"We can ask Worthington about the supplies, but the Paris connection is interesting." Lex sat and sipped her drink. In a little while, let's go see Adrienne. I think she opens at nine."

"Do you want to call first?"

Lex took another sip. "No. I want to see how she reacts to us."

▲

The Candlelight Gallery door was opened by Gil and Lex saw Adrienne setting a piece of art on an easel. The French woman turned. "This is a surprise."

Lex said, "We were in the area and decided to stop in. "Is that a new painting?"

"It is. Reminds me of Magritte. Are you familiar with him?"

"Can't say I know much about art," Gil said. "But I'm learning."

"I've seen his work at a couple of museums," Lex said. "I have a few questions for you?"

They headed to her office where Lex took out her pad to refer to her previous notes. "I'd like to follow up on a few things. We know Cambourd made several visits to Paris." She showed Adrienne the well-worn address book. "Your name and a Paris address is listed."

Adrienne saw the notation. "It does say Chandelle, but that references my father. The address is his gallery."

"You're not related to Cambourd, correct?"

"No."

"Was your father selling Cambourd's paintings?"

"My father died ten years ago." She flipped a few pages in the address book. "I don't know who he visited, but I recognize a few of my relatives."

"Did you know about the will?"

"Will? No. What will?"

Lex said, "He had a will. We talked to his lawyer. Cambourd was a rich man. He had more than a million dollars in the bank and some hidden away. He recently changed his will. You were to inherit his money."

Adrienne gasped. "What? It all belongs to me?"

Lex hesitated. "Well, not quite. It seems he asked his lawyer to amend the existing will and name you the beneficiary, but Cambourd never signed it. It's not valid."

Lex saw the glazed look on Adrienne's face. The woman said, "I don't know what to say. This is stunning news. He said he was living on the paintings he consigned to Jerry Davidson."

"There is one other thing. Every time he went to Paris, deposits were wired into his bank account a short time later. That's why we're interested in knowing what he might have been doing when he was there and who he might have visited. Could you take another glimpse at the address book? Any other names stand out?"

She glanced at the names. "No, just my family and most are with Dieu."

"Dieu?" Lex asked.

"God. They are deceased. They are with Dieu."

Lex had to know something else. "Is your relationship with Stefan Martine strictly business?"

Adrienne blushed and Lex knew the answer without her saying a word. "He's a very nice man. I do like him." She paused. "But since Fredrike is gone and there will be none of his paintings coming forward, I'm thinking of going back to Paris."

"Really?" Lex said. "Does Stefan know?"

"I'm telling him later. We still have some business to work out."

"How soon might you leave here?" Lex asked.

"I'm not sure. There's a lot to do before I go, if I go."

"Have a nice day," Lex said as the detectives exited the gallery.

They got back into their car. Gil said, "Nice, Lex. Are you satisfied your competition might be out of the picture?"

"Watch it," she said with a grin.

"Come on, you can't wait for Stefan to call you."

Lex ignored the comment. "Just drive."

They were headed back to the precinct when Lex received a call from Manning informing her they had a court date.

CHAPTER 39

Jerry Davidson had strolled by Mid-Manhattan Hospital many times. He knew the drug rehab clinic was only a few feet away. With his briefcase in hand, the well-dressed businessman glanced at the sliding glass doors and continued walking toward Fifth Avenue.

Reaching the museum, he went to the director's office. "Hello," Marcus said. "I was thinking about the Cambourds."

"That's why I'm here. I have six of his paintings at my condo. I'd like you to see them. If any are acceptable, then you can borrow them."

"Wonderful. I'd love to see them. Would you mind if Mr. Gastone comes with me? He will need to find an appropriate gallery space to hang them."

"Not at all."

Davidson fidgeted. He knew he needed a hit. "Altman was reluctant to part with them. That bastard almost shot me before my men came to retrieve the paintings."

"Shot you?"

"Damn right. It's a good thing my movers showed up when they did."

Worthington picked up his phone. "I want Gastone up here."

Several minutes later, Gastone was sitting in Worthington's office. "We have a lot of work to do in the next few months, and I want to go over every detail," the director said. "Jerry has several Cambourd paintings he'd like us to see before we decide if they are suitable for the exhibit."

Gastone nodded. "Very good. We should start receiving the first few masterpieces from abroad soon."

"Make sure that all the equipment is working," Marcus said.

"The scanners and X-ray machines are up-to-date," Gastone replied. "I will personally examine every piece, match them to the documentation accompanying the paintings, and make sure the immunities from the seizure papers are in order."

The director addressed Jerry. "Perhaps we can stop by in the morning."

"That would be fine. Have Artie call me when you arrive. I need to head back to Chicago later this week." Jerry shook Marcus's hand. Remembering Gastone's reluctance to touching, he waved at him.

The businessman exited the museum and walked back toward his condo, once again nearing the hospital. Jerry stopped momentarily and contemplated going inside to seek help. It was as if his white powdered demon were standing beside him, preventing him from going inside, so he continued walking. Sweat began to drip from his forehead and he picked up his pace. A few blocks from his building, paranoia struck, and he had the feeling he was being followed. Looking over his shoulder, he was sure he saw a strange, long-haired man in a pair of blue sweats keeping up with him. Jerry quickly glanced back, and the man was gone. Approaching the Zagrin Building, he sensed a shadow behind him and looked back again, only to see other pedestrians. He scanned the crowd and imagined the man in blue sweats standing across the street giving him a menacing look.

Jerry reached the front door and before opening it, he glanced back one last time and then entered the lobby. "Mr. Davidson," Artie said. "Are you alright? You're quite sweaty."

"Don't let him in," Jerry said.

Artie asked, "Let who in?"

The concierge never received an answer.

Jerry got into the elevator and rode up to his condo. He moved to the kitchen and leaned against the counter, grabbing the devil's canister. *What am I doing? This stuff is death.* Still sweating, he took a hit and then threw the container of cocaine against the kitchen wall. The white powder covered the counter and floor. Still sweating, he rushed to shower and changed into casual attire before relaxing in his chair, turning on the TV and dozing off. Soon afterward his phone rang.

CHAPTER 40

It was 9:40 a.m. There was no coffee to be brewed. Hutch entered the squad room carrying a bag of grounds. "Won't be long," he said as he started to make a potful."

Before the machine was able to produce drinks, Lex heard Pressley yelling to her and Gil, "Get in here!"

They hurried into his office. "You need to get over to the Zagrin Building right away. It's Jerry Davidson. He's dead!"

Lex froze, and Gil's mouth was wide-open. "Are you kidding us?" she shouted.

"Hell, no! I wish I was."

"What happened? Cocaine overdose?" Gil asked.

"He was shot."

The detectives stormed out to a squad car and sped to the crime scene, lights flashing and siren blaring. Emergency vehicles lined the street, leading Gil to park in back of a patrol car. They rushed past the uniform at the door to see Artie sitting on a stool with his head resting between his hands. Lex stopped. "Artie, what happened?"

He looked up. "All I know is that he was shot."

The detectives got into the elevator, and before the door closed, Lex looked back at Artie and the patrol officer standing beside him. "We'll be back," she said.

A few seconds later, Lex and Gil exited the lift. Two uniforms were standing in the hallway talking with a bald man who was dressed in casual clothes. Lex stopped and asked a uniform. "Is he a witness?"

"A neighbor," the officer said. "He got home last night a little before nine and when he came in, he says a guy wearing a Red Sox cap just left the building."

Lex asked the man. "Can you describe him?"

"Not really," the neighbor said. "I didn't get a good look."

"Thank you," Lex said. She turned to the officers. "Get his name and statement."

She and Gil entered the condo. Paramedics, Rusty's team, and Pam were already there. Lex noticed blood spattered on the carpet as she approached Jerry Davidson's draped body. "Hi Pam. What's it this time?"

"Single shot to the head." Pointing, she said, "There's a shell casing over there, and a pizza inside the box on the coffee table. Not a piece of pie missing."

Lex borrowed a pair of latex gloves and bent to inspect the expended casing. "Looks like a thirty-eight."

"Check out the kitchen. It's covered with white powder," Pam alerted. "Looks like cocaine to me."

Lex and Gil walked a few feet to the kitchen. "His stash of coke. All over the place and the canister is resting against the microwave," Lex observed.

Gil said, "The killer sure didn't get away with any drugs."

Lex moved toward the pizza. "I don't get it. He never touched it." She addressed one of the uniforms in the room. "Who found the body?"

The officer pointed toward the balcony. "They did. The one standing is named Gastone."

Lex saw Worthington slumped in a chair with his head between his knees. "Oh my God. It's Marcus."

She and Gil made their way over to the sobbing museum director. Lex said to the man with Marcus, "I understand you are Mr. Gastone."

"Yes, Edward Gastone."

Lex approached Marcus, and he lifted his head. "I can't believe it. First Fredrike, now Jerry. Am I next? You need to arrest that bastard now!"

"Who are you talking about?" Lex asked.

"Altman."

Gil fetched a glass of water for the distraught director, while Lex handed him a few tissues. He took the water, drank half, and put the glass down. "It had to be him. Jerry came to see us yesterday and told me he took back several paintings from Altman. We made arrangements to see them this morning. Jerry said Altman was so mad that he pulled a gun and threatened to shoot him right there at the gallery. I guess he meant business, and finished the job here."

Lex and Gil looked at each other. "He told us the same story," Lex said. "Let's bring Altman in."

Lex didn't waste time and called the captain to tell him they may have a suspect, Altman.

Marcus was pale and when he stood, he was unsteady on his feet. "Are you okay?" Lex asked.

"I think so." Marcus sat again. "I need a few minutes."

"How did you get in here?"

"The doorman tried to call to let him know we were here, but there was no answer. I thought maybe Jerry was in the shower or something, so we took the elevator. I knocked on the door several times, but he still didn't answer. Then I twisted the doorknob and next thing we saw was...." He closed his eyes. "Need I say more? Edward called for help." Marcus suddenly began breathing hard and the color drained from his face.

"I think he's going to faint," Lex said. She held him by the shoulders to prevent him from toppling to the floor.

Gil alerted a paramedic, and she rushed to Marcus. After a quick check, the EMT said, "I'm going to get some oxygen."

"I'll stay with him," Gastone said.

While Marcus was being tended to, Lex saw Rusty and she

pointed to the pizza box. "Don't forget to check for teeth marks in the pepperoni."

Rusty stared at her. "That frickin' pie was never touched. And for your information, it's just cheese. Damn you. I screwed up once, and you can't let it go."

Lex stared back. "Twice, shorty. You missed an earring in the art studio. Did you check the door? Any sign of a forced entry?"

Rusty replied, "Everything is intact. He must have let the killer in. Looks like he was expecting that pizza."

Marcus quickly regained consciousness but kept the oxygen mask on while the paramedic took the man's vitals. Several minutes later, the mask was removed. He breathed normally. Lex said, "Relax. I have to talk to the sergeant. I'll be right back."

She spoke with the officer who told her that there was only one other resident on this floor. "We talked to that neighbor on our way in here," she stated.

"We're checking units on the other floors too," he said.

Lex saw Marcus sitting up and approached him. "I'm better," he assured her.

Gastone offered, "I'll get him back to the museum."

Lex suggested to Gil, "Let's see what Artie can tell us."

Before heading downstairs, Lex noticed Davidson's cell phone and plane tickets on a table, and glanced at the tickets. "Looks like he was going to Chicago again."

Gil picked up the phone and checked recent calls. "Lex, the last call on this phone was one he received at seven-ten p.m. last night from Edward Gastone."

She and Gil approached him. "Mr. Gastone," Lex said. "Did you call here last night?"

He hesitated. "Oh, I did. I wanted to confirm what time to be here."

"Did he seem to be okay?"

"He was fine. Said he was going to bed and would see us this morning."

"Thank you," Lex said.

They headed back to the lobby. Artie was sitting alongside a patrolman. The concierge's head was still bowed. Lex stood in front of him, and he looked up. "When was the last time you saw Mr. Davidson?"

"Late yesterday afternoon. He came in, walked right past me and said something weird. Something like *don't let him in*. I had no idea what or who he was talking about, and he never answered me. He seemed spooked."

"Spooked?"

"Yes. Like someone was chasing him, but there was no one."

"What time was that?" Lex asked.

"It was a little after five."

Gil said, "We can get the lobby videos from last night and this morning."

Lex remembered seeing a business name on the pizza box. "Where is Vito's?" she asked.

Artie directed the detectives to the restaurant that was located around the corner on Thirty-Seventh.

When Lex and Gil entered Vito's, the smell of garlic was unmistakable. An employee greeted them. Lex asked, "Is Vito here?"

The employee pointed to the oven behind the counter. "That old guy is him. I'm Junior."

Gil flashed his badge. "Cops?" Junior asked.

"Yes, sir" We'd like to talk with him," Gil said.

The man yelled, "Hey, Pop, These are cops. They want to talk to you."

The salt-and-pepper mustached man stepped out from behind the counter. In his Italian accent, Vito said, "We get busy soon."

"We'll be brief. Were you here last night?" Lex questioned.

"Sure."

"Do you recall any deliveries going to the Zagrin Building last night?"

199

Vito looked at his son and Junior thought. "Not last night."

"Are you positive about that?" Lex asked.

"I'm sure."

Gil inquired, "Do you remember anyone picking up a pizza who might have been acting strange or suspicious?"

Junior recollected, "There was one guy that came in. He ordered a small cheese and waited for it."

"What time was that?" Lex asked.

"I remember it was a little after eight because I switched the TV to the Yankees game."

Gil asked, "What made him seem strange?"

"He wore latex gloves, and he was wearing a Red Sox cap, and I'd remember it if I saw it again. It was autographed by Yaz near the B on the cap."

"Do you have cameras?" Gil queried.

"No. Never had a problem."

"Can you tell us anything else about this guy? Walk, talk, tattoos, or distinguishing marks?" Lex asked.

"No, but I should have charged him double for wearing that cap in here."

"Thanks," Lex said. "You've both been very helpful."

"What's this all about?" Vito asked.

Lex replied, "It's about a homicide at the Zagrin Building. One of your pizza boxes with an uneaten pizza was inside the victim's condo."

Gil and Lex left the restaurant, and patrons began entering. The detectives walked back to their vehicle. Lex pondered whether Altman would really pose as a pizza delivery guy. "It doesn't fit his style," she said. "He's too slick. I'm curious to see what the camera will tell us. And what the heck was Davidson seeing when he told Artie to not let him in? I've heard of drugs making you imagine things. Was that it, or was someone really after him?"

▲

When they got back to the precinct, the detectives headed to Pressley's office. Gil said, "Jerry Davidson took a thirty-eight in the head. It appears a phony pizza delivery guy visited him last night. It may have been Altman."

Lex clasped her hands. "Marcus Worthington and Edward Gastone went to Jerry's place this morning and got the shock of their lives when they saw the body sprawled on the carpet. We know Altman had pulled a gun on Davidson a couple of days ago."

Pressley gritted his teeth. "You got any hard evidence?"

Lex said, "Davidson can't testify now, but he did tell us the same story he'd told Marcus Worthington about the gun. We're going to drop in on Altman. I'm assuming he's at the galley doing business as usual. Let's see how he reacts to us."

"Are you arresting him?"

Lex replied, "It's certainly not out of the question."

"Be careful," Pressley urged his detectives.

"How about getting on the security company. We need another lobby video."

"I'll get on it."

CHAPTER 41

Eager to confront Altman, Lex and Gil got back into their vehicle and headed to the gallery. Lex thought. *Altman's reaction may tell us everything. He should be sweating when he sees us.*

Arriving at the gallery, Gil rang the bell. They waited, and he rang it again. Peering inside, Lex saw Laura walking toward the door to open it. "We're closed because I'm doing inventory."

"Is Mr. Altman here?" Lex asked.

Laura said, "No. he won't be back for two weeks."

"What? Where is he?"

"He's on vacation. Leaving in a few hours for the Caribbean."

"A cruise? Do you have his itinerary?"

"Yes, he left a copy in his office."

"Please get it. We need it."

Laura retrieved the paper and presented it to Lex. "Can I keep this?"

"I'll make a copy."

Less than a minute later, Lex had the paper in her hand. "He's leaving on the Blue Islander later this afternoon. Let's get to Pier Six right now."

"I'm calling for backup. We need a couple of uniforms," Gil stated.

He called Pressley to tell him what was going on and where they were headed. "Captain said uniforms will meet us there."

"Wait," Laura interrupted. "What's going on?"

"Your boss might be in danger," Lex said.

A puzzled Laura uttered, "What?"

"Don't worry, we'll take care of him," Lex replied.

The smart detective realized Laura might attempt to warn him. "And don't try to contact him, it could jeopardize his safety."

The detectives headed to the pier and waited for their backups. It was only a few minutes before Gil spotted the cruiser. Pete, and another uniform named Felix, exited their car and joined the detectives. "What have we got?" Pete asked.

Lex explained the situation. "We need to see the ship's captain."

The police officers moved past a line of passengers boarding the ship. Reaching the entrance, they approached a steward. Lex presented her badge. "Where is the captain? We need to see him immediately."

"Captain Blair could be anywhere."

"Can you contact him and tell him to come here?"

"What's going on?" the steward inquired.

"There may be a dangerous person on board. Please get the captain down here."

They waited and a few minutes later, Captain Blair, wearing his classic white uniform arrived. "May we go somewhere private?" Lex asked.

"Follow me."

They walked up one deck into the captain's quarters, and Lex explained why they were there. "What is Altman's cabin number?"

"Heinrich Altman. Number two-ten."

Lex thought for a few seconds, and retrieved his itinerary. "Here's his cell number. Can you call him and ask him to go to his room?"

"Sure. What shall I tell him?"

"Tell him there's been a mistake. You booked his room twice. Do you have any suites available?"

"There are a few. We can use number four. It's the end suite."

"Great. Tell him to wait in his room for your crew to help him relocate to the suite."

Blair did as Lex suggested. Altman answered his cell. The ship's captain apologized for the mistake and told his passenger a free suite was waiting for him. "He bought it," Blair said.

"Take us up there," Lex said. "Once we're inside, have your crew bring him up." The captain led the way. Lex, Gil, and the two uniforms waited inside the suite with Blair.

A few minutes later, the door opened, and Altman stepped inside. Gil shouted, "Get your hands up and freeze, Heinrich. You're under arrest for murder."

Stunned, Altman yelled, "Murder?"

"Cuff him," Gil said to Pete. Blair told his employees to go back downstairs.

Furious, Altman said, "You can't do this. I didn't kill Cambourd. This is outrageous."

"Did we say you were under arrest for killing him?" Lex clarified, "You're under arrest for killing Jerry Davidson."

Altman appeared shocked. "What? Are you serious? You're telling me that someone shot Jerry?"

"Bingo, Heinrich. How did you know he was shot? We didn't say that," Gil said.

"You're making a mistake. I didn't kill anyone."

Lex stared the angered Altman down. "I think you did. We know you pulled a gun on Davidson and threatened to shoot him when he came to get the Cambourd paintings."

"We were arguing, and it got a little hot. I wasn't thinking when I pulled out my gun. I didn't shoot anyone."

"Not true," Gil corrected. "We have it on record that you once shot a robber."

Altman yelled, "This is outrageous. I should be on my way to Jamaica."

Lex said, "Right now, you're taking a trip downtown." She requested to Pete, "Please read Mr. Altman his Miranda rights."

After Lex thanked the ship's captain for his help, the detectives escorted Altman off the ship and into a patrol car. Lex and Gil rode back to the precinct in their vehicle. "Think we'll get a confession?" Gil asked.

"I think we'll be seeing his lawyer," Lex replied.

As soon as they got to the precinct, the detectives entered Pressley's office. "Altman is being booked," Gil said.

"Charged with what?"

"Murder one," Lex stated.

"One count or two?"

"One for now," Lex said. "Davidson."

Pressley inched forward and lamented, "You realize, all we have is circumstantial. No weapon, prints, DNA, or anything else except hearsay from the museum director. And what happened to the embezzlement? That you can prove. You can bet he's making a call to his lawyer."

"I'm sure he is," Lex said. "We had probable cause. We couldn't take a chance on him leaving the country. Let's see how this plays out. We had no choice."

Pressley rested his chin in his hands. "I suppose you're right, but I have a feeling this isn't going to end well for us. We'll see where the chips fall in the morning. He'll probably be arraigned then."

CHAPTER 42

Gil and Lex were in their workplace when Pressley approached his office. Gil asked the captain, "How's your dog, anyway?"

Pressley gave him a quick look. "Dog? What dog. I don't have a dog."

Lex chimed in, "The dog. I think I misspoke when I told Gil about the dog. It's your son's dog. The one you had to shell out three hundred for."

"Oh, yes. He still owes me," Pressley said. "Lex, can I see you for a minute?" She followed him and closed the door. He said, "Next time, how about cluing me in on what you say to your partner or anyone else around here? Thanks for keeping my son's stupidity between us."

"What should I tell Gil about this conversation?"

"Tell him I talked to you about charging Hutch with sexual harassment, but you declined to press charges."

"That's rich. He'll buy it."

The captain's phone rang and he excused his detective. Lex reentered her workspace, and Gil asked, "What was that all about?" She relayed to her partner the fabricated sexual harassment story.

A few minutes later, Pressley appeared at their cube. "We have to talk. My office, and close the door."

They all took seats and Pressley said, "Altman spoke with his attorney last night, and I just spoke with the DA, Tynes. Altman's attorney is Vance Richland."

Gil said. "If anyone can get Altman off, it's him."

Pressley stared at his detectives. "Look. Tynes is advising us to drop the murder charge. We have no hard evidence. Tynes doesn't want to waste taxpayers' money pursuing it, and he surely doesn't want a false arrest suit."

"When's the arraignment?" Lex asked.

"This morning sometime. I told the DA to drop the charges. Altman will be out later. Wouldn't be surprised if we hear from Richland."

"Oh, Altman will wind up in jail, one way or another," Lex said. "If we can't get him for murder, we'll nail him for embezzlement."

Benzinger knocked on the Captain's door. "Got another FedEx for you guys." He gave Lex the package.

She opened it, slid out a disc, and declared, "That was fast. Let's go get a look."

"I told them it was urgent, we needed it today. Let me know what you've got," Pressley said.

The detectives went to Lex's computer and she slid the disc in.

"Let this show begin," Gil said.

When the recording hit 8:33 p.m., Lex said, "There's the guy with the pizza. He's wearing gloves and a Red Sox cap." She froze the image and zoomed in to get a closer look. "I don't recognize him. Do you?"

"No," Gil said.

"I want to see when he left."

At 8:49 p.m., the same guy reappeared and exited the building. Pausing it, Lex asked, "Does that guy look like Altman to you?"

"No. Definitely not."

Lex reran it and stopped at 8:33. "Damn it," she groaned. "That's surely not Altman. You can alter appearances but not height and build. Who the hell is this? Damn it! Altman is off the hook."

"This is a game changer," Gil added.

Lex got up. "Wait. What if the two killings aren't related? What if Jerry Davidson was killed by a drug dealer? All that cocaine on the kitchen floor. Maybe he owed money, or a deal went bad."

"Anything's possible. Pressley needs to hear this."

They charged into his office. "Looks like you two robbed a bank," he said.

Gil held the disc. "This just blew holes into our theory that Altman shot Jerry Davidson. The guy in the video definitely isn't Altman."

Pressley said, "What are you saying? We have two murderers on the loose?"

Lex said, "I don't know if we have one or two. Davidson could be drug related."

They left Pressley's office, and Lex began to pace. *Was this killing drug related? Was it connected to Cambourd? Worthington knew both victims well. What don't we know?* She finished her lap around the room and neared Gil who was at his desk. "What do you think? Is Davidson's death drug related or is it linked to Cambourd?" she asked.

"Could go either way," Gil replied.

Lex grabbed Davidson's cell, looked through his contacts, and call history. She saw several calls to someone named Money. "This has to be his dealer."

"Money, good name for a drug dealer," Gil said.

Lex keyed in the number, and the guy answered. She was silent, and he said, "Jerry, you out already?"

Lex spoke, "Please don't hang up. I'm Jerry's friend. He asked me to call you. My name is Lex, and I need some good stuff, bad."

"Where's Jerry?"

Since the dealer answered, Lex was sure he hadn't heard Jerry had been killed. "He's away. Went to Chicago, left me dry. He'll be back in a few days, but I can't wait. I have cash. I can meet you anywhere."

"I need five hundred. It's a new customer minimum. You got that much?"

"Not quite. I can stop at an ATM. Where can we meet?"

"Grand Central, downstairs. Be there in an hour."

"Deal. How will I know you?"

"Easy. I'll be sucking on a Tootsie Pop. What about you?"

"I'm five-nine, dark hair. They say I look like Julia Roberts."

"Okay, good looking. Meet me near the bakery."

"Done."

Lex wiped her brow. "He's meeting me at Grand Central in an hour, downstairs by the bakery. He'll have a Tootsie Pop hanging from his mouth."

"Julia Roberts?"

"You have a problem with that? Would you rather I said Julia Child?"

Gil laughed at his resourceful partner. "That would be a stretch. Roberts it is."

They headed for the train station. "We should separate before we get there. Stay back and don't approach me until I need you. And stay far enough away not to be suspicious."

It wasn't long before Lex spotted a man with a long stick in his mouth. She knew instantly that he wasn't the pizza guy. Money was black and had dreadlocks. She approached him. "Come on, let's sit in the corner," he suggested.

Lex saw the pouch he was carrying. "I need to see the stuff," she said.

He sucked on the pop. "So do I, sweetheart. Show me the green."

Lex opened her purse and pulled out her badge. "Stay seated. My partner has his eyes on us. I just want to talk."

"What kind of shit is this? Where is Jerry?"

Lex leaned in. "Dead. Now can we talk?"

"Dead! That's crazy. I hate losing customers, and that other dude he was buying for got whacked too."

"Relax," Lex said. "I'm not here to arrest you." She waved to Gil. "My partner is joining us."

Gil pulled up a chair, causing Money to fidget. "I've played good cop/bad cop before. Is that the game we're playing?"

Lex stared at him. "I told you to relax. This is no game. Tell me about Jerry."

"What's to tell? He used to buy double, for him and his friend. Got pissed at me when I told him he had to keep buying the same way."

"Pissed? Like mad enough to threaten you?"

"He was mad, but we made amends. He was a good tipper. What did you mean, dead, like he overdosed?"

"No, more like he was shot."

Money removed the pop from his mouth. "Geez. I ain't never killed anyone."

Lex said, "With these drugs you're pushing, I bet you have, so let's not go there."

"Okay, fair enough. You know, you do look like Julia Roberts."

"Thanks. When was the last time you saw him?"

"Last week."

"Did he talk about anyone? Anyone he may have had a problem with?"

"I don't deal in small talk. Ain't a psychologist or nothing. Just a working guy."

"Understood," Lex said. "We're going now, but if we ever meet again and you're dealing, it won't be good for you. Get out of here."

Money left, and Lex's phone rang. It was Manning reminding her about tomorrow's proceedings. She announced to Gil, "I'll be in court tomorrow. I'm going to remind Pressley when we get back."

CHAPTER 43

Lex was up early. Sitting on the edge of her bed, she couldn't decide what to wear. The black dress she'd taken out of her closet last night didn't seem quite right for this courtroom battle. She showered, put on her makeup, and stared at the recently purchased matador red dress. *Oh, yes, we're going to slay that bull, and he'll be seeing red for a long time.*

Entering the courtroom twenty minutes early, Lex felt a sense of déjà vu. She walked slowly nearing the first table where Jon and Asino were seated. Noticing Jon's eyes on her as if it were the first time he was seeing her, she heard Asino not so quietly, whisper, "Drop-dead gorgeous."

She hid her smile from them as she passed by, joining Manning at the table on the opposite side. The attorney filled two glasses with water from the pitcher on the table. "Good morning, Lex." he said.

"I certainly hope so," she replied as she looked over to their opposition. "Can't wait to see them squirm."

Judge Fleming entered the room, and all rose while she took a seat. She pounded the gavel to start the proceedings. Opening the file in front of her, she glanced at Lex and her lawyer. "Mr. Manning, you may begin."

"Thank you, Your Honor." He stood and addressed the judge. "As you are well aware, Jon and Alexis Stall appeared in this very room a short time ago. Mr. Stall was awarded primary custody of their daughter Elizabeth, who had been residing with the previously awarded primary custodial parent, Alexis Stall." He reached for the glass of water and took a sip. "I'm here to prove while Mr. Stall was married to my client, he had several extramarital affairs."

Asino rose from his seat. "I object Your Honor. That has nothing to do with this case, and that allegation was dismissed at the previous custody trial."

Fleming said, "Mr. Asino. Objection sustained."

Manning approached the bench, and Asino followed. Manning quietly said, "Your Honor, I'm trying to prove a point by establishing previous behavior, which is why I'm asking for a paternity test to prove that Adam Baxter was born out of wedlock, and Jon Stall is his biological father."

She nodded. "The previous objection is overruled. You may sit, Mr. Asino, and Mr. Manning, you may continue."

He assertively stated, "The fact is, Your Honor, Jon Stall and his current wife, Julie Baxter, had a child out of wedlock while he and Alexis Stall were still married." He pointed to Jon who covered his mouth with one hand. Manning addressing the judge continued, "Your Honor, I am asking Jon Stall be given a paternity test to verify he is indeed the biological father of Adam Baxter. Mr. Stall perjured himself before you the last time we met." He held up a document. "This sworn affidavit states Adam is his stepson, and the paternity test will prove my argument that Jon Stall fathered Adam."

Manning presented Jon Stall's income tax filings to Fleming.

Asino appearing to be stunned, eyed his client, stood and protested. "Your Honor, I never received copies of those items and ask that you not accept them as evidence."

Fleming glared at him. "Mr. Asino, if you didn't see them, then I suggest you check your mail more often because copies were delivered to your office." She held up the signed receipt. "You do have a secretary named Eve Harrison, don't you?"

Asino sat, and Manning continued. "These tax returns were filed in consecutive years and show two child dependents: Elizabeth Stall and Adam Baxter as Jon Stall's children. Your Honor, either Jon

Stall adopted Adam Baxter, which he did not, or Adam is his child. I'm quite sure a paternity test would prove this so. Judge Fleming, Mr. Stall lied. He's either guilty of a federal charge of income tax fraud or lying to you in a child custody case. One way or the other, there is clear deceit and obstruction of justice."

An irate Asino again rose. "Your Honor. May I have a few minutes in private with my client?"

"Granted. You have five minutes."

▲

Asino and Jon left the courtroom and talked in the hallway. The lawyer pointed his finger at his client's face and stared at him. "What the fuck are we doing here? You lied to me too. Are you the boy's father?"

"I am," Jon said. "I never thought anyone but me and Julie would know."

Asino was angered. "Are you nuts? You mean you never intended to let the boy know who his father was?"

Jon grimaced. "We were going to tell him when he was old enough."

Asino's voice was filled with fire. "Do you see what you've done? What the hell am I supposed to do? Do you have anything else to tell me?"

Jon looked at the squat attorney. "No. I only wanted to have him and his sister in the same house, growing up together. What's wrong with that?"

Asino put his finger on Jon's chest. "You dumbass idiot, you may lose visitation rights altogether. I have no choice but to plead for a fair solution."

Jon grabbed Asino by the arm. "Wait a minute. Who the hell are you calling dumbass? You're the one who didn't bother to read your mail, and you were supposed to see Fleming beforehand, so what the fuck are you blaming me for?"

The lawyer jerked his arm back. "I didn't have a chance to. I had a jury case that went way beyond the normal."

Asino and his client reentered the courtroom. Jon took a seat and frowned at the radiant Lex while the attorney approached the bench to speak privately with Judge Fleming. "Your Honor," Asino said. "Mr. Stall is deeply sorry for his actions. He's a good father, always paid his support, and adores his daughter." Asino allowed a few seconds to pass. "Jon Stall is also an outstanding high school teacher." Whispering, he pleaded, "Your Honor, we will make a quiet exit from the courtroom if you will grant us the same privileges that existed prior to the previous lawsuit."

Judge Fleming leaned over the bench and spoke softly. "I need to know very clearly that you and your client are admitting guilt."

Asino icily glanced at Jon. "Yes, Your Honor, we are," he said.

"Mr. Asino, please return to your table and have your client stand with you."

He walked back and ordered Jon to rise. "What's going on?" he asked.

"Get up and do what the judge says."

Jon did as he was instructed, and Fleming addressed him. "Mr. Stall, will you plead guilty to perjury in the previous court appearance?"

Jon hesitated and had a blank look on his face. Asino nudged him and whispered, "Say yes, right now!"

"Yes, Your Honor," Jon stated.

Fleming ordered them to sit for the delivery of her verdict. "This is not a difficult decision for me to make, even though it is disturbing to know someone deliberately lied in a court of law," she said. "Mr. Stall, you had sworn in a written statement that Adam Baxter was your stepson. A statement that was made to mislead the court. That is perjury in the second degree and carries a punishment of four years in state prison and or a hefty fine. I'm torn between charging you with perjury and letting you off the hook."

Jon sat at the defense table with his head in his hands. Asino interrupted, "Your Honor."

Fleming barked at him, "Sit, Mr. Asino. I made my decision, and it's final." Silence came over the sparsely filled courtroom when she spoke. Speaking directly to Jon, she said, "Mr. Stall, all indications are that you're a fine teacher, but there are concerns about your honesty. Rather than putting you in prison, I'll let you continue teaching. However, I'm fining you one thousand dollars for committing perjury. This is to be paid within seven days, or a warrant will be issued for your arrest. Do you understand?"

"Yes, Your Honor."

Fleming ordered Jon to make arrangements to move Liz back to Lex's home and reinstated Jon Stall's child support payments. Asino stood. "Thank you, Your Honor," he said.

Creighton Manning rose and politely addressed the judge. "Your Honor, there is one more issue at hand. We are also asking restitution for all court costs and attorney's fees, including those incurred from the previous hearing."

"Granted, Mr. Manning. All of the necessary paperwork will be drawn up later today. This court is adjourned." Fleming hit her gavel on the wood block.

▲

Lex was beaming with joy. She hugged Manning and when she did, she saw Asino and Jon hastily leave the room. Manning held Lex's hand, and she said, "Creighton. I can't thank you enough." The victorious attorney closed his briefcase and walked out of the courtroom with his elated client.

As soon as she got into her Corolla, Lex called Gil. "It's over. We won. Liz will be home soon. Tell Pressley. I'll see you tomorrow."

When Lex got home, she went upstairs to her daughter's room where Van Gogh was in her usual spot on the bed. *Can't wait to have Lizzie back.*

After changing, Lex went back downstairs and called Elaine, who was still at work and told her what had happened. It was too early to call Liz, so Lex took a walk to the record store and stood at the window smiling broadly as she explained to her father that Liz was coming home.

Later that afternoon, Lex called her daughter. Liz already knew because Jon had told her. The teenager's emotions were going back and forth, but she was happy to be coming back to the village to be with her mother, Van Gogh, Shannon, and her old school.

CHAPTER 44

Starbucks was Lex's first stop and when she got to the precinct, she headed to the stable with her cup in hand. After a short visit with Butterscotch, Lex entered the squad room.

The smell of her cinnamon latte caught Hutch. "I'm gonna have to try one of those someday," he said. "

Pressley came out of his office. "I'm very happy for you," he said.

"Thank you, sir. It couldn't have gone better."

Gil joined them. "You sleep good last night?" he asked.

"Actually, I was so elated, I had a hard time falling asleep. I'm wide awake now and ready for action. Let's get to work."

She set her drink on her desk and dove right in. "If Altman didn't kill Davidson, then he likely didn't shoot Cambourd either, but we still have the crook on embezzlement." She paused. "So, we know it wasn't a drug deal gone bad, what's missing? If Altman didn't kill them, then who did?' I really don't think Adrienne is a suspect."

Gil said, "Yesterday, I dug into some of Cambourd's things. Marcus Worthington may have some answers about the trips to Paris, and I want to show him that little address book. I wonder if he would recognize any names."

"Great. Let's pay him a visit."

217

Edward Gastone was with the director when the detectives arrived. "Have a seat," Marcus offered the detectives. Gastone moved for the door.

"Wait," Lex said. "We have a few questions, and you might be able to help us."

Gastone turned around. "It's okay," the director assured.

Gil opened a tote and placed items on Marcus's desk.

"Take a look at these receipts," Lex said. "Why would Cambourd buy supplies in Paris and have them sent here? There is no shortage of art supply stores in New York. Does this seem odd to you, and were you aware of his purchases?"

Gastone looked at the receipts. "I can think of only one reason. He was a master restorer and certain pigments can only come from Europe. Exact matches to original paintings are often difficult."

Marcus hesitated, then he said, "True, Edward. Restoration work involves great detail. Correct?"

"Yes," Gastone replied.

Marcus continued, "But isn't it true you cannot bring a painting back to originality? All restoration work must be reversible, so my understanding is that you cannot use the old pigments."

Gastone nodded. "Yes, but he was a perfectionist, and I wouldn't put it past him to break the rules. In fact, there were times he wouldn't even let me in his room."

Lex showed Gastone and Marcus a notation that had been written on the bottom of a ledger. "ISG 180390 KU-EGG. Any idea what this means?" she asked.

"I have no idea," Gastone replied.

Marcus raised a hand, "There is something about it that's gnawing at me, but I can't figure it out."

"Cambourd made several trips to Paris and subsequently, deposits were wired into his bank account," Lex said. "Any idea who he went to see or what he did when he was there?"

"No," Marcus said.

"He once told me he'd go to the Seine and paint there. He could have been marketing his artwork," Gastone suggested.

"But his trips were only one to two weeks," Lex clarified.

"He was a master," Gastone said. "He could finish a great painting in a few days."

Gil pointed to the address book. "Take a look at these names. Are any familiar to you?" he asked.

Marcus perused the book and came to a name that made him gasp. He raised his head in disbelief and looked again to verify what he had seen. His jaw dropped open in shock, and he stood, placing his finger on that listing. "This name. This person, Gabriel Bergeron. It can't be him."

Gastone knew the name as well. "What?"

Marcus was speechless. Lex and Gil were waiting for him to give an explanation. The director brought his hands to his chin as if in prayer. "Detectives, if this is the same Gabriel Bergeron I think it is, he's the best art forger the world has ever seen. He's been in hiding for years, and even Interpol can't locate him."

Gastone gasped. "You don't think...."

Before Gastone could say another word, Marcus held his hands to his head and uttered, "He couldn't have. He wouldn't have...forgeries? There can't be forgeries here. Do you have that ledger with the masterpieces Cambourd restored?" he asked the detectives. Lex removed it from the tote. Marcus browsed the list. "Edward, drop everything!" he commanded. "I want you to remove all these paintings from their galleries. Take them downstairs and examine every one of them. Heaven help me! They can't be fakes. Go now. Do whatever you have to do and tell no one."

"What will I tell my staff?" Gastone solicited. "They'll need to help me."

Marcus took a deep breath. "Tell them you will be cleaning them for the exhibit. Start immediately." He retreated to his bar and poured a bourbon. "This is utterly unbelievable. Cambourd and Bergeron. My lord."

Lex saw the dazed director slouch back into his leather chair and take a drink. Gil started to say something, but Lex cut him short. "Let him be," she said.

Marcus rubbed his forehead. "My museum, my job, my credibility are all on the line. I pray we have no forgeries."

Lex responded, "We understand."

Marcus asked, "Have you arrested Altman?"

Lex replied, "As a matter of fact, we did, but all we had was circumstantial evidence. Your statement, as well as ours, would be seen as hearsay in court, so we couldn't hold him."

Gil placed all the items back into the tote. "Let us know what Gastone finds."

The detectives exited the office. "I want to go to the museum shop. Liz will be home soon. Our rooms were recently painted, and I want to get her a few posters," Lex said. She browsed the store and eyed an umbrella that had a Monet design. "What do you think?" she asked her partner.

"Lovely, Lex."

"You should get one for RayAnn. I'm getting one for Liz." Lex also picked out three posters from a bin, all Parisian scenes she knew Liz would like. The cashier rolled the posters, placed them into a long cardboard tube, and put the umbrella into a plastic bag. Gil wisely took Lex's advice and bought his wife an umbrella. They exited the store, and Lex said, "I have an idea."

"Don't you always?" Gil remarked. "What great brainstorm have you got now?"

"I'm going to bring the posters to Stefan Martine and ask him to frame them."

"Now I know why we really came to the museum shop," Gil said.

"Hey, I happen to know a framer. Why go somewhere else?"

Gil laughed at his partner. "You know, lady, you're something else."

"I'm going to head there after we get back. Want to come?"

"Oh no. I don't want to spoil the fun."

Once they reached the precinct, Lex headed for her car and drove to Stefan Martine's shop.

CHAPTER 45

"I take it things went well with your new friend," Gil said.

Lex knew he would be curious about Stefan. "I'd say it went okay. He's going to frame Liz's posters."

"That's it?"

"That's it. It was all business."

Gil smugly said, "Right. When's the first date?"

"Go get a doughnut."

"Oh no, what's the story?"

"There's no story. He does appear to be a nice guy. Will you go get a doughnut? I'm going to the ladies' room."

Gil did as he was told and, indeed, grabbed a chocolate frosted. Lex couldn't avoid Hutch when she exited the bathroom. "You sure you want to go back to Gil? Starsky isn't here. You can have his seat."

"Smooth, Hutch. Real smooth. You sure know how to attract the ladies. Gil has me booked for the day. Thanks." Rejoining her partner, she saw him eating and doled out a Kleenex. "You don't look so good in chocolate."

"Where's your expensive coffee?"

"Not today. I wonder how Gastone is doing with those paintings."

"My guess is it could take him a while to check them."

"You know, if there are forgeries, Marcus will have a heart attack. I'm calling him."

The director's phone rang and rolled over to voicemail. "Marcus, this is Detective Stall. I was wondering how Gastone was making out with the verifications. Call me."

"What about Gastone? How about calling him?"

Lex obtained his extension number. He didn't answer, and there was no recording. "I think that means real trouble. We should head over there."

"Good idea."

Lex's phone rang. "Marcus. Where are you?"

"I'm here with Edward. He's examined several of the paintings Cambourd had cleaned or restored. Right now, they all appear to be legitimate. Edward has worked through the night. He'll continue examining the others."

"That's good news," Lex said. She breathed a sigh of relief as she ended the call. "All the paintings Gastone has examined are real. He still has more to do." Lex watched Gil wipe his face. She left the cube and began to pace the floor. *Why didn't Cambourd sign the will? Did he know something? Is that why she's really going back to Paris?*

Lex veered back, quickly whisking past Gil. She opened the box that contained Cambourd's items, retrieving the bankbook that showed a balance of over a million dollars. "There's something about this money trail I don't like."

"What are you talking about?"

"It's the unsigned will, all this money, and Adrienne Chandelle, who suddenly decided she might head back to Paris." Lex studied the bankbook and all those wired deposits. "Know what? This is only a bankbook. It's updated when it's physically presented. The last posting was over a year ago. There might not be any money in here at all. We never asked if this is current. We assumed it to be. We need to see the bank manager, Gayle."

▲

223

The detectives entered the bank and proceeded to the manager's office. The door was open, and Lex asked, "May we come in?"

Gayle raised her head. "Please do. How may I help you today?"

Lex showed her the bankbook. "Tell me something. Is this the current balance in Mr. Cambourd's account?"

The manager entered the account number into her computer. "No. There was a large wire transfer to a bank in Paris recently, February 28. Someone named Brigitte Chandelle."

Lex closed her eyes and reopened them. "Adrienne's sister. All the money?"

"No, there's a hundred dollars left. That's the minimum in order to maintain an account."

Lex said, "I knew it. We need to see Adrienne right now. Thank you, Gayle."

Outside the bank, Lex said, "She knew about the money and the will. It didn't matter whether it was signed or not. She already had his money. I'm guessing he never told her about his secret stash here and in his apartment. Let's get over to Candlelight."

Lex opened her purse to remove her phone, and Adrienne's card. "She better answer. Damn it, voicemail. Let me call Stefan. He may know where she is." Lex quickly dialed his number. "Hi," she said.

"Hi, Lex. I have your framed posters."

"Thank you. Listen, have you seen or heard from Adrienne?"

There was a long pause. "That's really strange. She called me last night. She's gone. Took a red-eye back to Paris with her sister."

Lex gasped. "Are you serious?"

"Very. What's going on?"

"I'll explain it to you. I'm coming to see you with my partner right now."

"What's happened?" Gil asked.

"She's gone. She went back to Paris last night with Brigitte. I think we scared Adrienne enough to make her quickly exit the country. One smart lady. Makes me wonder if she had killed Cambourd."

224

"It's possible," Gil said. "We don't have any evidence pointing to her as the shooter."

"No, but she may have been in on it. She was there that night. Let's go see Stefan."

▲

Stefan greeted them. "You sounded miffed?" he said to Lex.

They entered his office. "Miffed isn't the word. Stunned is better." She asked, "What exactly did she tell you when she said she contemplated moving back to Paris?"

"She mentioned how sad it was that Cambourd was murdered. She knew he didn't leave behind any paintings, and we certainly couldn't obtain any. I tried to reason with her. I mentioned there are several other artists who could make us one of the largest and best galleries in New York, New Jersey, and Connecticut combined. She told me she'd think about it, so I continued looking for a larger space. Luckily, I never contracted with anyone."

Lex commented, "You were blindsided by her last night, correct? She told us she was thinking of returning to Paris, but this sudden exit is very bad. There's more to her story than we know at this point." After a breath, Lex said, "She took Cambourd's money. He wasn't the pauper everyone thought he was. She may have even planned his murder."

"What? She seemed so nice."

"I agree," Lex said. "She is attractive and sounded charming with her French accent, but she has a dark side. You're better off without her."

Stefan nodded. "I don't know what to say."

Gil suggested, "I think we better go."

"Wait," Stefan said. "The posters. I have them. Take them with you." He reached back and pulled out the framed artwork.

"They're perfect," Lex remarked. "Thank you, Stefan."

Gil said, "I'll carry them."

When they got into their vehicle, Gil teased, "I saw him smile at you when you made that crack about him being better off without her. Slid it right in. I'm sure he got the message."

"You do like him, right?" Lex grinned.

"I suppose so. Those pictures are nice. How much did he charge you?"

Ignoring the question, Lex said, "I can't wait for Liz to see them."

Gil shook his head. "I knew it."

CHAPTER 46

Lex was on her way to Creighton Manning's office. The phone call she received from him the previous evening was vague but urgent. He asked her to come see him. *What is he going to tell me? Was Fleming reversing her decision? Did Jon and Asino fabricate some garbage that she fell for? What the heck is going on?*

Before arriving at the lawyer's, Lex called Gil to inform him she'd be late. Gil said, "You'll be surprised when you get here."

"Surprised? What do you mean?"

"Can't tell you. You'll see."

Entering Manning's office, Lex said, "You have me going crazy. What's this all about?"

Manning told her to sit. "Keep calm. It's nothing to do with you or Liz. Well, not exactly. Asino called me yesterday afternoon, and he's filing a petition for reduced child support."

Lex stared at Manning. "What? How dare them!"

"Wait, Lex. Hear me out. It's the whole reason Jon sought custody of Liz."

Lex countered, "I don't understand."

"It's Julie. She has pancreatic cancer, probably won't make it more than six months. Jon will be alone with Adam, and he desperately wanted to have Liz be with him permanently."

Lex bowed her head. "They went through all of this instead of telling the truth?"

"Well, it's a little deeper than that. It seems Julie had filed for divorce but didn't pursue it after her diagnosis. Remember the school incident when Jon was fired, but the charge was later dropped because the kid admitted nothing happened?"

"What are you telling me?"

"Turns out the kid made up the story to get back at Jon. Seems his mother and Jon were having an affair, and the kid wasn't happy about it, so he held his mother and Jon hostage until he came clean."

"Really. All over again. He'll never change. Then what's with the new petition?"

"Asino hasn't filed it yet. He wants to amend the agreement out of court."

"No way," Lex said. "I feel for Julie and Adam, but Jon has never learned, and he deserves what he gets...except for Julie's death sentence."

"I needed you to reject the proposal. I'll get back to Asino and tell him there won't be a meeting of the minds. There's no way he'll file the petition. He knows there's too much dirt on Jon." Manning paused. "Asino insists he didn't know about Julie until after the court proceeding. He did know Jon had another infidelity issue."

Lex shook her head, and Manning removed an envelope from his drawer and handed it to her. "What's this?" she asked.

"A revised bill. You owe nothing. I'll get my payment from the court, courtesy of Mr. Asino."

"Thank you," Lex said. She left the building and went to the precinct.

▲

Approaching her partner, she saw a long box sitting on her desk. The name of a local florist was written on it. "It looks like flowers to me," Gil remarked.

"Really," she softly said.

"You gonna open it?"

She untied the bow and slid off the ribbon. Inside were a dozen yellow roses. "These are beautiful." A card was visible, so she opened the envelope and smiled.

"Need I guess?" Gil chided. "I know it's not Altman. Must be your new boyfriend."

Lex sat and read the card again. It was an invitation. "Give him a break. Stefan is a nice guy. He wants me to attend an exhibit at his gallery."

"Attend? You mean the first date."

Pressley entered their cube. "Who's the lucky guy?"

Without hesitation, Lex replied, "They're from my attorney. Don't worry. He's a happily married man, and he's thrilled we won Liz back."

Gil reacted to another Lex spur-of-the-moment lie. "Nice one. I couldn't have thought up anything believable that fast. Watch out, I think he's a smooth one."

"Really? Because he's good looking? You know, you act like I'm your daughter."

Gil shook his head. "I'm sorry, Lex. More like my sister. I don't want you to get hurt. You and Liz are family to me and RayAnn."

"I appreciate that. I do think it's time I start dating again." Lex grinned at him. "I need a vase." She thought for a second. "Go to the paddock and get a bucket. There should be some there." Gil did what he was asked and minutes later presented her with a silver pail. "Go fill it."

Gil reluctantly walked to the men's room and came back with the water-filled bucket. "Here, my fair lady."

"Thank you, you clown."

Hutch and Starsky walked toward their own cube, and Hutch spotted the flowers. He looked at Gil. "You two really are something."

"She appreciates a good man," Gil said.

"So, what's the story, Lex?"

She repeated what she told Pressley, and Hutch walked back to his partner.

Gil quizzed, "What's with the urgent lawyer visit?"

"I had to sign a few papers, and he gave me a revised bill. Zero." Lex switched the topic. "We need to check on Marcus Worthington. I'm calling him to find out how Gastone made out with the rest of the paintings."

Worthington answered. "Detective Stall, it's a wonderful day. Edward has checked all the paintings. I'm happy to report we have no forgeries."

"That is good news. I'm happy to hear it. Now you can concentrate on the exhibit."

"Yes, Edward is a busy man."

"Have you been able to make heads or tails with that notation?" Lex asked.

"No, but I swear there's something familiar about it," Marcus replied.

"If you think of it, please call me."

"Surely, I will."

Gil said, "Sounds like everything is legit."

"Yes, Gastone checked them all. They're real." Lex eyed the flowers. "I need to call Stefan."

"Go ahead."

She got up and grabbed her cell. "I'll be in the conference room."

"Keep the mushy stuff down."

Lex turned on the lights and called Stefan. "Hi. The flowers are beautiful. Thank you very much."

"I'm glad you like them."

"What's not to like about roses? And I'd be happy to attend the gallery exhibit. I'm thrilled. You have my number; call me."

Lex came back to her partner. "I bet he's happy," Gil said.

"So am I."

Lex's cell phone vibrated. She answered and heard a stranger's voice. "Detective Stall, this is Duane from Kelstrom's."

"The wine shop?" she asked.

"Yes. Mr. Kelstrom, you might remember, is a little hard of

hearing and sometimes forgets things. I forgot something too. There's a small storage unit here; a closet-sized room that's kept cool. Mr. Cambourd had been utilizing it. He has a key, and so do we. I opened the door and found black tubes stored inside. I placed a couple of them on a table and pulled one out. There are rolled up paintings inside. Canvases."

Lex rose from her chair. "What?" she shouted. "Gently roll them up and put them back inside the tubes. Try not to touch the paint. We'll be right there."

Gil asked, "What was that all about?"

"The key. Get the key. It's for a closet in that wine shop. We need to get over there right now. They found paintings inside. If I'm correct they may be valuable."

A steady rain had started to fall. Lex grabbed Gil's arm. "I have my umbrella. You can squeeze in." They rushed out back to get into a car. "This could be huge," Lex said. "He had many secrets, but this may have been his biggest."

They arrived at the wine shop in what seemed like seconds and went inside. Lex closed her wet umbrella, and Duane led them to the back room. Kelstrom was sitting at a table. Two black tubes were on it, and the door to the closet was open. Gil took out the key and inserted it into the lock. "It fits," he announced.

Lex opened one tube, eased out the canvas, and slowly unrolled it. The signature in the lower right corner was unmistakable. "My God," she said. "This appears to be a Monet. Are these forgeries?"

Gil studied the painting he'd removed from the second tube and glanced at the signature. "Renoir."

Lex looked at both canvasses, and turned to Gil. "Do you suppose…Is there any way these can be the real? Remember, Cambourd got supplies from Paris, and Gastone told us those pigments are rare. If Cambourd was going to forge a masterpiece, then I imagine he would use the proper materials. He may have somehow been able to create forgeries at the museum, steal these, and replace them with his fakes. Why else would he keep these in a cool, safe place?"

Lex took pictures of the two paintings before she and Gil carefully rolled the canvasses back up and placed them inside their tubes. Gil said, "I remember Gastone also saying there were times when Cambourd wouldn't let him in the room."

Lex was stunned. "Are these paintings, or what's left of them, what he took on his trips to Paris? Was he selling them? That would make the large wire deposits sensible." Lex turned to Duane and Kelstrom. "Do you recall when he last visited this locker?"

Kelstrom shook his head, indicating he didn't know, while Duane thought about it. "I really don't remember, but I'd say it had been some time. We forgot about it."

Lex counted sixteen tubes. "I'm not comfortable with loading these into the car. It's raining too hard."

She asked Kelstrom, "Can we put these back into the closet? We'll return to get them. I don't want to take them out in this rainstorm."

They placed the tubes back inside, and Gil shut the door. He locked it and said to Duane, "Would you mind if we took your key too?"

Duane gave it to him, and Lex retrieved her umbrella. They got back into their car and headed toward the precinct where they filled Pressley in on what they'd found at the wine shop.

CHAPTER 47

Lex managed to get her roses home and into a vase. She admired the flowers and freshened the water. Relieved to see there was no rain in sight, she headed to the precinct. She knew retrieving the rolled canvases was a job she and Gil would have to do as soon as possible.

She was curious about something else. If Gastone examined the masterpieces at the museum and verified they were the real paintings, then the ones in the wine shop closet must be copies, but what if they weren't and Gastone was fooled.

Gil was at his desk when Lex walked in. Setting her latte on her desk, she saw the coffee and half-eaten doughnut on his desk. "You're addicted to those things. You're all addicts."

He looked at her. "I could say the same about that drink."

Lex sipped her beverage. "Okay, fat boy. Eat up. We have to go get the paintings from the wine shop."

The one thing Lex didn't consider was that Kelstrom's didn't open until 11 a.m. She learned that by calling and listening to a recording. "They're not open yet. We need to see Worthington, then we could go back to the wine store," Lex said. "I have a strange feeling that Gastone may not be telling Marcus the truth about his verifications." She called the director.

"Good morning," Marcus said.

"Good morning," Lex replied. "We need to see you now. It's urgent."

"Urgent? You've found something?"

"We have. We'll see you shortly."

"Let's go," Lex said as Gil swallowed the last bite of his doughnut.

⋀

Twenty minutes later, the detectives entered the director's office. Lex began, "We have interesting news to tell you, but I want to ask you something first. How can you determine a forgery from an original painting?"

"There are two processes: stylistic analysis and technical analysis. In the latter, we use methods and techniques such as carbon dating, white lead testing, and X-ray scanning to determine the legitimacy of works of art. Come take a walk with me. I'm going to show you what few people have ever seen." Marcus retrieved a lanyard with a key attached from inside his desk drawer.

Lex asked. "Have you made any headway with that notation?"

Marcus replied, "I'm still thinking about it. I just can't seem to figure it out. We're going downstairs."

They walked to an elevator and got in. Marcus used the key to unlock the control that permitted the car to descend to the lower level. They exited, and Marcus guided the detectives past a maze of rooms. One was marked "Asian Artifacts," and another was labeled "Egyptian Artifacts." Several storage rooms contained antiques, paintings, and a variety of other valuable items. They walked past a few offices, saw staff members busily at work, and viewed a room that housed ultraviolet cameras, as well as other expensive equipment. The high-tech machines were impressive looking, and Marcus stressed that each room was climate-controlled for heat, light, and humidity. "This is where Edward examined the paintings to certify their authenticity," Marcus said.

He led them to the examiner's office. The door was open. Edward was seated, and he appeared to be studying something on his computer. He stood when he saw the detectives with his boss. "Showing them around," Marcus explained. "They were curious to know how you examine artwork to determine authenticity."

"It takes a lot of training," Gastone said. "I was taught by a master. Fredrike knew what he was doing."

Lex took a minute to study the office and her eyes caught an interesting item on a table to the left of Gastone's chair. She also spotted another conspicuous item on his desk. Carefully slipping her cell phone out of her purse, Lex discretely snapped a few pictures. Marcus and the detectives left the area and made their way back to the director's office. "Thank you for the tour," Lex said as she turned to leave.

"Wait." Marcus asked, "What's the news you were going to tell me?"

"I forgot something. I'll explain it to you later," Lex responded. She nudge her partner. "Come on, we have to get back to the precinct."

Gil followed her out the door. "What was that all about? What's the rush?"

"Gastone said all of those paintings are originals."

"He should know."

"You're right," Lex said.

"You've lost me. What are you getting at?"

"You didn't see what I saw, did you?"

"Okay. What exactly did you see?"

"I took a few interesting pictures with my phone."

"Of what?"

"I'll show you when we get back. You'll find them more than interesting."

They arrived at the precinct, and Gil could hardly keep up with her. She stormed into the squad room ahead of him, and he finally joined her. "You gonna tell me now, Miss Marple?" he asked.

Lex had a scowl on her face. She pulled out the second disc from Davidson's lobby and inserted it into her computer.

"What's going on?" Gil asked.

"You'll see in a few seconds." The footage ran until 8:33 p.m. "There," she said as she froze the image. "Look at that cap and the gloves." She showed Gil the pictures she'd snapped at the museum. "That's the hat. The same Red Sox hat. Yaz. And here's a shot of a box of latex gloves. The same kind he was wearing in the lobby. It's Gastone, he killed Davidson. I'm sure he shot Cambourd too. What do we really know about Gastone?"

"But why would he kill them both?" Gil asked. "It's not like he wanted Cambourd's job because he already had that."

"True," Lex agreed. "What did they know that would cause Edward Gastone to kill them? I think he knew about those masterpieces we just found. He was after them. We better get back to the wine shop and retrieve them now."

"We need to tell Pressley first," Gil replied.

Stepping into their boss's office, Lex stated, "We've got the murderer. Cambourd's successor, Edward Gastone. He delivered the pizza. We just got back from the museum and saw his office. I took snapshots of his Red Sox cap, and gloves. They match what the pizza guy was wearing. We ran the video again. It's him."

Lex knew there were times when she'd jumped the gun, like the case with Altman; there wasn't enough concrete evidence to convict him. She wasn't going to make that same mistake with Gastone. She literally needed that smoking gun. Lex said, "We need to know everything about Gastone. I'm sure Marcus can tell us. But we need to return to the wine shop and rescue those paintings."

Pressley said to Gil, "Get Benzinger to go with you."

"I'm calling Duane to let him know we're on our way back," Lex remarked.

Gil and the rookie detective approached Pressley's office. "Let's go," Lex said.

▲

Duane was waiting for the detectives, and he led them back to the locked closet. Gil opened the door. With Benzinger's help, they loaded the tubes into their vehicle and headed back to the precinct. They placed the merchandise on the conference room table. Pressley entered. "What's in the tubes?"

Lex said, "Canvasses. I'm positive these are masterpieces worth millions. We need to tell Marcus Worthington what we have. Gastone's a liar, an outright liar. He never examined those paintings at the Met, because he knew they were forgeries done by Cambourd, and he was sure Marcus wouldn't question him. These paintings are what Gastone was after, and I think he killed Cambourd because the cagey old artist wouldn't tell him where they were hidden. Cambourd knew he had to keep these in a cool place. He died rather than giving them up."

"But why Jerry Davidson? What made Gastone kill him?" Pressley asked.

"He must have thought Jerry Davidson had known where Cambourd hid the paintings, but Gastone was wrong."

Pressley said, "Mark these for evidence. We need to keep them locked up."

Lex focused on Pressley. "These need to go back to the museum. There's no time for evidence tagging. I need to call Marcus."

"Lex, these tubes are evidence," Pressley said.

She glared at the captain. "Of what? We have priceless masterpieces here. They need to be where they belong, not in some property room."

Pressley shook his head. "Get them back there."

Lex called the director. "We're coming back to see you now. I'll tell you everything when we arrive."

"Fine," Marcus said.

Lex looked at Benzinger. "Let's get these to the museum."

Pressley requested, "Take a couple of uniforms."

"Not yet," Lex replied. "I want to get these back now and have Worthington identify them. We'll get Gastone, but first I want to

237

know as much about him as possible."

Twenty minutes later, Lex, Gil and Benzinger hauled the tubes up to the director's office. "What the heck are all of these?" Marcus asked.

"I think you better sit. This is going to sting," Lex said. "This is Detective Benzinger."

"Nice to meet you," Marcus said. "What's going on?"

Gil closed the door before opening a tube and carefully rolling the canvas onto Marcus's desk. The director stood with his mouth agape and examined the canvas closer. "Holy Jesus! Is this what I think it is? This is Renoir's *By the Seashore*. Are you telling me all these tubes contain original masterpieces?"

"Yes, we believe they are," Lex answered. "We found them in storage at the wine shop near Cambourd's studio."

Marcus was flush with disbelief. "What do we have hanging here? Edward verified the authenticity of every one of the paintings."

"I don't think so," Lex said. "He knew they were forgeries, and he went through the motions to appease you."

"But why would he do that?"

"We don't know yet, but we think he was looking for these. Cambourd wouldn't tell him where they were, so Gastone killed him."

"What? I'm totally confused. It can't be Edward. He idolized Cambourd. I need a drink."

"Try to be calm. We need to know more about Gastone before we make an arrest," Lex explained. "As long as he doesn't suspect anything, he shouldn't go anywhere."

"What do we do now?" Marcus asked.

"I want you to store these tubes in a safe place before Gastone sees them," Lex said.

There was a small room to Marcus's left. "In there. I can lock the door, and no one can get in." They carefully placed the tubes inside the room.

"Do you have a file on Gastone?"

Marcus opened his bottom drawer and took out a folder. "Edward Garrison Gastone graduated from Yale and worked at the Museum of Fine Arts in Boston for five years before coming here in ninety-one." Marcus stopped reading as though a light went off in his head, and he froze. "That's it," he declared. "Those initials in that ledger, ISG and EGG." He opened his top drawer and pulled out the note he'd written. "I copied the notation so I could think about it." He stared at the piece of paper, removed his glasses and rubbed his eyes. "ISG 180390 KU-EGG. EGG: Edward Garrison Gastone. ISG is Isabella Stewart Gardner and that number is a date. A significant date. It's March 18, 1990, the date of the museum heist. I think he was trying to say that Gastone had something to do with it."

"Tell us more about the heist," Lex said.

"If I remember it correctly, two men dressed as police officers entered the museum early that morning. They tied up the guards and stole a dozen or so paintings. They've never been caught, and the paintings are still missing." Marcus turned to his computer and brought up the details. "Here's pictures of the stolen paintings." He paged down to a vase, and Gil's eyes lit up.

"What's that?" he asked.

"It's a Ku." He looked at the notation again. "Here it says KU. That's a priceless Chinese bronzed beaker," Marcus said. "It was taken too."

Gil commented to Lex, "That's the one in Altman's office."

Lex agreed, "It sure looks like it. Can you print a picture of it?" she asked Marcus. He obliged, and a color copy of the beaker slid out of the printer.

Lex said, "Listen, we have some unfinished business with Heinrich Altman. I'm sure we'll be at the bottom of this within the next twenty-four hours. Stay calm. We can't alarm Gastone now. Gil and I need to see Altman first. Don't say anything until you hear from us. Act normal."

CHAPTER 48

With a sense of urgency, the detectives headed to Altman's, but were surprised when the gallery was closed. No lights, no Laura, and no Altman. "Damn it," Lex said. "Closed. No one is here. He better not have booked another cruise. I still have his itinerary in my desk. His cell number is on it. I'll call him when we get back."

▲

Lex and Gil got back to their workplace and she pulled out the itinerary. "Wait," Gil said. "What if he's involved? What if he knows the Ku was stolen?"

"We'll have to take that chance. I need to call him, now."

Altman answered. "Hello detective."

"Mr. Altman. We have to see you as soon as possible."

"Really? Let me give you my lawyer's number. You can talk to him."

"It's important. You are not in trouble, but we need your help." Lex reached into her bag of tricks. She hid the fact that he may well be in trouble. "Meet us at your gallery as soon as possible. Now if you can."

"What's so urgent?"

"It's about your prized possession, your beaker."

"The Ku?"

"Yes, sir. Please meet us at the gallery."

"Christ sakes, I'm in Philadelphia at a friend's place. I'll never make it back in time to meet today. How about tomorrow morning? I can be there by nine."

"Thank you. We'll be there."

Lex let out a sigh of relief. "When I mentioned the Ku, he nearly freaked out. I don't think he knows anything about it being stolen. He'll be able to tell us where he got it."

Pressley entered their workplace. "What's going on? You tore in here, like lightning."

"This is bigger than we could have imagined," Lex said. "Gastone not only killed Cambourd, he was involved in the biggest unsolved museum heist in the world. Gastone stole from the Gardner in Boston."

"What? We have two major crimes?" Pressley rocked back in his chair and then leaned forward. "The FBI and Boston Police need to be contacted."

"Later," Lex said. We should have a lot of answers tomorrow."

CHAPTER 49

Lex was more than elated to have Liz back home, and it seemed as if she'd never left. The teenager had gotten back into her old school and Shannon was hanging out at Lex's again.

Van Gogh was settled on the floor and Lex entered the kitchen. "How's it going?" she asked the kids.

"Great Mrs. Stall," Shannon said. "I have my BFF back and I love our kitty too. Mom said you helped pick Smokey out."

"I was there. She did the picking."

Van Gogh purred and stretched before moving to her empty food dish. "I'll feed her," Liz said.

"I have to go," Shannon said. "See you."

Liz asked her mother if they could eat at the pizza place on Bleecker and Lex didn't deny the request. They took their walk to the restaurant and after eating, they proceeded to the record shop. Liz waited while Lex stared into the window. *Hi, Dad. You were right. Everything worked out fine. Liz is back with me, and I couldn't be happier, of course, unless you could hug us both. I still love you. I mean we still love you.*

And I love you both too.

▲

Once they got home, Lex changed the water in the vase containing her yellow roses. She picked up Stefan's invitation and read it again.

"Mom, you look so happy."

"I am. You know I haven't really dated since the divorce. Stefan Martine seems like a nice man."

"Is he handsome?"

Lex smiled. "I think so. I've never been to a gallery exhibit. I hope everything goes well and you can meet him sometime. In the meantime, how about us hanging the posters?"

They headed upstairs with the four-legged adoptee trailing them. "There are hooks attached to the picture wires," Lex said. "We need a hammer. There's one in the linen closet."

Liz retrieved it and Lex glanced at the barren walls. "What do you think?"

Liz looked at the posters, and directed her mother to where she wanted them hung.

After completing the project, Lex said, "Done. We still have time for Jeopardy."

CHAPTER 50

The detectives and police officers Pete and Felix arrived at Altman's at 8:50 a.m. and Lex rang the bell. Altman opened the door and upon seeing the uniforms, he said, "What are they here for? What kind of bullshit are you pulling now? I'm calling my lawyer."

"No," Lex said. "Wait until you hear what we have to tell you. Again, it isn't about you. It's about the Ku."

He glanced at the uniformed policemen. "Then why are they here?"

"Settle down. Let's go to your office to talk. My friends will remain out here."

Inside the office, the small Ku was still sitting encased in the center of the display cabinet. Altman picked up a cigar, and smugly snapped, "I don't suppose you're sending me on a vacation to Jamaica. What about the Ku?"

Lex pointed to it while Gil placed the picture Worthington had printed in front of Altman. "It's about this."

Staring at the photo, Altman glanced back at the beaker. "That's my Ku," he said.

"Is it your Ku?" Lex asked.

"What are you getting at? I bought that years ago, and I paid a small fortune for it."

"Tell us about that purchase. Who did you buy it from?" Lex asked. "Actually, it was Edward Gastone, wasn't it?"

"Yes, but what's that got to do with anything?" Altman went to his file and pulled out a receipt. "I paid twenty grand for that beautiful antique. And here's a certificate of authenticity."

It was apparent to Lex that Altman had no idea about the true identity of the Ku. "How long have you known Gastone, and how did you come to buy it?" she pressed.

"I knew Gastone from the Met. He said he used to work in Boston, and his wife had divorced him. The Ku came from her antique shop. He thought I might like it, and he was right. I've seen Chinese vases go for thirty grand, and more. I bought it."

"Alright, Heinrich. Sit back and take a deep breath," Lex said. "That Ku is the one that was stolen from the Isabella Stewart Gardner Museum in Boston over twenty years ago." Lex pointed to the artifact. "This has to go back to Boston."

Altman stared at the Ku. "What? Are you serious? He stole it?"

"I'm afraid that's correct."

"Now what?"

"Excuse us. Gil and I need to talk privately. We'll be in the gallery."

Altman poured himself a scotch as Lex and Gil stepped out of the room. "I think he's telling the truth," Lex said.

"We need his help, don't we?"

"Yes, and I think there's only one way he'll cooperate."

"I agree, but can we do that?"

"It's worth a try."

The detectives reentered the office, and Lex said, "Heinrich, we believe you had no idea about the Ku, but we need your help. We're prepared to not seek an embezzlement charge in exchange for your assistance."

Altman gulped the drink and leaned forward. "What do I have to do?"

"First, don't have any more liquor," Lex said. "We need to set up a confrontation with Gastone. I want you to call him."

"What do I tell him? It's not like we're close friends. I can't remember the last time I spoke with him."

"No, but you do have that Ku in common. Tell him it has a crack, and insist he look at it. Sound upset and say you're bringing it to the museum to see if he can repair it."

"What if he says he can't?" What if he says take it somewhere else?"

Lex assured Altman, "He's not about to let anyone else see it. He knows it's stolen."

Altman found Gastone's cell number. "When do you want me to bring it to him?"

"Today. It has to be today before the crack spreads."

Altman took out his cell and made the call, while Lex and Gil listened. They could only hear Altman, but it was obvious to Lex that the call wasn't going well. Quickly, she wrote on her pad. *Tell him you're going to bring it whether he likes it or not.* Altman raised his voice. "Don't hand me that shit. I'm bringing it over right now."

A few seconds later, the call ended and Altman wiped his forehead. "He said to meet him in the lobby around one p.m." He reached for his liquor. "One more. I really need this one."

Lex called to Pete and Felix and they entered the office. "You two stay here with Mr. Altman." She redirected her conversation to the gallery owner. "Please wrap the beaker and have it ready to take to the museum." She then looked back to Pete. "Make sure he has no more alcohol."

Altman placed the Ku on his desk and stared at it. "I'll pack it real good."

Lex said to Gil, "We need to see Marcus and tell him what is going to happen." She then turned to the officers again. "We're taking a cab to the museum. Get Mr. Altman there at noon, and bring him and the Ku to Marcus Worthington's office. That's where we will be."

Lex said to the frazzled Altman. "Good work, Mr. Altman. We'll see you in a little while."

"Wait," Altman said. "Did he killed Cambourd and Jerry?"

"We believe he did," Lex said. "We hope to find out why when we confront him."

Altman eyed his scotch bottle and Pete made sure it stayed where it was. "I want to see the look on that bastard's face when you arrest him. I don't suppose you could have him write me a check for twenty grand before you take him away?"

"Wish we could, but that's one deal we can't undo," Lex said. She turned Gil. "Let's go."

It only took Lex a minute to hail a cab and they were on their way to see Marcus Worthington.

⋏

The detectives purposefully walked to the director's office. He stood. "I'm a nervous wreck."

Lex said, "Please sit and try to stay calm. We were just at Heinrich Altman's. That Ku from the Gardner museum is in his possession. We recognized it from the photo you gave us. Altman had purchased it from Gastone. Altman and the Ku are going to be here along with two police officers at noon. A little while ago, Altman called Gastone and they are supposed to meet in the lobby at one p.m. I've instructed the police officers to have Altman and the beaker brought here to your office. We will then set up a confrontation with Mr. Gastone right here."

Marcus slumped back in his chair. "Are you going to arrest Edward?"

"Yes."

"My hands are shaking."

"You'll be fine," Lex reassured.

Gil said to Lex, "We should tell Pressley what's happening."

Lex called the captain and explained the situation and the plan. "He's okay. Glad we'll have Pete and Felix with us."

247

CHAPTER 51

Gil and Lex sat in Marcus Worthington's office waiting for the police officers, and Altman to arrive with the Ku. Lex got up and stood at the door. "I hope they get here soon."

"It's still early," Gil said.

"I'm calling Pete." She took out her cell and then she saw them heading to the office. "I was getting worried," she said to Pete.

"We're right on time," he replied.

"Thanks. You and Felix hang out in the lobby until we need you."

Altman placed the Ku on Marcus's desk. "This is it?" Marcus said.

The gallery owner unwrapped it and it stood on the desk. "It's magnificent," Marcus said.

Lex directed Altman to a chair in the corner as she took her seat beside Gil. Marcus placed two black tubes on his credenza and then sat behind his desk.

They waited until 12:45 p.m. Lex said to Altman. "Call Gastone and have him come up here rather than meet you in the lobby."

"What do I say?"

"Tell him you were early and decided to see Marcus."

Altman took out his cell and connected with the murdering thief while the detectives listened. "Edward, I was early. I'm here in Marcus's office. I haven't seen him in a while. I thought I'd say hello." After a pause, Altman spoke again. "Yes, I have the Ku. I know you said the lobby, but I'm here with Marcus. He wants you to join us."

Altman put his phone in his pocket. "He'll be here in a few minutes."

"You did a great job. Thank you," Lex said. "Sit tight when he enters the office."

Marcus was nervously tapping his desk when the conservationist entered. Gastone stopped and stared at the unbroken Ku. Then he saw the detectives and Altman. "What's this?" he asked Lex and Gil. He looked at Altman. "What's going on, Heinrich?"

Altman smugly said, "You tell us. You stole that beaker, you son of a bitch. I'm out twenty grand. I don't suppose you can write me a check?"

Gastone had a blank look on his face and stood almost motionless.

Lex suggested, "Why don't you start with the Gardner heist? We know that's where the Ku came from."

Gastone turned red, hesitated, and blurted out, "Should never have sold that thing." Then, appearing to be relieved to get the story off his chest, he began talking. "My ex-wife was once a guard there; she knew the place inside and out. They never suspected she was in on it. It was Saint Patrick's Eve, and the cops had their hands full with parties and bars, just as we thought. We were dressed as Boston Police and we got lucky because of the fog. We were out by three a.m. and drove away as silently as we came with a trunkful of paintings and that Ku."

"When you say, 'we'. Who do you mean?"

"Us. Me and my brother, he was an ex-cop and still had a few uniforms. He died several years ago."

"Why did you do it?" Lex asked.

"That's the funny part. I'd been across the street at the Museum of Fine Arts for a few years. I loved that place and always thought the Gardner was a poor sister. One thing my boss knew was that Isabella Stewart Gardner had vowed if anything were ever moved inside her museum, Mrs. Gardner would send everything over to the MFA. I always thought those masterpieces belonged there anyway."

"Where are they?"

Gastone smiled. "I can't say, but they may not be far from where they had been."

Lex took that to mean, the stolen pieces might be at the Museum of Fine Arts.

"Wait," Marcus said. "Are you saying Maxine Simmons was in on the heist?"

"Who do you think planned it?" Gastone asked.

"Why the beaker?" Gil queried. "It doesn't fit with the rest of the heist."

"Good observation. It wasn't on the list. I grabbed it at the last second. Interesting how no one ever mentions it. I waited and then figured I could sell it, and no one would know because no one seemed to care about it. It was always the paintings that were missing."

Lex said, "You had a list of paintings to steal?"

"Maxine gave us one."

"Why'd you kill Fredrike?" Lex demanded.

Gastone was silent for a second. Again, as if being cleansed, he said, "He knew I was involved in the Gardner, and I knew his secrets too. He was going to fess up and I feared he'd tell the police about me. Stubborn old bastard. He wouldn't tell me where he hid the canvasses. I had to kill him." Gastone glanced at the black containers that were on the credenza. "What's in the tubes?" he asked.

Marcus retrieved one, put on a pair of latex gloves, and unrolled a Renoir. Gastone immediately recognized it. "Where'd you get that?"

Lex asserted, "We'll get to that. All those paintings you verified are forgeries, right?"

"Yes, he was a master. I knew he hid the real ones."

"That's correct," Lex said. "The rest are in tubes inside the small room in back of us. He stored them in the wine shop down the street from his studio."

"Sly old man."

"Why Jerry Davidson?" Lex asked.

"I thought he might have known where they were. I figured if anyone knew, it would be him, but he didn't. He went for my gun. I shot him."

"As I recall, you had said you phoned him the previous evening to confirm your meeting."

Gastone nodded. "He'd been here the day before and I knew he was going to Chicago. I decided to strike before he went. I did call him, but I told him Marcus was ill and we couldn't make it in the morning. I told him Marcus had left me an envelope he wanted Jerry to take to Chicago, so I arranged to bring it to him."

"The pizza?" Lex asked.

"As it turns out, I really didn't need that. I remembered there was a doorman, so I knew I couldn't just walk in and go up to the Condo without being seen. I figured delivering a pizza was a clever disguise. He wasn't there though, and Jerry buzzed me in. He thought I was bringing him that letter from Marcus."

Lex looked directly at Gastone. "You didn't know the doorman only works until six, but there was a camera in the lobby and it captured you." She paused. "When we toured your work area with Marcus, I saw that Red Sox cap and latex gloves in your office, and I knew it was you. How did you know to wipe your prints from the bullet casings?" Lex queried.

"I clean everything. I'm obsessed. I have OCD."

Lex continued her questioning. "You said there were times he wouldn't let you in his room. Was that when he was doing his forging?"

"Yes, but I knew it. Gabriel Bergeron was his mentor. A master like no other. Fredrike wanted to prove to the world that he was the greatest of them all; not Bergeron, Monet, or Renoir. He knew he could forge those masterpieces and fool every art patron and critic alive. He could match the masters, stroke for stroke, color by color. He needed the right pigments, and Bergeron supplied him with aged canvases from the period and all the proper minerals. Those two were a perfect pair."

"But how did he get them out of here?" Lex asked.

"Easier than you could imagine. He'd buy posters from time to time in the museum store. He had them rolled into those cheap cardboard tubes, took them to his workshop, emptied the tubes, and walked out with the real masterpieces rolled inside the same tubes. Judging by the black archival storage containers, he stored them properly."

"And Bergeron?" Lex questioned.

"He was very elusive. Interpol never caught on. He lived in Paris for years under the name Dieu Tenom, and died two years ago. Monet spelled backwards, and Dieu...The god of forgers."

"Explain something," Lex said. "Cambourd made several trips to Paris and subsequently, large deposits were wired into his bank account. Sounds like Bergeron may have wired them. What was he doing when he visited Bergeron?"

A strange glow came over Gastone. "That's the best part. He even fooled his mentor. He brought Bergeron what the master forger thought were originals, and they were sold on the black market for large sums. Buyers trusted Bergeron, but Fredrike fooled even him. And here's a kicker, Dieu's niece is Adrienne Chandelle."

Lex turned to Gil. "Now it fits. She knew her uncle gave Cambourd all that money, and she came here to take it back." She refocused on Gastone. "So you knew Adrienne and you knew she was there the night you killed Cambourd."

"I knew her. If it wasn't for me she never would have found Cambourd."

Gastone had a menacing look on his face, reached into his pocket, pulled out a Glock, and pointed it at Lex. "Very smart, lady." He eyed the detectives. "Both of you. Put your guns on the floor, right now!"

"You're making a big mistake," Lex said. "There are police officers in the lobby waiting for you."

"Then that's your mistake, because I don't see them here to save you. Now do as I say." Gil and Lex placed their guns on the floor. "Now, boot them over to me." Gastone rotated to Lex. "Get up, Wonder Woman. You're my way out of here. I'm taking you with me."

Lex didn't budge. "Put the gun down. I told you there are police waiting to take you away. You'll never leave here alive," she assertively said.

"We'll see about that. Now get your ass up before I shoot those pretty brown eyes out."

Lex still didn't move and stared into his crazed eyes. "So, shoot. Shoot me. I dare you to shoot."

Gil nudged his partner. "Lex. Shut up! Do what he says before he pulls the trigger."

Without warning, a shot was fired. The sound was deafening, and blood spewed from the forehead of the fallen body. Edward Gastone was sprawled on the carpet. In that shocking moment, Lex saw Altman standing with a gun in his hand. His arm dropped to his side after firing the deadly shot. "He deserved it," Altman said as he observed his kill. The uniformed officers rushed into the office, and Pete pointed his weapon at Altman. "Drop the gun," he barked as Felix looked around the room with his gun drawn.

Altman let his Sig Sauer hit the floor. "He's okay," Lex said. "Put your weapons away."

Marcus Worthington fainted, and Gil immediately called for medical help. "Are you guys okay?" Pete asked.

"We're fine," Lex reassured. "Thanks for the quick backup."

Minutes later, EMTs arrived to tend to Worthington, and he soon regained consciousness.

Gil put his arms around his partner. "Damn it! You scared the living shit out of me, Lex."

"I didn't think he'd really shoot."

"Oh really? I thought he would. What the hell were you thinking?"

"To be honest, I was thinking you might be gentlemanly enough to jump in front of me and take one for the lady in the room."

Gil squinted hard at her. "Lex, Lex, Lex. What am I gonna do with you?"

"For starters you can let me go." She opened her purse. "Good thing he didn't shoot this." She took out her phone. "It's all on here. I recorded everything." Lex veered toward Altman. "Thanks. I guess we're friends now."

Altman nodded. "Are you making a peace offering? I am still out a vacation."

"Sorry about that," Lex replied. "We all make mistakes. You need to stick around until I write up a report. We'll need to seize your gun. It's only temporary. It is registered, right?"

"I told you it was. Learned that lesson."

Lex worked on the incident report, and waited for the medical examiners to come and remove Gastone's body. She dismissed Altman and asked Pete and Felix to drive him back to his gallery.

When the detectives arrived at the precinct, they entered Pressley's office. Lex told him what had happened and what they learned about the Gardner heist. "We need to get in touch with Boston Police," she urged. "They'll have to contact the FBI. The director of the Museum of Fine Arts, Maxine Simmons, was behind the robbery."

"Can you prove it?"

"I was recording everything. It's on my phone."

Pressley picked up his phone. "Wait," Lex said, "Gastone indicated the paintings were not far from the Gardner. The FBI may want to search the Museum of Fine Arts." Pressley called Boston Police and put the call on speaker. She recited the entire story. "I have proof. I recorded everything," she said.

"Thank you. We'll get in touch with the FBI."

After the call ended, Lex sighed, "Never expected anything like this. I'm ready for a long weekend."

They headed out. "You forgetting something?" Gil asked. "You have a hot date tomorrow."

Lex smiled at her partner. "Don't worry, I'll have my weapon in my purse the entire evening."

CHAPTER 52

The flowers from Stefan Martine were in full bloom. Lex smelled the sweet aroma and glanced at the invitation. *Should I wear the red dress or the blue one?*

"What are you thinking about, Mom?" Liz asked.

"Tomorrow night. I've never been to an art exhibit before, and I don't know what to expect."

"I hope you have a good time."

"Thanks, sweetie. Elaine said you can sleep there. I don't know what time I'll be getting home. Want to go see Shannon? I have to talk with Elaine."

"Sure. I want to see Smokey."

They walked to Elaine's. The teenagers and the cat went to Shannon's room while the two mothers went into the kitchen. "You want some tea?" Elaine asked.

"Sure." The host got up to put water into her teapot. "I need your opinion," Lex said. "Which dress do you think I should wear to the gallery? The blue or the red?"

"I like them both." Elaine smirked. "Honestly, I think the blue one shows a little too much cleavage. She paused. It's a beautiful dress. Remember what happened the last time you wore it? Unless you plan to sleep with him, I'd be a little more conservative. The red one is stunning on you."

Elaine poured the teas, Lex sipped her drink, and flashed back to that night at the bar. "I'm not sure it was the dress. I had too much to drink. I have no intentions of having sex with Stefan tomorrow night, and I will be watching my drinking. One cocktail, two at most."

"Wear the red one," Elaine said.

"I will."

"Hair?"

"I have an appointment."

Liz, Shannon, and Smokey appeared. "Looks like he belongs here," Lex said.

"I love him," Shannon cooed.

Lex got up. "Time to go," she said to Liz.

They went home, and Lex studied her closet. She took out the red dress and hung it on the door. *Elaine's right.*

▲

Date day was here, and Lex kept the appointment with her hairdresser. It was midafternoon when she got home.

"What time are you leaving?" Liz asked.

"I have to be at the gallery at seven-fifteen. Stefan is sending a limo to pick me up."

"I love your shorter hair. You're really going in a limo?"

"Thanks, sweetie. I like it too, and yes. He has to stay at the Gallery, so he's sending a limo."

"Mom, that's awesome."

"I'm glad you're okay with me going. What time did Elaine say to come over for dinner?"

"Six, but Shannon said to come earlier."

"Come upstairs. I'm going to start to get ready."

Lex placed the red dress on her bed. "It's beautiful," Liz said. "Put it on."

"Okay, but I'll have to take it off again. I want to take a bath before I really get dressed." Lex slipped into the dress.

"You're pretty, Mom."

"Thank you," Lex replied. "Go get your bag. I'll take you to Shannon's in a few minutes."

Liz got her overnight bag, and having put jeans on, Lex walked her to Elaine's.

Once home again, Lex drew herself a bath and then dressed. While waiting for the ride, she received a call from Stefan. "Hi. Are you all set? The limo is on the way. I can't wait to see you."

"I'm all set except for my lipstick. I'll be waiting. Looking forward to being there."

Forty minutes later, the fancy vehicle dropped her off at the gallery, and Stefan was waiting. He stepped outside to take his date's hand. "You look amazing. The staff is almost finished setting up the food. Let's go inside."

"You look quite handsome in that tux."

She perused the gallery. Several tables draped with white linen displayed an assortment of foods and drinks. Guests started to arrive, and soon the event began. Stefan made sure to introduce Lex to his invitees. She nursed a cocktail and observed Stefan expertly describe paintings to the guests and negotiate sales with clients.

At 11:00 p.m., the last of the guests exited the gallery. Stefan and Lex were alone. She said, "You are very eloquent and quite the salesperson."

"Thank you. I think I could have sold more items if you weren't here." He grinned at her. "Half my guests were more interested in you than the artwork. Come, I have champagne in my office. Let's drink a toast." Keenly aware that she'd finished one drink, she let Stefan pour her a glass of champagne. "A toast," he said. "To a lovely lady. I'm so glad you came."

"I enjoyed the entire evening," she replied.

They clicked glasses and drank the champagne. Stefan offered up another, and said, "May I ask what you are wearing? It's very nice."

Lex answered, "Chanel." She wasn't sure if that was an innocent question or was it an attempt to be a little more intimate. Though the second drink was tempting, she said, "You know, it's getting late, and I should go. My daughter will be waiting. I had my neighbor sit with her."

"I understand," Stefan said. "Let me take you home. I apologize for sending a limo to pick you up, but as you saw, I couldn't leave here."

"That was quite thoughtful. I'd never been in a limo before. Thank you."

He took her hand. "I'm very happy you came." After he locked up, they headed toward his Jaguar.

When they got to Lex's house, he walked her to the door. "Would you like to have dinner sometime soon? There's a terrific French restaurant a few blocks from my gallery. I'd love to take you there."

Lex unlocked her door. "I'd love to."

With the porchlight on, their eyes met. "May I kiss you goodnight?" he asked.

She smiled at him. "I thought you'd never ask." They leaned into each other and shared their first kiss. "Thank you again for a lovely evening," she whispered.

Lex watched Stefan get into his Jaguar and drive away. Stepping inside the house she thought, *I really like him. I hope he's as nice as he appears to be.*

Chapter 53

L ex had a large latte in her hand as she strode toward her partner.
"Hey, like the hair," Hutch said.

"Thanks," she said as she continued to her desk.

"You look like a happy camper," Gil said as he tried to slide his doughnut under a napkin.

Lex laughed. "Eat the damn thing. I am happy. Maybe for the first time in a long while."

"I guess it's fair to say you and Stefan hit it off."

"Good guess. He was a perfect gentleman. He even sent a limo for me."

"You are going to invite me and RayAnn to the wedding, right?"

"I plan to take it slow."

"So, when's the next date?" Gil asked before biting into his doughnut.

"Soon. He asked me to dinner at a French restaurant, but we didn't set a date. He'll call me. Wipe your face when you're done."

"Smooth transition, Lex. What's on your mind besides Stefan?"

The captain approached Lex and Gil. "Boston Police let me know they raided the Museum of Fine Arts last night along with the FBI. They found the stolen paintings in a remote locked storeroom. Maxine Simmons confessed to the theft and the FBI arrested her."

Lex took a sip of her latte, and began walking the squad room floor. *Is it even thinkable? Anything is possible. That would be the ultimate deception.*

"Uh-oh," Gil uttered to the captain. "What on earth is she thinking now?"

A few minutes later, Lex said to Pressley, "We need to think about this. I have a bad feeling. Gastone confessed way too easily to the Gardner heist. He never did say the paintings were at the Museum of Fine Arts in Boston. He said the paintings might not be far from where they had been. He did implicate Maxine Simmons though. I think they need to authenticate those paintings. I sense something isn't right. The originals could still be somewhere other than the Boston museum. And you know what? It's possible Simmons had no idea what was going on behind her back."

Pressley challenged, "What? That's the wildest theory I ever heard."

"Is it? Call the Boston Police and have them get back to the FBI so they can authenticate the paintings they confiscated from the Museum of Fine Arts."

Pressley retreated to his office and made the call.

CHAPTER 54

One week later, Lex and Gil were inside Pressley's office, and the captain, holding his encased bullet, stared at Lex. "Tell me again. What exactly were you thinking? You could have been killed?"

She felt the captain's angst. "I knew he wouldn't pull the trigger." She tried to maintain her tough exterior. "I'll admit that I almost peed my pants."

Gil teased, "Your pants? Mine were nearly brown."

"Never again, Lex. You hear me?" Pressley insisted. "By the way, I heard from Epstein. His father's settled in at the nursing home and his mother is okay. Her sister is moving in next week and Epstein will be back."

"That's good to hear," Lex said.

"Gil said, "The cash we took from the apartment and deposit box is still in the property room. There is no one who can legally claim it. What will happen to it?"

"I believe it goes to probate, and a judge decides where it goes," the captain said.

"The signed will is valid, and the museum will get the money after it clears probate," Lex said.

Entering the squad room were two men dressed in dark suits and heading toward Pressley's office. One man appeared to be about six feet tall, the other a few inches shorter; both men were clean-cut. "Who the hell are they?" Gil asked.

"They look like feds to me," Lex replied.

The mysterious men walked into to the office. "Captain Pressley," one of the men presented his badge, "may we come in? I'm Special Agent Sheldon Murdock."

"I'm Special Agent Terrance Gaines," the other man announced.

"Close the door, gentlemen," Pressley said. "These are Detectives Gil Ramos and Lex Stall."

"Wonderful," Murdock said. "Thank you for having that Chinese Ku returned to the Boston Police. And thanks for tipping us to the Museum of Fine Arts."

Lex had a puzzled look on her face. "I don't think you came here to congratulate us. Why are you here?"

"Good observation," Murdock said. "We've known for years there were several accomplices in the Gardner heist. There are mobsters who have been under suspicion, but none have ever been arrested. Leads have led us nowhere, until now. We have checked Edward Gastone's background. He'd mentioned his ex to you. We found her. Amazingly, she was in Cambridge running an antique store two blocks from Harvard."

"That's great," Lex said.

"She and Maxine Simmons are in custody, but neither one is willing to give us the names of the other participants. It's possible if we cut them a deal, they may talk, but I doubt it," Murdock paused. "What can you tell us about Fredrike Cambourd, Gabriel Bergeron, Adrienne Chandelle, and Brigitte Chandelle?"

Sensing her suspicions may have been correct, Lex replied. "Why do you ask?"

Murdock shook his head. "Because the paintings recovered from the Boston Museum of Fine Arts are forgeries. Maxine Simmons had no idea they were fakes. She claims she doesn't know where stolen pieces are."

THE END

MEET THE AUTHOR: MARK L. DRESSLER

A former corporate manager and successful businessman, Mark began writing in 2014. Born and raised in Hartford, Connecticut, his mysteries featuring Dan Shields, "the detective who breaks all the rules," are set in his hometown. His first novel, *Dead and Gone*, was published in 2017. The follow-up story, *Dead Right*, hit bookstores in 2019 and was named a most notable 2019 book by the Hartford Courant. Both novels are local best sellers.

Mark has appeared on New Haven's News 8 WTNH with Teresa Dufour and Hartford's Fox 61 with Stan Simpson, who described Mark as "an internet sensation." He was honored by the Boston Children's Hospital for his generosity. Mark donates proceeds from all his books to that incredible hospital.

He is a member of Mystery Writers of America and Connecticut Authors and Publishers Association.

You can find Mark on Facebook at:
www.facebook.com/MarkLDressler
Write to him at: mark.dressler17@gmail.com

What's next for author Mark L. Dressler?

Up next is a return to Hartford with "the detective who breaks all the rules," Dan Shields, in another suspenseful thriller titled *Dead Air*. Dan goes back to college to investigate the death of a student disc jockey, who was broadcasting a late-night jazz show when the music suddenly stopped. Many witnessed the killing, but no one saw the killer.